RITES OF OBEDIENCE

Across the darkened room, the white flesh of the girl in furs shone eerily back to Penny from the exquisite oil portrait. Penny slipped her fingers into her punished and still-wet sex, and moaned beneath the velvet canopy protecting her solitary rapture. The girl embodied the desire in some universal woman, imprisoned by convention in every soul. At Whitehead, Penny knew, a woman could become anything. Here a girl could discover her true passion, no matter how obscene or excessive; she could be lashed and bound, taken mercilessly, or lose herself in an endless cycle of exploration and deviant lust.

A NEXUS CLASSIC

RITES OF OBEDIENCE

Lindsay Gordon

This book is a work of fiction.
In real life, make sure you practise safe, sane
and consensual sex.

This Nexus Classic edition published in 2005

First published in 1998 by
Nexus
Thames Wharf Studios
Rainville Road
London W6 9HA

www.nexus-books.co.uk

Typeset by TW Typesetting, Plymouth, Devon

Printed and bound by
Clays Ltd, St Ives PLC

ISBN 0 352 34005 3

One

'A uniform? The trainees wear uniforms? It just seems so odd.'

Penny's green eyes refused to blink. Her pretty face wrinkled with surprise and she felt her mouth drying with apprehension. She stared at the carefully folded garments beside her on Miss Barbusse's red velvet couch.

The wardrobe had been made to measure in preparation of her arrival. The black, patent, Cuban heels were at least five inches high. The tailored, knee-length hobble skirt seemed unnecessarily tight and the white silk blouses were distinctly old-fashioned. Her shock, however, focused on the underwear: there were seven black, whalebone brassieres and seven gauzy panty girdles with suspenders dangling off each leg. Penny rarely wore skirts, let alone an undergarment, even managing to reach the age of twenty-five without ever wearing stockings. It had all been packaged in slim brown boxes, with a French script on the top of each thin parcel. Panties had been supplied as well, and Penny sensed their expense. They were all dainty and black, with the satin shining as they drifted beneath little hangers.

Miss Barbusse smiled at Penny's astonishment and rose elegantly from behind her desk. She turned away from Penny to gaze through the large bay window. The rays of bright sunlight streamed around her slender

1

silhouette, enticing Penny to stare at the dean's smooth pale shoulders and the rear of her sleek head, her raven hair having been tied into a tight and shiny bun.

Miss Barbusse turned her head to light a black cigarette and Penny watched the dean's flawless aristocratic profile with admiration: the small chin raised imperiously and the high cheekbones enhanced by subtle rouge. The dean's blood-red lips pulled gently on the cigarette and her heavily lidded eyes fluttered. Penny had never seen such a sophisticated woman; she even smoked with style.

The dean's husky voice, rich with a continental lilt, sounded beautifully melodic to Penny as she said, 'My dear Penny, the fortunate students at this Academy set standards. One must be a genius and an enthusiast to even gain access. Only the brightest minds and most determined captains of industry will graduate from Whitehead. A formal, though chic, dress code brings out the best in my students.'

She teetered gracefully towards Penny and assumed an elegant pose beside her on the couch. The dean's long and shapely legs crossed with a whisper. The smile vanished from Miss Barbusse's face as she raised one immaculate eyebrow and peered at Penny's appearance with disdain.

Her long white fingers raised the cigarette to her mouth and her crimson nail varnish glinted. A reprimand flowed from the beautiful mouth in a plume of smoke: 'The trouser-suit will not do, the low heels are a travesty and your make-up is inappropriate.'

Penny gasped and the dean softened her voice to a condescending tone: 'Your employers at Polycorp have paid a small fortune to put you through our rigorous paces. You will find your ten-day experience at the Academy both rewarding and, shall I say, enlightening. One must, however, abide by the rules to win the game.'

Penny nodded, unsure whether to laugh or cry. She

was twenty-five and about to wear a school uniform again. The thought seemed monstrous, but how could she argue with a woman who had the style of Audrey Hepburn?

The dean continued, as if tired of Penny's inhibitions, 'And, you will agree, commitment and loyalty are vital for harmony in any institution.'

'Of course, but the heels seem so high and the skirt . . .' Penny stammered.

Miss Barbusse raised her eyebrow again to further endorse a belittling tone. 'You never know, you may even enjoy the transformation. It is my experience that a woman will learn to love elegance, especially amongst the antiquity and finery of an eighteenth-century manor. That even goes for a tomboy.'

The seamed stocking crept up Penny's leg; the sensation of sheer black nylon on her soft skin made her shiver. At first she had felt ridiculous wearing the half-cupped bra and the black girdle, but now, with the fine nylons secured to the suspenders, a curious feeling seeped through her. Something came alive deep inside of her; it was like wearing high heels for the first time in senior school. This feeling, though, was more sultry: it purred, uncoiled and made her skin tingle. She had always resisted the ultra-feminine look, refusing to obey tradition; even shaving her legs used to make her feel guilty.

The transformation continued when Penny slipped her nylon-swathed feet into the restricting high-heeled shoes. She imagined it would take days of wear to stretch the tight leather and to escape the sensation of walking on stilts. Desperate, however, to see the final result, she teetered towards the full-length mirror.

Penny's jaw dropped with surprise. It was impossible to deny, her sex appeal had rocketed: her seemingly longer legs had developed new contours and the stiff bra pushed her white breasts into tempting mounds. Her blonde shoulder-length bob was tied up to reveal a slender throat. Her pretty face flushed beneath the make-up. She felt like a high-class hooker – the similarity appealed to her.

Penny allowed one hand to descend to her sex, now damp and tightly hugged by sheer satin. She tickled it through her panties with her middle finger and bent over to stroke her shimmering stocking-clad legs with her other hand. She thought of the history, grace and culture of Whitehead and an image of a long and wealthy cock slipping inside her flickered behind her half-closed eyes, as the rubbing fingers, at play between her legs, increased their tempo.

Penny licked her freshly painted lips. She was alone and no one could see her – she swallowed her pride and allowed the underwear to offer its thrill.

She gazed about the richly furnished room and devoured her new surroundings; the high ceilings and carved wainscoting, the warm sunlight on polished wood, the thick red rugs beneath her heels, all combined to fill her spirit with a sense of decadence.

Penny gazed at the vast double bed and continued to play with her sex. She eyed the crimson velvet canopy with wonder, and stared at the dissolute artwork hung on the walls. There were shapely nudes with insolent eyes; some of the faces were masked and one pair of breasts had been graced by a black see-through veil. Ankles had been cuffed together and sensual mouths had been gagged with silk ribbons. It was the slender silhouette of a pretty dark-eyed girl, languishing amidst the thick folds of a fur coat, that appealed to Penny the most. Her sullen face, eclipsed by shadow, seemed oddly familiar. The girl had stretched her slender body across a chaise longue. Her long pale legs seemed to have been sculpted by some perverse god's hands. The downy hairs on the back of Penny's neck prickled at the sight of the

4

black riding crop, held lightly between the model's fingers. The grainy texture of the photograph suggested age. The seductive girl must have been captured by a photographer as her pubescence flourished into early womanhood. Despite her allure, Penny detected a suggestion of danger.

Her fingers pressed on, circling and exploring her glowing sex. Her body, uptight from so much research and preparation, demanded a release. Little moans of pleasure erupted from inside her as she teetered back towards the bed. She had thirty minutes to indulge in private rapture before the introductory seminar began. Penny moved her fingers in quick little flurries over her swollen clit and her mouth began a rhythmic gasping, in tune with the sparks of arousal that shot through her body.

It was only when she slumped back on to the bed and disturbed her bag that the masturbatory frenzy wilted. Her eyes had picked out the notebook and dictaphone, which were spilling out of her hand luggage like some disciplinary caution. The unwanted intrusion of reality and the reminder of her purpose jarred. Penny suddenly felt ashamed, even unprofessional, indulging an impulse on her first day at Whitehead. She had been warned. She had read the biography. This instant susceptibility annoyed her.

She took a deep breath, relaxed, and talked herself back into composure: Penny, you are doing your job, just assuming the role and exploring your emotions. It is all part of going under deep cover.

. She had already acquired enough evidence to place a massive question mark above the validity of the Whitehead Academy. She began to marvel at how it had ever managed to stay so discreet. It would be a delight detailing Miss Barbusse's rudeness and insistence on dressing the elite student populace like fifties movie stars. The dean's comments had hurt and Penny still smarted from the humiliation, unsure whether she hated or admired the woman.

Miss Barbusse's Academy, however, astonished her. She could not completely assuage the tingles of excitement exploding in her stomach: the prospect of a bizarre adventure, in such a remote Cornish setting, aroused her journalistic instincts. She imagined her investigative feature headlined on the cover of *Inquisitor* magazine, even allowing her ambitions to soar towards book and film rights. She considered herself lucky. Besides her colleague Sebastian, who had failed to return from Whitehead, she had been the first investigative reporter with access to Miss Barbusse's mythic Academy. It had cost the *Inquisitor* ten thousand pounds for one short ten-day term and six months of developing her fake Polycorp alibi.

Penny crossed her slippery thighs and looked down at her freshly painted fingernails. She smiled to reassure herself and acknowledged the need to play the part like a skilled actress.

She picked up her dictaphone and began whispering her priorities into the little whirring machine:

'Discover the Academy's secret of producing the world's top executive class. Detail any irregularities in teaching methods, and investigate alleged use of corporal punishment. Find the whereabouts of Sebastian. Is Miss Barbusse the notorious author of *The Deviants*?'

The sound of two male voices snapped her concentration. Penny jumped up and tried to approach the window, immediately loosing balance on her new heels and falling on to the Persian rug. She tried to kick off the heels but they clung to her feet like manacles.

'Damn it!' she whispered through gritted teeth. The outfit was going to be a big restriction: how was she going to sneak around in extreme heels and directoire corsetry.

The men laughed below her first-floor window and Penny rose to her knees and crawled forward on all fours to peer over the window ledge.

She inhaled sharply at the sight of two naked chests. The torsos were smooth with youth and exposed through floppy linen shirts open to the waist. The two young men wrestled with each other, play fighting over a cricket ball on the bright-green lawn below. Penny eyed the young blond, admiring his lean and tanned physique.

The cool summer breeze and blossom scents stirred memories. She remembered her undergraduate days, at Hereford University, and the rich pickings of young men eager for experience, when away from home for the first time in their lives. She had been wicked: manipulating, teasing, breaking hearts, and Penny missed those games and opportunities. Three years of unsociable hours, labouring on the *Inquisitor* gossip column, had left her with a sad parody of her former social life.

Another voice, this one female, Germanic and simmering with rage, killed the boys' game. It erupted from a ground-floor room: 'Louts! That is hardly the behaviour befitting grown men. You have been here for two days. Have you learnt nothing? To my room immediately!'

The two young men looked at each other, anxiety spreading across each handsome face. The blond tried to make amends; 'Forgive us, Doctor Kloster, we were on our way to the showers –'

The harsh Prussian voice interrupted the panicking blond: 'I will give you two something that will make you damn well skip to the showers!'

Penny frowned with disbelief. The lads must have been in their early twenties, probably Oxbridge high-flyers with a merchant bank picking up the tab for their training. The furious woman below had spoken to the students as if they had been nothing more than errant public-school boys. Penny was incredulous – there would have been a riot at Hereford University if a lecturer had even raised his voice.

As the boys disappeared from view, she heard one of them giggle.

Penny rose to her feet and peered down through the open window, just catching sight of a delicate hand resting on the window ledge with its lacquered fingernails tapping impatiently.

Within minutes Penny had frozen to the spot.

The sound was unmistakable: an open palm meeting a bare backside with some vigour. The swish and smack drifted from the open window below.

Penny gulped with fear – they beat the students! The thought raced through her frantic mind. She wanted to tear the new clothes off and rush for her car; she had heard enough.

A groan of pleasure forced her to drop her suitcase.

She tiptoed back to the window and leant out.

Following a quick succession of blows, the moan rose again as if the young man were lost to his arousal. Penny's eyes widened. Flight was still an option. The flogging, her clothes, the way she had felt, all struck her as sinister, even perverse. But the story. What a story! No more hearsay from the London scene; she had the scoop of the century unfolding before her. Her mind spun through the depraved possibilities. The Fleet Street rumours concerning the unorthodox methods applied to the exclusive students could be true.

If only she were able to peek into the room below. She thought of the bare tight buttocks, the cricket whites ruffled around the ankles, the other boy fretting and about to take his turn.

Penny's curiosity propelled her from the room in her stocking-clad feet. She carried her high heels in one hand and stuffed a slim-line camera inside her blouse.

She crept through the oaken hall and slipped down the marbled steps to the palatial reception.

Penny held her breath and felt her heart hammering beneath her tightly secured breasts as she made a cautious approach to the window beneath her room.

The sounds of the spanking grew louder, cracking through the still summer air. Penny inched her face around the corner of the window frame. Her hand instinctively rose to her pretty oval mouth in shock.

The blond youth's backside was beetroot red.

He clung to the back of a leather-bound armchair, peering behind him at the svelte punisher as her long hand rose and fell in a quick succession of blows. The stainless-steel heels on her stilettos seemed cruel and unnecessarily high, even dagger-like. Thin black seams ran up the back of the doctor's shapely calves and her dark shiny hair had been razored into an immaculate bob. An elegant black dress, tight fitting and just off the knee, completed the dark academic's outfit. It struck Penny that she was dressed to kill and probably could.

Penny looked at the other, darker-skinned, man, possibly a foreign candidate. He eyed his colleague's plight with glee, wetting his lips and massaging his bulging groin. Penny watched his sinewy fingers unbelt his baggy white slacks. She drew in her breath sharply as his erection sprang into view – the head of his cock already beaded with pre-come.

Penny slipped her right hand up and across her tingling nipples. She stopped herself with the thought that she should not delight in the punishment ritual.

The lecturer paused for breath. She raised one of her long legs, allowing the hemline of her skirt to slide up her shiny thigh, before pushing the blond man off the chair with her spiteful heel.

Her tone was sharp and demanding. 'When will you learn, Rupert! Sometimes I suspect you enjoy the discipline. Be careful, my boy. Have you ever wondered why they exiled me from Berlin?'

9

She eyed the swarthy man disdainfully. He released his quivering erection and attempted a weak smile.

'I do not recall giving you permission to bare your wretched cock!' the doctor spat out, before her voice changed tack, descending to a cruel whisper. 'Did you think that I would grant a favour? Allow you to touch my silkies or enter my delicious pussy? I have no use for your rigid vanity today, my boy. A far more worthy disciple will enjoy my insatiable appetites. You are little more than a badly behaved dog. On your knees, boy, and clean my shoes with your tongue.'

The man hesitated, looking to his cowering friend for support.

'I will not repeat myself!' the woman screamed.

The dark youth fell to his hands and knees. The lecturer reclined on her desk and offered one high-heeled foot. The man crawled across to her, perspiration beading his forehead. Penny shook her head with disbelief as he gently cupped the woman's ankle and began a slow and methodical lapping of her shoe. He kissed the pale tan sole affectionately and allowed one hand to slip on to her shimmering nylon stockings.

The lecturer bent down and slapped his hand off her leg with annoyance, before beginning to yawn, seemingly bored with his devotion. She pulled her skirt up to her stocking-tops and readjusted her shiny black PVC suspender straps. The young man's cock pulsed and strained eagerly as his soft brown eyes lifted to peer at the knickerless sex above him. The blond youth nursed his own erection while still wincing at the heat generated from his spanked buttocks.

The lecturer wrinkled her thin nose with disgust and sneered at the two hapless pupils. She pushed the dark youth away and beckoned to the blond with one long finger. He shuffled, hesitantly, towards her.

The doctor reached out a hand and began playing

with his thick ash-blond fringe, entwining her fingers in his hair. The hand suddenly clenched and she forced the whimpering blond to his knees.

She turned her head to smile at the swarthy youth, offering her other hand. Penny watched him gulp and take the hand with his own shaking paw. She yanked his arm downward, placing him in a sprawl before her glinting heels.

'Roberto. Lick my arse!' she demanded.

He hastily obeyed, crawling round behind her and raising her hemline. The lecturer unleashed a sinister laugh, throwing her beautiful face back. She stood with her long athletic legs wide apart. She dragged the blond youth round to her dark thatch and pushed her sex on to his gasping face. Her thin red lips broadened across white canines, showing her pleasure at the young tongues licking her from two angles.

'Yes. Oh, yes, that's good. Deeper, Rupert, tickle my insides. Eat me, Roberto.'

The woman's heavily painted eyelids closed as she sighed deeply.

Penny wanted to turn away, to hide her own shame at the voyeuristic thrill she was feeling, her repulsion combining with desire. Her mind screamed 'No!' but her own sex warmed and moistened. She was thrilled and hypnotised by the spectacle, her thrill-seeking at war with her better instincts.

Overcome by a light-headed sensation, Penny had to force herself away from the window and push her tingling body along the stone wall, taking deep breaths in between her staggers.

A bell chimed. The austere sound resonated across the wide acres of immaculate lawn and bounced off the manor's ancient walls. It was midday; Penny had ten minutes to compose herself and find the induction room.

* * *

11

Amongst the ten new female trainees in the lecture theatre, Penny sat next to a girl she recognised as Lucy Harrington. The beautiful debutante seemed to spend more time on the front cover of the *Inquisitor* than she did between the sheets of her own bed. Lucy Harrington was a notorious member of London's young and wealthy wolf pack, even distantly related to a prince. Penny's stomach tingled with excitement – her story was fattening far beyond her original expectations.

The lights dimmed in the lecture theatre and a video began to play. Her mouth fell, in time with a gasp from the other girls.

On the wide screen before them, a woman had been cuffed and chained between two vertical wooden posts. A shiny leather blindfold, stretching down from her smooth forehead to her little freckled nose, confined her long auburn hair. She had been stripped down to a pair of laddered stockings and her make-up was streaked with tears. The captive girl bucked and writhed between her tight fastenings as she was lashed from behind. She bit her bottom lip, her pretty features contorting into a combination of anguish and ecstasy.

Behind her, and against the shadowy stone walls, two smiling figures moved into view. They strutted across the damp flagstones in thigh-high boots. Each blonde dominatrix had unzipped her skin-tight rubber top to reveal an expanse of creamy cleavage. The peaks of leather police caps covered their eyes. They clenched square jaws to pout their glistening lips with a sultry determination. Beneath each tight rubber miniskirt, a long black appendage protruded, oiled and straining.

The two rubber-clad Amazons loosened the chains that creaked through pulleys on the apparatus, and gently bent the redheaded girl over. One dominatrix took up position behind the captive. She gripped her black dildo with one shiny hand, which was gloved in

PVC to her elbow, and tickled the bound girl's soft white buttocks with the tip of the false cock.

The captive quivered, her small mouth pursed. She shook her head from side to side, whispering barely audibly. She hissed the word 'Yes' into the dungeon air. The dominatrix behind smiled and pushed her false cock between the girl's buttocks, nudging it against the tiny puckered rosebud of her anus before sliding it into the slippery vagina. The captive moaned and pushed backward with her tiny hips, greedily consuming the phallic intrusion. Her tormentor slipped it back slightly, frustrating the girl's desperate need for deep penetration. •

The second dominatrix moved round to partially obscure the chained girl. She bent down and lovingly sucked the captive's hard pink nipples before offering her own sinister black cock to the smeared and panting mouth. The bound girl devoured the rigid morsel, slipping her parted lips up and down the shaft.

The pumping from behind grew in intensity – the hips of the first dominatrix banging on and off the captive's quivering behind. She moved the captive's feet further apart with the pointed toes of her thigh-high boots and clutched the girl's small waist, purchasing a grip for a harder lunge.

The image on the screen froze. The silhouette of Miss Barbusse appeared against the backdrop. 'Submission leads to power! Know your enemy. Watch their arrogance and confidence from afar, accept the reprimands and lashes, feign subservience. You will learn more on your hands and knees than you will with a head-on attack!'

Miss Barbusse stepped back from the screen, assuming her position beside the wooden podium. She nodded to the projectionist to continue.

The film sped through a quickly cut rollercoaster of erotic images: beautiful feminine ankles above shiny high heels, soft rounded buttocks enhanced by taut suspenders that ran down white thighs and grasped shimmering black stocking-tops, thin laces, on a black PVC dress, crisscrossed a tightly trussed pair of firm breasts, thickly painted lips drank from wine glasses before sliding up and down anonymous erections. The collage spun and rolled across tight knee-length boots and pretty painted toenails. The film slowed down to reveal the image of a middle-aged man as he crawled on all fours with a silver ashtray strapped to his face. A disinterested woman, beautiful and insolent, sat on a stool before him. She moved her high-heeled foot slowly, before nonchalantly flicking her cigarette ash on to the man's mouthpiece. The film paused on her cold smiling face.

Miss Barbusse appeared before the screen again to address her novices. 'At Whitehead you will discover the subtle techniques of elegance and the speeding train of total seduction. You will discover a will to power. Your new purpose will lead to success in the boardroom and bedroom, the frontlines for the new millennium. Your God-given graces will lead the mighty into blind alleys of complete adoration.'

The film restarted, revealing a line of girls of all shapes and sizes, dressed in an identical Whitehead manner, walking in step. Their Cuban heels clicked out an intoxicating rhythm.

The scene changed, revealing the same girls standing to attention before black leather chairs. The haughty Doctor Kloster stood with her back to the camera, her beautiful pale body finely tattooed around the shoulders, and naked except for the shiny stiletto sandals on her long feet. She clapped her cold white hands and the girls eased down into the waiting chairs, flicking their skirts up quickly and provocatively, revealing white thigh amidst rustling black undergarments. Doctor Kloster clapped her hands twice more and each pupil crossed her legs slowly, sliding one stockinged calf across her shiny knee.

Miss Barbusse gripped the oak podium with both hands and stared down at her new female trainees. 'You will taste subservience before rising to the heights of excellence. Failure is not an option. When you leave Whitehead, the men who sent you here will quake and squirm. Woe betide he who dares to underestimate you!'

The film stopped on an image of a naked Cathérine Deneuve smoking a French cigarette. Her heavily lidded eyes lowered seductively and her mouth parted.

The new arrivals slipped and struggled, on their unfamiliar heels, towards the grand dining room for the first evening meal. The petite American girl behind Penny dabbed her blue eyes and sniffed. 'There must be some kind of mistake. Is this some crazy European thing? They told me this place was going to complete my education. I cannot believe my aunt sent me here. I'm going to phone the embassy after dinner!'

A tall raven-haired girl, a natural on her heels, laughed before answering the sobbing American. 'Forget it, haven't you read the handbook? No phone privileges. Whitehead is in complete isolation. You are here for the duration and I wouldn't even think of rocking the boat.'

The small blonde from across the Atlantic gasped. 'It is illegal, surely! What kind of government would allow such a . . . such a prison? I have rights.'

The raven-haired girl shook her head with disbelief, seemingly incredulous of the American's naivety, as she replied, 'Half of the politicians in England have been students here, most of the army's top brass and a couple of Republican senators too. Didn't your aunt tell you anything? I know there is a secrecy clause, but didn't she offer so much as a hint?'

The American sobbed through her answer: 'No, she

came here in the seventies. She told me I would have the time of my life.'

Penny's confidence soared at the prospect of so much material. 'What's your name?' Penny asked the red-eyed American.

She sniffed as she replied, 'Amber. I'm from New York. My aunt's company wants me to manage a new department store. What's yours?'

'Penny Chambers. I work for the Polycorp entertainment group, in creative development –'

The sight of the dining room stopped Penny's introduction.

The oak-panelled hall opened out before her as she passed under a red-brick archway. Two long tables covered in thick lilac tablecloths and candelabras filled the centre of the vast refectory. The male students were already seated on the second banqueting table, their young bodies shifting uncomfortably before the silver and crystal finery. A great fire raged in the hearth and the two blonde dominatrices, from the introductory film, stalked between the tables. They had dressed in stylish leather waitress outfits, and appeared gigantic in their fishnets and thigh-high boots. As they ladled hot soup into bowls, Penny heard them ordering the slouchers to sit up straight.

At the head of both tables, raised on a small platform, Miss Barbusse sat with her staff. Penny's eyes caught Doctor Kloster's briefly. The severe Prussian's gaze swept up and down Penny's tightly corseted figure. Penny felt as though her stare had the ability to plunge itself inside her soul; the cold eyes seemed to scour her for vulnerability as if probing for an entrance. Penny blushed and took her seat beside Amber. She peeked back across at the lecturers' dais to check out the male tutor. He sat stiffly, gazing at each new girl with a brooding pair of slowly moving hazel eyes, as if to arrogantly survey and discard his new quarry. Penny

16

thought him handsome, brutally so, but found herself resenting his stare. She turned her head to guzzle some wine and deflect his attentions, but still sensed the smouldering eyes lingering upon her face.

Miss Barbusse rose elegantly from her chair and proposed a toast: 'I would like to wish the new intake a warm welcome to Whitehead.' She raised her sparkling crystal glass. 'To imagination, discipline and success.'

The girls followed the men's lead and lifted their glasses. Penny picked out Roberto and Rupert with her eyes, wondering if Rupert had a pillow to cushion his punished haunches.

The scent of hot food pulled her attention down to her meal, and Penny started on her asparagus soup. It was good, heartening and warm after the day's continual barrage of shock and surprise.

Penny wondered why Lucy Harrington was missing from the table. She made a little nervous small talk with her neighbours: a plump girl from a mining corporation and the quaking Amber. Neither could shed any light on the young heir's disappearance. No sooner had Penny started to relax, while devouring the delicious main course, than something brushed her leg beneath the table. She ignored it and continued to nonchalantly eat her meal.

The contact had not been accidental; a slippery leg was brushing up and down her own nylon-clad calf. The pressure was gentle and slowly moving, beginning at her ankle and pushing upwards to her knee. Penny gulped and panicked. She glanced at the girls across the table from her.

Her eyes picked out the striking raven-haired girl sitting immediately opposite, the confident young woman who had been amused by Amber's plight. The girl winked at Penny, her blue eyes glinting with mischief.

Penny ignored the insistent advance, adjusted her

whispering legs beneath the table and continued to eat, unsure of the depths of her current bewildering environment. The raven-haired lovely subtly removed her shoe beneath the table and Penny felt a stocking-clad foot slip between her knees, sliding upward to tickle her inner thigh. Penny coughed to hide her surprise.

It had been three years since Penny's clumsy and confusing fumble with her best friend, Janis, at the Hereford University Valedictory Ball. Penny had fought her curiosity before and since that incident, but was unable to completely eradicate the urges. She and Janis had both been in relationships with men at the time but had slipped away, both giggling on a champagne high, in their silk gowns. Beyond the gaze of the other drunken undergraduates, the farewell hug between two companions had quickly developed into a passionate kiss. In the dark, beneath the perfumed rose bushes, three years of mutual curiosity had suddenly blossomed between the best of friends. Penny had been unable to stop the passage of her trembling hands all over Janis's firm breasts. They had looked so tempting at the dance, tanned and swelling beneath the pink shoulderless gown. Janis had whimpered with pleasure when her large brown nipples had been teased into two rigid pebbles by Penny's feverish fingers and flicking tongue. It had been the far-off voice of Brad, Janis's fiancé, that had killed the spontaneous rapture. Janis refused, the following morning, to discuss the incident. She eventually faded away to the north of England, unable to deal with the disappointed and baffled Penny.

The same emotions surged and peaked inside Penny now, as the foot between her legs slipped about gently, reaching for her damp sex. She stared into her stroganoff and allowed her legs to part themselves as far as her tight skirt would allow. The girl's big toe found her tingling slit.

18

The raven-haired goddess spoke to Penny in a friendly manner, the tone of voice hovering between the sultry and tarty: 'Hi. My name's Amanda. I thought I had better introduce myself, especially as we are practically neighbours. I am just down the corridor and I saw you arrive. A girl needs a friend in a place like this.'

Penny struggled to look the girl in the face, but it proved easier to bite her bottom lip and close her eyes.

The foot continued to move expertly in the dark and secret place, beneath the table and her skirt. Penny pushed her tiny backside further down the wooden seat, wanting to impale herself on the long toes. She wanted to moan and kiss the girl's wide sensual mouth. Her composure began to wilt as her arousal peaked, and she covered her tightly shut eyes with one hand.

The foot was withdrawn and Penny's wet mouth released a small sigh, of relief as much as disappointment. Amanda held her stare and mouthed the word 'later' across the table.

Penny curled up on her bed with her notes lit by a porcelain bedside lamp. The warm sun had finally disappeared and it was time for the shadows and night scents to drift in through her open window. When a small envelope slid beneath her door, she stopped whispering her first impressions and observations into the tiny dictaphone and hid her equipment beneath the bed. As she approached the letter, Penny heard the sound of quickly retreating footsteps in the hall. Must be Amanda, she thought, disappointed that the girl had run away.

She opened the elegant linen envelope and pulled the sky-blue notepaper out.

Dear Penny
Whitehead is a very strange place. No doubt you are
aware of that after only one day. I could not, however,

*stop myself from noticing you at dinner. I am writing
because you intrigue me. If you are curious about a new
friend then meet me after tomorrow evening's eleven
o'clock curfew by the rhododendron bushes, beside the
tennis courts. I know fraternisation between the male
and female students is strictly forbidden, but do not be
frightened. In our first week, a friend and I have
already managed to bend several rules without
detection.*

   Affectionately yours
   Rupert

Her pulse sped up. The thought of sneaking around
to pursue an illicit midnight rendezvous made her skin
prickle with fear. Penny knew that arousing suspicion
could be fatal to her purpose.

Penny's eyes swept across the wide four-poster bed
and another hot flush seemed to rise up from her collar.
She thought of Rupert's tight chest. She found her
hands unconsciously tidying her hair.

It was almost too much to consider. After so long at
the coalface of the *Inquisitor*, Penny found herself in a
position she had only been able to fantasise about.
Which one? Rupert or Amanda? A man or a woman?
Both tempted her equally but the voice of sanity warned
against either.

She thought again of Rupert's slender boyish body
and obvious appetite for forbidden fruit. The thoughts
clashed with those of the striking Amanda; Penny
imagined the girl undressed, the tall athletic body
pressed against her own soft shape, the long hair and
even features close to her own mouth.

A quiet knock at her door roused Penny from her
frantic thoughts.

She unlocked the bedroom door, wincing at the sound
of the heavy bolt sliding back, and eased the creaking
door open to peer through the gap. Amanda smiled

back at her from the corridor, holding a bottle of wine in one hand and her high heels in the other. Penny noticed how the tall girl had re-applied her make-up and she could smell the lashings of perfume all over her pretty head. She invited her in.

'Hi, gorgeous, look what I swiped from the kitchen,' Amanda whispered, swinging the wine bottle about. 'These rooms are so beautiful. Don't you think?'

'I know,' Penny nervously replied. 'I want to transport all of this back to my flat when it's over. That is, if I survive the ordeal.'

Amanda's blue eyes dazzled her. Penny stared up at the lovely face, admiring the thick, dark eyebrows and bright-red lips – lips, she imagined, capable of a fierce and passionate touch.

Amanda giggled, pouring the wine, her retort gushing with an easy confidence: 'They don't scare me. They are smart, all right, with unusual methods, but I think we can learn a great deal here.'

Penny frowned. 'You don't honestly believe that?'

'Why not?' Amanda replied. 'I have a lot of natural ammunition, and I say that without immodesty. What is the harm of an enhancement? If it gets me to where I need to be, then so be it. Take the rough with the smooth and enjoy the view.'

'And where do you want to be?' Penny asked.

'Somewhere nice, with a glass of wine in my hand, retired at thirty-five, under a palm tree with someone hot. With a nice dick, of course.'

Penny smiled and said with something approaching relief in her voice, 'So you like guys too?'

'You bet, but why restrict yourself?' Amanda countered. 'I have never been insensitive to the charms of pretty girls either. It is as natural to me as enjoying a hunky guy. Oh, I'm sorry for being so blunt, it's just my way. You know, I see everything from two angles. That is why I am on the fast track at Hedonism

Couture: the leading buyer at twenty-four. I got a first in drama and physics. My right and left brain hemispheres combine effortlessly. Sex with guys and girls is just a wicked extension of my nature, another duality. I am even ambidextrous.'

Penny gaped at the girl's onslaught, but decided that she seemed harmless enough. She had to admit it: she liked Amanda; the girl excited her.

The pass Amanda had made at dinner and this late-night appearance made Penny think that she should clear the air. 'I am impressed, and it was nice at dinner, you know, the contact beneath our table. You just took me by surprise. I didn't know a woman could be so . . . forward. Not that I'm criticising you. I'm flattered. I am, though, a little shy with girls. Something happened once that ruined a friendship.'

Amanda strode across to Penny and offered her a glass of wine. Her long crimson nails brushed softly against Penny's delicate wrist and she seductively pushed a tiny pink tongue out of her wide mouth to lick her top lip. She leant forward, brushing her cheek against Penny's face before whispering in her ear, 'Life is no dress rehearsal. You have to seize every moment. And don't look so nervous, you are in good hands tonight, Penny Chambers.'

Amanda's softening eyes calmed Penny, and something gentle started to flutter about inside her stomach. She is younger than me, Penny thought, and yet her confidence and style make me think of wasted opportunities and too much time spent dithering over choices. Amanda just went for exactly what she wanted, dazzling her prey with her beauty and clever tongue.

She continued to saunter around Penny, devouring her body with those eyes and flirting shamelessly. 'I think you are simply delicious. So prim and smart in your tight skirt, I just had to make a pass at dinner. I wanted to eat you alive.'

Penny swallowed and closed her eyes after a mouthful of dry sparkling wine. She wanted to float away in a stream of Amanda's perfume and feel the girl's soft red lips all over her body. A warm sensation spread between Penny's legs. She wanted to start all over again, go back to the glorious place where Janis left her three years previously.

Penny emptied another glass of wine for courage, as she watched Amanda wander over to the bed. Amanda stroked the velvet canopy before slithering on to the mattress, smiling at Penny and offering her hand.

Penny's throat was dry. She was unable to speak or take the hand. Her girdle seemed to tighten around her soft belly and the neck of her blouse ruffled uncomfortably against her skin. She sat down on the thick goose-feather duvet, away from Amanda, at the other end of the four-poster.

Amanda shuffled across the mattress and whispered into Penny's ear, 'Close those pretty green eyes.'

Penny found herself automatically refusing. 'Er, I'd rather not.'

'Why?' Amanda quizzed.

'Things are moving a little too fast. It's the first night, and you know the rules. If we were caught . . .'

'We won't be. Just relax, I don't bite. That's better. Now close your eyes.'

Penny complied and shivered with expectation. She felt Amanda's soft lips gently kissing each of her closed eyelids. The hot mouth kissed its way down her snub nose and eventually found her slightly parted lips.

Amanda kissed her mouth tenderly. The sensation of shiny lipstick sliding between their eager mouths fired a bolt of lightning up Penny's spine. She found herself returning Amanda's kiss and her entire body seemed to be gripped by a wave of tremors.

The kiss grew more passionate. Amanda sucked at her panting mouth while sliding her slender arm round

Penny's back, pulling her close. Penny felt insignificant within the embrace of the tall long-limbed girl, relishing the sense of powerlessness and dependence before the confident raven-haired seductress. She kept her eyes tightly shut and listened to her heart pumping its fiery blood through her veins. Tingling sensations spread across her skin and she desperately wanted to be free of her clinging garments, to have them unwrapped by Amanda's long fingers. 'Undress me, please,' she panted with her eyes still tightly shut, unable to hold back any longer.

She heard Amanda softly moan and quick fingers began unbuttoning her flimsy blouse. Penny opened her eyes to see Amanda's face light up at the sight of her neatly trussed breasts, her eyes completely transfixed by the soft swell of Penny's buxom cleavage as the white mounds rose and fell, in time with her quick breaths, over the half-cups of her black satin brassiere.

Amanda unclipped the tight garment, threading the thin black straps down Penny's compliant arms. Penny watched the girl's growing excitement, the dreamy look in those blue eyes and the quivering lips.

She felt Amanda's breath across her pale throat and whimpered with excitement as Amanda slid on to her knees before the bed.

Amanda moaned, whispering huskily, 'Ooh, you little fox, I thought it would take a week to seduce you.' Amanda's hot tongue began lapping at Penny's large pink nipples, coaxing them up and out, making them rigid as they glistened with saliva. Suddenly she bit at them. The delicate pain was exquisite to Penny. It was so strange and yet undeniably erotic watching another woman's mouth busy on her naked breasts.

Amanda caressed and massaged Penny's small waist with her strong fingers as her mouth fed: lashing, scooping and squeezing the warm flesh. Penny reclined on the wide and luxuriously soft bed, shaking her blonde hair free from the grips and pins. She felt it fall in a shiny torrent, down and across her naked shoulders. The sight of her relaxing seeming to increase Amanda's desire.

Amanda gripped Penny's taut little backside, pulling her off the bed and back on to her high-heeled feet. She slipped her arms around Penny's narrow hips, reaching behind her to find the clasp and zipper on the black hobble skirt.

Amanda spoke to her between gritted teeth: 'I want your little pussy. I need your little wet pussy on my face.'

Penny moaned loudly, tottering, unable to remove her wide eyes from Amanda's flushed and determined face. The girl yanked her skirt down to her shapely ankles and slid her open-palmed hands up and down Penny's seamed nylons, forcing the delicate stockings to swish and glide over Penny's shaved skin.

Amanda pressed her face against Penny's sex and inhaled before whispering up to her, 'I do like to take a girl in her undies, but I can't get my tongue inside your pussy with this girdle in the way.'

Amanda unclipped Penny's nylons and rolled them down into a dark ruffle around her ankles. She forced the girdle and tiny panties down next, slipping them over Penny's heels in one swift movement.

Penny gasped at Amanda's frenzy of passion. She stared down between her sticky breasts and watched the shock of raven hair nestle between her naked goose-pimpling thighs. She lost her balance as Amanda's hot mouth engulfed her sex, her tongue lapping at her clit. Amanda reached up and steadied her with strong and supple hands, gripping her narrow white waist with glinting crimson talons. The dark-haired girl's wet mouth sucked and nibbled in the blonde bush, frantic and thorough in its desire for soft female fruit. Penny adored the little hot thrills and spasms raging through her, coaxed forth by Amanda's circling tongue and hard teeth.

Penny needed to be utterly consumed by Amanda's passion; she wanted to writhe and thrash on the bed under that delightful mouth. She slithered backward out of Amanda's tight clutches and on to the mattress, catching sight of herself in the mirror – her face had flushed, and glistening trails of lipstick had been smeared wantonly across her wet mouth and little white teeth. The afternoon's glorious self-indulgent feeling throbbed through Penny with a new force.

Penny watched Amanda slide out of her hobble skirt, gasping at the sight of her lover's long stocking-clad legs. They seemed to never end. Amanda tore off her blouse and unhooked her bra, allowing a pair of small but firm breasts to quiver into freedom. She whipped her corsetry, nylons and shoes off eagerly, before swaying back to the love-nest, naked and flushed. The soft hair and smooth face was soon nuzzling back between Penny's thighs.

Penny quivered and shook on the bed. She stretched out her arms and raked the bedclothes with her shiny nails, shuddering, already feeling the first tremors of orgasm. She had waited for so long, yearning for another girl to make a pass and initiate this forbidden love. Within minutes, Amanda's exquisite mouth and teeth, busy on her frustrated and neglected sex, pushed her into a rhapsody of pleasure.

Amanda pleaded with her, 'Come on, Penny! Come! Let go! You know you want to.'

Penny groaned, while shivers wracked her body. She felt dizzy, almost passing in and out of consciousness, before climaxing with an intensity she had not experienced in years.

Amanda continued to suck and lap at her wet sex, easing her through the intense peak.

'Amanda, that is so beautiful. I want to taste you too'.

Amanda straddled Penny's face, and sank her trimmed black bush on to Penny's open mouth. With the scent of Amanda's moist sex in her nose and the weight of her lover's groin on her face, Penny found herself surging towards another orgasm.

She found Amanda's swollen clit and lashed it repeatedly with the tip of her tongue, servicing the more experienced sex, watching Amanda's soft backside buck and writhe above her. She relished the taste of Amanda's clean intimacy, as soft as a delicate sweetmeat in her mouth. She heard Amanda groaning with ecstasy and watched her reach out for something beside the bed. The scrabbling hand returned clasping the neck of a jet-black rubber dildo.

'Want to get fucked, Penny?' Amanda asked.

Penny groaned, too far gone to be surprised, and tore at the bed sheets with her nails, shouting, 'Yes!'

Within seconds, the thick implement that Amanda had concealed inside her skirt was slipping into her soft insides.

Penny moaned from the sensation of the rubber penis's solidity gently slipping in and out of her sensitised slit. Amanda must have angled the dildo well, because Penny could feel it in the farthest reaches of her sex, forcing her entire frame to peak and surge with delight. Amanda's sticky mouth worked around the slippery toy, sucking on Penny's stretched clit.

The combination of an attentive mouth and the pumping cock drove Penny into a wriggling frenzy. She thought of Amanda tasting the warm honey seeping out of her. Penny started to shout with excitement, swept away by her second orgasmic peak: 'Fuck me! Put it in to me! Just fuck me!'

Her lapping mouth and trashy language must have swept Amanda to a similar high. She heard Amanda sobbing as a climax raged through her stretched body. The rubber dildo slipped out of Penny's sex and fell to

27

the rug. She saw Amanda's hands gripping the bed linen and heard her lover croaking rhythmically in time with every orgasmic pulse that fired through her body.

Amanda collapsed around Penny. She sobbed quietly and gripped Penny's knees. When her face finally turned towards Penny, the dark-blue eyes were damp with tears.

Penny smiled down at her tousle-headed lover – after so many years of denial and timidity, a secret desire had at last been satiated between another girl's warm thighs. She made herself comfortable in a nest of cool pillows, feeling as if a great knot had been untied inside her.

Amanda followed her up the mattress and picked up one of Penny's feet. She kissed the high-heeled shoe and removed it, before peeling the ruffled stocking off the foot.

'You seem fairly knowledgeable about the Academy,' Penny said, as Amanda's insatiable mouth busied itself on her toes.

'I like the place, it suits me,' she replied, removing Penny's toes from her smeared mouth. 'I know that after only one day. We have danger and pleasure mingling freely and exquisitely, nice clothes, good pussy, new experiences.'

Penny shook her head and laughed. 'But what do you make of Barbusse? I mean, where is that bitch coming from?'

Amanda peered down at her thoughtfully, casting her gaze through and beyond Penny's questioning face. She spoke after several seconds of contemplation: 'I can only go on the rumours, you know, the stuff I heard at work. This place is tight, hardly any information seeps out, but I heard that she was some kind of famous French society girl in the sixties or seventies. I don't really know anything else. But just think, after a term here they put you at the top of the class but have so much smut on you it guarantees discretion on your behalf. It's really clever, Barbusse gives but Barbusse can take away. Rumours are the only thing you have left.'

Penny knew it would be tough grasping any real evidence on the Academy's proprietor beyond hearsay. She wondered what would happen if a crack appeared in her Polycorp alibi.

'Don't let her bother you,' Amanda whispered, continuing to caress Penny's smooth thighs.

'Unless, that is, you want her to,' she added with a wicked smile, winking at Penny's baffled expression before continuing to suck on her little hot toes.

Two

The tight leather corset, beneath her elegant outer coverings, never failed to secretly thrill Miss Barbusse. Sabrina had been busy for half an hour that morning lacing her mistress into the tailor-made garment. The attentive handmaiden had stood behind Miss Barbusse, with one knee in the small of her back, pulling at the fine laces to thread her mistress into the constricting device. Satin panties, sheer flesh-coloured nylons from Paris, and a mummifying dress completed her formal Academy outfit. It was the start of a new term and a fresh gathering of nervous pupils awaited her.

The gravel path crunched beneath the new leather soles of the dean's patent mirror heels. Her tight, black, hobble dress restricted the length of her dainty steps on the narrow path as she went over to the second, eighteenth-century building on the Whitehead estate. It ran parallel to the main manor and contained the male quarters, old ballroom and utility rooms, all palisaded by bright-green lawns and towering oaks.

Doctor Kloster joined her on the path. The elegant doctor nodded to Miss Barbusse over her black-rimmed pince-nez. 'Good morning, dean.'

'Good morning, my friend,' Miss Barbusse replied, staring straight ahead, lost in thought.

'You are a little pensive this morning?' the doctor asked.

'Yes, my dear. There is something about the new intake that concerns me. I sense unruly elements.'

'Oh. There will be trouble, you think?'

'My intuition warns me against that pretty young Penny Chambers. And the tall girl, Amanda, is far too self-assured.'

'Yes, I too am aware of Amanda's attitude, but she excites my interest for a different reason. The haughty madam did not sleep in her room last night, I was informed by our source. I must acquaint myself with the girl.'

Miss Barbusse smiled at her ally, lowering her voice to reply: 'Do as you see fit, good doctor. I too find myself drawn to a specific pupil. I see potential in Lucy Harrington.'

The doctor's eyes narrowed 'She has inherited a fortune.'

'It is not her wealth that interests me. It is something far more noble than money I see at stake,' Miss Barbusse answered, her cold face suddenly illumined by a flush of excitement.

'She is unruly and has been exposed by the press at every turn,' Doctor Kloster warned.

'Yes, I am aware of her past,' Miss Barbusse replied. 'But her breeding is so captivating. Have you not observed her sense of elegance? And her history suggests a taste for debauchery. But what if the two can combine? Her disapproving guardian warned me of the girl's mischief and wayward habits, which only served to entice me further.'

Doctor Kloster smiled at her dean and whispered, 'You see yourself in the girl?'

'Yes, my astute friend. She has ripped hearts from the most eligible bachelors and spike-heeled her adversaries. I recognise the cold intelligence behind her blue eyes. I sense her desire for the peaks of endurance, where exquisite pain converses with pleasure. I hope to show her the twilight world where most fear to even take a glimpse.'

31

'Can she be tamed? Will she understand?' the doctor queried, with concern furrowing her pale brow.

'She is worth the risk. Did you notice her reaction during the introductory film? She bit her bottom lip with curiosity while her fellow pupils just gaped.'

'But she missed the first meal? Why did you prevent me from sending the twins to seek her out?'

'I had my reasons.'

Lucy's absence from the first meal had not surprised the dean. Miss Barbusse imagined the slender beauty alone in her room while the others ate. Had her hands been busy between her legs with something long and slippery? There had been a specific purpose behind the planting of an onyx dildo in Lucy Harrington's quarters.

'Has she the potential to be a chosen one?' the doctor pressed, with one eyebrow raised.

'We shall see. Maybe the girl will awake to a new vocation here, as you did, my friend, so many years ago. I can only hope she has your discipline.'

'That is the test, my dean. Will she disown everything? Does she have the strength to avoid *that* place?' the doctor added.

Miss Barbusse let her gaze drift over to the distant gamekeeper's cottage. She hoped that Lucy Harrington was made of sterner stuff, that she would delight in and yet shun the imprisonment of the gimps.

Miss Barbusse took the women's first lesson herself. She glided through the ornamented ballroom alongside the column of teetering blindfold girls, pleased that the new batch of perfumed femininity had progressed from the twisted-ankle stage, most of them having learnt to tread warily in a straight line on their ultra-high Cuban heels. In the afternoon session she would teach them how to sway their soft hips; impart instruction on how to glide through a crowded restaurant and polished hotel lobby, or how to march to a seat in a pressured boardroom or approach a new client in an airport.

Penny and Amanda lagged behind the others, giggling. Miss Barbusse frowned at their misbehaviour, noticing the immediate gulf between their lack of agility and Lucy Harrington's effortless mince across the gleaming dance floor. A session with Doctor Kloster might be due, even at such an early stage in the term. That might, she mused, remedy their lack of focus.

'Penny and Amanda! Stop right there!'

The sound of her heels echoed up to the vaulted ceiling as Miss Barbusse approached the girls to gently remove their blindfolds. Her stern and beautiful face greeted their eyes, swiping the grins off both faces in an instant. The dean placed a small red card in each of the girls' hands. It looked like an invitation, but the blood-red colour of the stiff laminated paper created several lines on each brow.

'Go immediately to Doctor Kloster's study and wait for her there. You will find her room on the ground floor of the main manor house. It is better in the long term if an undisciplined approach is curtailed at the start of your training.'

She watched both stunning faces quiver with apprehension before they exited the hall. Miss Barbusse promptly turned to face the other astounded girls and ordered them to take seats around the dance floor's perimeter.

'Now, ladies, I would like you all to observe Miss Harrington and to use her as an example. She is a natural on five-inch heels and her posture is an aesthetic delight. Observe the angle of her chin and the baring of her delicate neck, see the dainty steps and delightful sway of her hips. Remember, size and weight are irrelevant, it is your deportment and the execution of your technique that will count.'

Miss Barbusse approached the sullen Lucy

Harrington, who was seemingly unmoved by her tutor's flattery. Miss Barbusse knelt down behind the young girl and straightened the seam running down the rear of her shapely left leg. She traced two fingers up Lucy's inner calf, gently brushing the toned muscle beneath the clinging nylon of her stocking. She allowed her hand to caress Lucy's pert behind as it travelled up to the girl's supple lower back. Lucy's straight spine trembled beneath her white blouse.

Miss Barbusse spoke quietly to the girl, her breath teasing the shiny blonde hair concealing the girl's right ear. 'I would like to invite you to my rooms this evening after dinner. Will you come?'

Lucy nodded, and Miss Barbusse hesitated by the girl long enough to see her beautiful eyelids flutter, detecting a new light dancing inside her star pupil's gemstone eyes.

'This will be fun,' Penny heard Amanda whisper.

Penny trembled behind Amanda's confident strut, their heels clattering through the oak-panelled corridor that led to the doctor's study. Penny's throat tightened and anxiety fluttered deep inside her as she remembered Rupert and Roberto reduced to slaves in that very room, receiving strict lashes from a quickly whipping hand. If only she had behaved herself. A fit of giggles had consumed Amanda and quickly spread across to Penny during their very first lesson with Miss Barbusse. Penny had to assure herself, despite her fears, that this was an ideal opportunity to learn a great deal more about the mysterious German doctor.

'What will she do to us?' Penny asked Amanda with a quivering voice.

'Oh, six of the best, I should imagine,' she replied, calmly smoking, and smiled over her shoulder.

'Will it hurt?' Penny queried, incredulous of Amanda's calm.

'A little bit, but don't worry, you will probably get a kick out of it.'

'What! My parents never even spanked me,' Penny exclaimed, as they stood outside the ominous door with the shiny brass plaque engraved with Doctor Kloster's title.

Amanda seemed genuinely excited. 'Oh, come on, it is so kinky. It was a regular occurrence for me at boarding school. I was touching my toes at least twice a week, in front of the gorgeous history master, of course. You soon develop a taste for it. But discipline from a woman? Now that is new for me. They say a woman is more thorough, less tolerant.'

Penny felt her stomach loop as Amanda calmly reached forward to knock on Doctor Kloster's door.

'Enter!' a voice commanded from within.

With a pallid face, Penny looked at Amanda's serene and sultry pout. Amanda winked before turning the brass door knob and waltzing into the study. Penny had no choice but to follow, gulping, with her face lowered.

When Penny looked up, the doctor greeted her pale face with a smile. There was, however, little warmth in the smile: the teeth were strong and glinting, bright and wolflike between dark crimson lips. Her blue eyes narrowed: two stone-cold pools shrouded by long black eyelashes and delicate shades of deep-purple eyeshadow.

The sunlight fell through the wide bay window behind the doctor's desk, shining through her jet-black bob and fading the Spartan wooden interior of the study. Penny's flitting eyes stole a glance at the doctor's leather-bound books, which were stacked neatly in a glass-panelled book case. Three titles seemed to almost shout back at Penny: *An Anatomy of Discipline*, *Professor Neretva's Almanac of Correction* and *A Treatise on Disobedience*.

Penny winced and felt a little faint, her body shuddering beside the statuesque Amanda, who stood tall with her chin and breasts pushed out in defiance.

Kloster spoke, cracking the silence: 'Well, let me guess, a red-card offence on your second day. This is not so unusual, not for two pretty headstrong girls adjusting to the regime at Whitehead. Let me think, the pretty little blonde is Penny and our giantess is Amanda. Amanda did not sleep in her bed last night: the sheets were undisturbed. The walls at this Academy have eyes, my dears. I wonder where she slept.'

Penny heard Amanda gasp. It was the first time she had seen her friend's confidence shaken.

The doctor seemed to be enjoying their discomfort. 'But you are both so well turned out, positively adorable in your heels and hose. Miss Barbusse, though, will stand for little nonsense and silliness amongst her girls. I am surprised she did not want to deal with you personally. Still, I am overjoyed with her referral.

'Penny, I would like you to take a seat in the corner. From the look on your face, you may have been punished enough. But you, Amanda, my leggy beauty, I believe you are the bad influence. I knew you were going to be a handful as soon as I saw you yesterday.'

The doctor's expression suddenly changed; a sheet of ice appeared to have formed behind her refined bone-structure, freezing her natural beauty into a haunting glare. Shivers rippled up and down Penny's spine and she took a seat, behind Amanda's back, in the corner closest to the door.

The doctor rose to her full height and strode round her desk. She stood before Amanda, moving her handsome face within an inch of the girl's nose. 'Dearest Amanda. Will this be difficult? Will I need restraints? Or do you wish to comply with the corrective treatment? I can assure you it will be swift and clinical.'

Penny observed a shudder beneath Amanda's sheer blouse as she replied, 'Good, doctor. I wish to comply with whatever you have in mind.'

Penny gasped at her new friend's tone of voice: there

36

was something haughty and challenging on the edge of her words.

Doctor Kloster continued to stare into Amanda's eyes and Penny began to wonder about the expression on her friend's face; something in it must have appealed to the doctor: Kloster's eyes had flashed wide open with surprise. Her cold face thawed into a broad flush of excitement.

Doctor Kloster stretched her arms behind her back and Penny heard a zipper open. Kloster is stripping for action, she thought with a mixture of dread and excitement. The doctor allowed gravity to aid the fall of her thin black dress down to her leather-hugged ankles.

Penny gasped at the sight of the doctor's slender body, her eyes immediately drawn to the fine, black, boot-lace-thin tattoos circling around either shoulder. Her tiny waist had been pulled into a tight hour-glass shape by a shiny black PVC corset, which was buckled by steel on one side. Her breasts seemed unusually heavy: the buxom white flesh pushed upward and bulged over the top of her corset.

Penny sensed Amanda's surprise and delight; she watched her shoulders tremble while her pretty head lowered to survey the doctor's outfit.

'Disrobe!' the doctor ordered, staring at the side of Amanda's head.

Amanda hastily unbuttoned her blouse and unzipped her hobble skirt.

It was the doctor's turn to stare, her eyes lingering on Amanda's pert half-cupped breasts before sweeping down her long and shimmering nylon-clad legs. Doctor Kloster walked around Amanda slowly, inches from the girl's body, her long legs rippling with a dancer's muscle-tone beneath her own sheer black stockings. Her eight suspender clasps, four to each leg, were gold and shone with a dull lustre in the morning sunlight, while the tight knee-length leather boots gripped her shapely calves and long feet in a neat but severe manner.

Penny imagined the doctor's cool breath brushing against Amanda's suddenly naked shoulders and she shivered, a curious feeling seeping through her body, moistening her sex beneath the girdle and satin panties. Penny was feeling almost envious and started to imagine herself stripping before the haughty doctor, offering her own young body to the strict and handsome tutor, impressing the severe woman with her own soft curves.

She watched the doctor take a seat in the leather armchair before Amanda; the same item of furniture that Rupert had clung on to for support. Doctor Kloster pulled her shapely tight-booted ankles together and hissed at Amanda, 'Lie across my knees, girl!'

Amanda teetered over in her underwear and heels. She stood on one side of Kloster's chair before elegantly bending over the doctor's long legs and placing her hands on the floor. Amanda's body created a beautiful arch: her high-heeled feet on one side, her long painted fingernails sustaining the weight of her upper body on the other. Amanda, as if on cue, let her stomach fall gently on to Kloster's shiny thighs, her thick raven hair falling down to her elbows and obscuring her face from Penny.

Doctor Kloster smiled wickedly and placed one hand on Amanda's curvaceous bottom, smoothing the palm over the sheer girdle fabric. Her long taloned fingers moved in slowly narrowing circles until the hand stopped, marking the spot.

Doctor Kloster withdrew her hand, pulling it at least a foot from Amanda's tempting backside. Penny tingled with anticipation and noticed Amanda's entire body trembling from some private thrill.

The first blow fell in a flash of white forearm and crimson nail polish. The muffled slap startled Penny, but Amanda only moaned, raising her pretty ankles off the floor and wiggling her backside for more.

Doctor Kloster sucked the warm air in through her

gritted teeth and her cold eyes flashed with an acetylene flame. The doctor began lashing her hand down quickly and methodically, vigorously spanking Amanda's soft bottom again and again. Penny jumped at every slap; the sound echoed off the study walls and landed inside her like sparks from a beautiful firework.

Penny slipped her right hand inside her white blouse and began massaging her hard pink nipples: she had to do something to ease the hot urges shooting from her sex. Amanda groaned more deeply, still trying to raise her bottom off the doctor's slippery legs to meet the hard lashing hand.

'Little slut! Where did you sleep last night?' the doctor hissed.

Amanda squealed and shook her head, refusing to answer the doctor. She tossed her silken hair about and wiggled her hips, deliberately baiting the punisher.

Penny winced at the sound of a heavier slap as Kloster's arm descended from a full stretch.

'Were you sucking a cock?' the doctor screamed through a maelstrom of lust and anger. 'Maybe you were eating that pretty blonde's pussy! Which one? Tell me, girl! I demand to know!'

'Pussy,' Amanda whispered.

'Louder!' the doctor shrieked, slapping her again.

'Pussy! I had my mouth between a girl's legs.'

Doctor Kloster closed her blue eyes and whimpered with pleasure before issuing her next command. 'Bend over my desk! Your misbehaviour demands more than a slap. It requires a determined and scientific re-education.'

Amanda skipped over to the doctor's desk to bend her body at a right angle, with her high-heeled feet wide apart and long arms stretched across the mahogany expanse. Kloster raced to a dark cupboard behind her desk and swung the panelled doors wide open. Penny shuddered at the sight of so many canes, paddles and cuffs. Kloster dipped her ghostly hands into the dark confines of the cupboard and produced a thick black implement, a series of silver buckles and leather straps falling from it like oily tentacles. Penny recognised the sinister device from the introductory film and the memory ignited a violent throbbing in her sex.

The doctor held the strap-on penis up to the light and admired its length and wide diameter before turning to face Penny. Penny suddenly felt ashamed playing with her breasts as her friend received a spanking. The doctor spoke to her as if in a daze: 'Leave those warm puppies alone and strap me into this.'

Penny shuffled across the office, feeling more light-headed from her arousal as each tense second passed. She slipped the straps around Doctor Kloster's tightly corseted hips and secured the implement tightly in place. She then sank to her knees inches away from the doctor's legs, able to smell the leather of her tight boots, wanting a good view of the hard black tool widening the sex that her own mouth had ravaged the night before. Now she knew how Roberto had felt as Rupert received the doctor's wrath, how he had been unable to leave his desperate cock alone when confronted with such a shocking display.

The doctor began her careful preparations, bending over to unclasp Amanda's stockings and gently roll the dark nylon down to the girl's white knees. She proceeded to pull the girdle up and inside out, over Amanda's waist, revealing a pair of tender and ruddy cheeks.

The doctor's stare became transfixed by the figure stretched over her desk: the warm backside and long slender arms spread wide across the wood, the fingernails clawing the smooth varnish in anticipation, the feet rising on to tiptoes, unable to stay still.

The doctor wasted no time in delivering her sentence. 'You seem fond of unconventional acts and of shameful night-time secrets. It will not be tolerated at Whitehead and I will show you what that errant little pussy is for!'

From the floor, on her knees, Penny saw Kloster clutch Amanda's hips. She stared fixedly at the long cock easing itself between her friend's shaking thighs. Amanda shuddered and let forth a whimper.

Penny bit her bottom lip, imagining the passage of the thick baton between the mouth of her friend's flushed sex. Penny could even smell Amanda's arousal: a rich and musky aroma mingling with Kloster's perfume and the shiny leather of her boots. She inhaled the delicious bouquet and sighed, her pretty face wrinkling with regret at not having been selected to receive the doctor's rigid correctional implement.

Penny wanted to touch the beautiful women, to caress their breasts and satin skin. She needed to reach out and stroke Amanda's shuddering body and kiss Kloster's ecstatic face. Just one long night of female love had not been enough; Penny knew she would pine for this experience over and over again, demanding a woman's primal sexual rage – equal in ferocity and intensity to any man's, but always longer lasting.

Kloster failed to even notice Penny, who was flushed and panting beneath her: she was too busy slipping her length in and out of Amanda's moist sex, sliding the thick appendage with a slow and sensual rhythm.

Amanda moaned with each stubborn thrust into her sex, slapping her hands down on to the desk and shaking her wild mane about at the point of maximum penetration. Penny eyed her friend's ecstasy with an almost uncontrollable envy. She longed for something thick and rigid pushing itself deeply into her own aching sex, knocking her inhibitions over and remorselessly piercing her inexperience.

Kloster sped up her action, banging on and off Amanda's smarting cheeks with all the power her thighs could muster. Amanda screeched with pleasure and her knees sagged from the barrage, but Kloster held her upright, grinding her hips into the girl's bottom and slapping her cheeks when the false cock could impale itself no further.

Penny could only guess that Amanda had lost sense of place and time in her shuddering and squealing approach to orgasm.

'Yes! Yes! Yes!' Amanda cried, mesmerised by the hip-thrusting onslaught from the esteemed Doctor Kloster.

The lecturer grinned, maniacally adoring her own role. 'What is that pussy for? Tell me!'

'For a cock. A hard cock, doctor!'

'And what are you?'

'A bad girl, doctor. A naughty slut!'

'And when you need a cock, my girl, where will you run?'

'To you, doctor. I'll run to – to you –'

Amanda collapsed on the desk top, her entire body quaking from an all-consuming climax.

Doctor Kloster flicked her own stylish hair back and inhaled deeply, having worn herself out from the exertion of the impromptu delivery.

Penny could only find solace with thoughts of the boyish Rupert. It is all just research, she told herself over and over again, rubbing her slippery thighs together in anticipation of another thrilling encounter at the Academy.

Back in her room, after the delicious evening meal, Penny massaged her aching feet. The afternoon's posture and hip-placement session had every girl groaning for the dinner bell. Penny, however, had to marvel at Miss Barbusse's intricate knowledge and specialist technique. In one day she even had the plump Bessy, from Amtex Mineral Inc., striding around the dance floor like an irresistible nineties Jane Mansfield.

42

The girl's clumsiness and shrinking confidence had blossomed into something dynamic and sexy. Penny hated to admit it, but she had been unable to prevent her own active mind from imagining several scenarios in which her fledgling technique would create wonder at work. She was already picturing her high-heeled legs striding into the editor's office, with her hips mincing suggestively and her glossy lips demanding the pick of feature-length interviews.

Penny made detailed notes on the second spanking session in Kloster's office. She already had enough material to place a refugee camp of reporters outside the gates of Whitehead, to satellite link her into the lucrative heart of the celebrity world. It would be the scandal to end the millennium. Even the *Inquisitor* chiefs would be stunned with the report on her first two days. Every successful company director and public figure would be asked on every chat show, for years to come, about a possible attendance at Whitehead. It would blow the country's success-stories wide open for speculation. Penny's pulse raced at the prospect.

She remembered to keep Amanda's name out of the research. She adored her new friend and balked at the prospect of exposing her. It created a conflict of interests, however, and Penny struggled with her fresh doubts. Did she have any right to pick and choose those identities she revealed and possibly ruined? She told herself to remain professional at all costs, to focus on the acquisition of evidence, to unveil the dark past of Barbusse and her perverse Academy. But what had it summoned from her own depths in only two days? Penny blushed when thinking back on her repeated arousal and her illicit behaviour with Amanda. Was she just as guilty as Kloster and Barbusse? Or was she playing the role? Should there be any guilt involved?

Penny shook the questions from her busy mind and prepared for her date with Rupert. She needed some exciting male company and intended to make a very special effort. She would leave her bra at home base, allowing her soft breasts some air beneath the flimsy blouse. She decided to open a fresh packet of rustling nylons, too, repainted her toenails and spent an age on her make-up.

The night promised to be warm and moonlit: perfect for slinking and pouting around the gorgeous Rupert, making herself irresistible, re-creating the allure of the sultry dean.

Sabrina disappeared through the side portal and an oak panel closed silently behind her. Only a delicate trace of the stunning redhead's perfume remained behind in Miss Barbusse's private chambers.

Miss Barbusse had noticed how Sabrina had been particularly attentive that evening. Her handmaid had run a steamy spiced bath in the private bathroom, retouched her mistress's flawless make-up and gently laid her evening wear out on the bed. Sabrina obviously understood the gravity and importance of the evening – it was a rare occasion when her mistress discovered a potential prodigy.

Miss Barbusse reclined languorously on her velvet chaise longue. She looked down at her tight-skirted legs, admiring the soft kid-skin boots gripping her calves and feet. Sabrina had lovingly laced her shapely legs into the tight boots; the specially tailored footwear from Milan stretched up to her knees from the points of the six-inch spike heels.

Lucy arrived at eight and Miss Barbusse smiled before she invited her in through the unlocked door. She had heard the young heir dithering outside, perhaps gazing at her lovely reflection in a vanity mirror, or adding final preparations to her charming apparel, determined to impress the mistress of every ceremony at Whitehead.

Miss Barbusse had trained two of Lucy's male cousins. The first had been smitten with her, forever gazing after her tiny swaying backside or staring at her cold face with puppy-dog eyes. She remembered his devotion fondly and wondered whether this tendency ran in the family.

Lucy walked almost arrogantly into her study. Miss Barbusse took the time to admire the girl's narrow hips, which tapered down towards her slender ankles. She spotted a delicate gold chain around the girl's right ankle, almost invisible beneath her sheer black stocking. She decided to allow the slight liberty with the strict dress code. It was such a pretty ankle, after all, and was only enhanced by something thin and metallic around its gentle contours.

'Good evening, my dear. Will you take a seat beside me?'

Lucy returned Miss Barbusse's smile and sat down.

Miss Barbusse stared, for several seconds, at Lucy's beautiful yet impassive young face. She tried to guess at the depths behind the sparkling dark-blue eyes, having found Lucy's eyes mesmerising from the day she saw her application photo. They were like little crystal lagoons beneath delicate eyebrows, which appeared on her smooth white forehead as if left by the deft stroke of a grand master's brush. She knew the hypnotic power within such gentle feminine orbs. But the eyes, she guessed, could also become glacial diamonds shining above another's servitude.

'You are probably wondering why I have asked you to come to my rooms, but there is something I wish to discuss with you. I know you experienced a resentment towards your guardian for sending you to Whitehead. It may seem like an untimely interruption in your hectic young life, but I know we have much to offer you here. This is no ordinary school, Lucy. Yes, it has rules and a uniform, and the strict regime may seem like a step back in time for you. But, given time and a special tuition, I think you will become aware of the renaissance it will create within your rare soul. I believe we may be kindred spirits, Lucy. You too, I think, are curious about certain practices. Your yearnings mirror mine when I was your age. What you need is a mentor and the occasional private tutorial to accelerate your progress here at Whitehead.'

Lucy's blank face broke like a sunrise into a faint smile. She stared back into Miss Barbusse's delicately lined eyes. Her cultured voice replied softly, 'I am sure you know about my wild youth, but everybody experiments when they are young. I have no doubt that my guardian delighted in exaggerating certain instances from prep school. I have just never been able to find a role. I suppose that is why my guardian sent me to you.'

Miss Barbusse smiled sympathetically. She admired the girl's full sensual lips; their continental shape appealed to her. She even tried to imagine the flavour of Lucy's shiny crimson lipstick.

'I too was such a girl, a long time ago in Paris. I had the good fortune of meeting someone very special. Someone who made me, shaped me, by showing me forbidden things.'

'A woman?' Lucy asked.

'No. A very dear man. I tell very few people about my past. So few would understand. But I will tell you that he became my master. He reduced me to a seedling before letting me blossom like an exotic orchid.'

'What did he do to you?' Lucy questioned, leaning forward.

'Let me just say that my second skin, my outfits, are always there to summon an irresistible wealth of memory. My tight shoes and clinging nylons remind me of Paris, where my young limbs delighted my master's special guests. They would lean forward in their chairs and strain their ears to catch a whisper from between

46

my thighs. My waist is always trapped by a leather corset to remind me of tightly bound days in the Loire Valley chateau.'

'But the discomfort?' Lucy queried, her eyes wide, her mouth slightly parted as she tried to understand.

'Discomfort, when applied by expert hands, is a rare thrill, my girl. I often sleep in my crucifying garments, alone in the dark between black silk sheets. Sometimes I can even hear the tinkling music of thin silver chains and smell the cold dungeon stone. My body was young and soft and white. It could tremble as I know yours is now, but it quickly learnt to love contortions and their pleasures, practices beyond the narrow imaginations of the uninitiated. Sometimes I can even taste rubber, as if it is still clasped between my lips.'

Lucy shifted her position on the couch and Miss Barbusse thought she heard a sharp intake of breath.

'Is this the purpose of Whitehead?' Lucy asked.

'Whitehead could never be the same as my master's world. A twilight world of secrecy, speeding from city apartment to country residence, forever listening to our hearts. It does, though, serve certain needs and imparts a very beneficial lesson to those lucky enough to attend.'

'But how?'

'My dear, I know from experience that so many individuals possess the hidden desire to descend into the folds of tight leather, clinging rubber, cold encircling chains and sheer entrancing nylon. Those fabrics and tools demand roles. They uncover strengths. They are vital to the subtle craft of submission, seduction and eventual domination. It is a dangerous path, my girl, but a thrilling one. It has led so many to the summits of their worlds, the worlds of commerce, military service and of politics. I have seen my students preach from pulpits and raise millions for charity.'

'It is not all just clothes and discipline, and sexual titillation?'

'No, my sweet. It is the harnessing of the greatest power of all, the original fire, the original sin, the beguiling and hypnotising power of sexuality. I expose talents as my master exposed mine. The realms of erotica are limitless; the possibilities endless. Sex brings meaning to a life, and meaning provides knowledge; knowledge in turn creates success.'

A glimmer of a smile, too faint to judge, hovered around Lucy's mouth as she studied the dean for several seconds before replying, 'Miss Barbusse, I think I would be very grateful for your guidance.'

It was as if an orchestra tuned up inside Miss Barbusse's stomach.

'It is a long and dangerous journey, my dear Lucy. Be warned, you will see sides to your character that will crush you with shame. But be strong, pain will lead to pleasure. You may discover the paths that I once crossed. There may be nights behind china masks when anonymous lovers prise your young thighs apart and enter your intimacy, when you are used according to my limits and desires. You may be left longing for the meticulous switches of canes and rods.'

Lucy lowered her eyelids gently and wet her lips with a small pink tongue.

Miss Barbusse reached out and clasped one of Lucy's hands, squeezing her cool skin before whispering to her, 'For some this is hell, deviant and perverse. For us it is paradise, an adventure in body and spirit.'

Lucy sighed and Miss Barbusse leant across the velvet couch and kissed her forehead, making the girl shiver from the contact of bright-red lips on her cool skin.

Lucy slid off the couch and curled around Miss Barbusse's shiny boots, placing her hands behind the dean's smooth calves and caressing the leather. She raised one heel towards her mouth, slipping her thick lips across its rigid dagger-like shape. She closed her beautiful eyes and sucked the heel, breathing gently through her tiny nose.

Miss Barbusse shuddered and little sparks of fire danced along her spine. She reclined on the soft couch and closed her eyes, imagining the girl's soft and fragrant skin pressed close to her own.

Miss Barbusse felt Lucy's long manicured fingernails at work on her boot laces: unlacing them slowly and gently, unthreading the thin laces one hole at a time. When both boots had been unlaced, Miss Barbusse opened her eyes and watched Lucy ease them off her hot legs. She watched the rear of the girl's blonde head and felt her soft lips kissing her feet. The girl began to stroke her legs, slipping dextrous fingertips up and down her slippery powder-grey nylon stockings, tracing the seams up to the rear of her hot knees.

Miss Barbusse surveyed the girl's face with an immense feeling of satisfaction, enjoying the sight of the girl's eager eyes and relishing the soft ministrations from the moist young mouth sucking her toes.

She decided it was time for Lucy's first lesson.

She removed her dainty foot from Lucy's busy mouth and spoke to the girl in a quiet but assertive tone: 'My dear Lucy, I would like to take you on a special journey tonight. I would like to uncover your innermost thoughts, the thoughts you have when you are alone, when your mind travels off at the speed of light until it finds the right lover and situation. A place where you can completely be yourself, without restrictions.'

Lucy narrowed her eyes seductively. Her cheeks had flushed with excitement and she pouted up at Miss Barbusse. 'Show me the way.'

Miss Barbusse rose from the couch and took Lucy's hand. She led the coyly smiling girl to a door on the far side of her study, guiding Lucy through the open portal to reveal her ornate bedroom. She watched Lucy's astonished eyes travel around the dark walls. They had been decorated with crimson silk and hung with precious oil paintings that depicted depraved and passionate scenes of seduction and submission. Lucy's stare soon fell upon the Imperial-sized bed.

The vast bed was in impenetrable darkness, behind black satin drapes. It called to Miss Barbusse. She sensed its inviting softness and secret memories. She led Lucy to the mysterious altar, inviting her to recline along it with a sweep of her manicured hand. Lucy relaxed on the bed, curling her pretty legs up beneath her, while Miss Barbusse moved silently towards the black dresser in the corner of her room.

She opened the second drawer and dipped one slender arm into its depths. Her delicate hands returned to the subdued light, gently cradling tinkling cuffs and chains. She heard Lucy's sharp intake of breath behind her. Miss Barbusse turned and approached the trembling captive, smiling at the svelte creature curled up like some pedigree kitten on her bed.

She spoke quietly to the girl in a tone that few ever heard: 'Have you ever placed your inquisitive mind and body in another's hands?'

'No,' Lucy replied.

Little tremors of glee passed through the dean's body. She could see the girl's shiny lips glistening in the dark and the bright whites of her big eyes tempting her with their innocence.

'Have you ever wanted to prostrate yourself before another woman's desire?'

Lucy released a sigh. She closed her eyes and wet her lips with the tiny pink tip of her tongue. 'No. But it is something . . . something I dream about.'

Miss Barbusse, her slender arms entwined within the thin silver chains, moved towards Lucy, whispering, 'Stand up and close your eyes.'

Lucy complied, slipping off the bed without any sound save the rustle of her expensive undergarments. Miss Barbusse stood in front of Lucy and reached around the small hips to unzip the girl's skirt. She could not prevent a moan of delight: Lucy wore a boot-lace-thin suspender belt decorated with tiny red flowers, and, beneath the wispy garters, the girl's knickerless sex lay exposed.

Had she come to her dean with seduction in mind? Did she desire correction for flaunting the strict dress code? Miss Barbusse felt her pulse quicken as she mused on the girl's intentions. She bent down and licked along the compliant Lucy's slippery nylon-encased legs, feeling the girl's body shiver when her tongue discovered the narrow strip of soft pale skin atop her thighs. The faint aroma of Lucy's young sex wafted under the dean's expectant nose and she closed her eyes to savour the scent of arousal.

Miss Barbusse found the girl's slender ankles with her steady fingers, caressing their delicate lines and curves before slipping a cold silver cuff around each joint. She ran a chain between the little round fixtures on the cuffs before securing the chain to the heavy foundations of her bed. The chain pulled Lucy's legs apart, leaving little slack for any movement. Miss Barbusse performed the same swift manoeuvre on Lucy's slim wrists, this time attaching the chain to the upright posts on her bed canopy.

She stood back for a moment and surveyed Lucy, who was now spread-eagled at the foot of the bed.

In her next deft move she unbuttoned Lucy's blouse, immediately gasping with surprise at the sudden and intoxicating sight of two hard brown nipples revealed by a non-regulation peephole brassiere. The bra cups had been fashioned with a transparent black gauze, enhancing the soft buxom contour of her firm young breasts.

Something snapped within Miss Barbusse and her slippery mouth fell upon the girl's chest. She licked and bit at the little hard nipples and passionately massaged the full breasts with her open palms, making Lucy jerk and moan within the restraints. Miss Barbusse traced her mouth down the girl's flat stomach to play with her creamy navel, flicking her tongue over the skin in a tiny circular motion.

Lucy began to moan and push her groin forwards; her stocking clad legs pulled at the chains as she became desperate to thrash them about. Miss Barbusse smiled at the eager young fox that she had crucified in chains on her bed frame. She placed her hands on Lucy's thighs and caressed the supple limbs, running her fingers down to the cuffed ankles, her fingertips making sure they savoured every slippery curve on the shapely legs.

'Take me,' Lucy hissed, her eyes alight with lust.

Miss Barbusse stood beside Lucy's secured body and gently kissed the beautiful reddening face.

'Take me!' Lucy demanded, yanking her arms around and making the ancient bed frame creak.

Miss Barbusse promptly removed her own skirt and unrolled one of her sheer stockings. She gripped it between her two fists and gagged Lucy's mouth, tying her stocking around the girl's head and running the wispy nylon between the parted lips. Miss Barbusse removed her blouse and the remaining stocking. She stripped down to her unfeasibly tight leather corset and blindfolded Lucy with the second warm stocking. Lucy's head moved from side to side as she tried to peer over the edges of her blindfold. Miss Barbusse walked back to the dresser to remove a flat black case before proceeding to flick open the silver locks.

The black instruments, displayed on the red velvet lining, began to shine in the dim light. Miss Barbusse selected a small hide whip, remembering a time when she would tiptoe in her own slave bracelets to fetch the implement at her master's bidding. He had bought them for her from a count in Budapest. Miss Barbusse slipped the makeshift gag out of Lucy's mouth.

'Lucy! You will speak only when spoken to. Do you understand?'

'Yes,' Lucy whispered.

'Yes, what!'

'Yes, miss?'

'Not good enough!' Miss Barbusse trailed the nine hide tails of the whip across Lucy's bare backside. The girl shivered but kept silent. 'You will refer to me as mistress.'

'Yes, mistress,' Lucy quickly added.

'I have some questions for you. Why did you not wear your regulation girdle and brassiere?'

'I wanted to feel comfortable,' she answered.

'Liar!' Miss Barbusse volleyed back at her and whipped her backside with a short and sharp blow. Lucy's entire body stiffened and then relaxed.

'I wanted to impress you,' Lucy said.

'How? And tell me the truth. You must learn to comply frankly with any of my questions.'

'I thought . . . I thought you would make a pass. I wanted to tease you.'

'With your young body and sluttish underwear?'

'Yes, mistress.'

Miss Barbusse smiled. Humour, however, was absent from her tone of voice. 'You must learn to curb your forward nature. I have no use for good-time girls.'

Miss Barbusse whipped Lucy's backside three times. The girl bit her bottom lip and released a gentle sigh. Miss Barbusse put her hand on Lucy's sex; the lips were damp and she sucked her moist fingers before continuing to flog the girl. She made sure her strokes were even and perfectly placed, landing across her cheeks, lower back, gartered thighs and partially exposed sex. She softened her blows to raise no more than a blush to the girl's backside but gave her thighs longer and more severe strokes.

Lucy's stifled moans filled the dark room; her slender limbs writhed and pulled within the unmerciful restraints. Miss Barbusse sensed the girl's passion – the crack of the whip created a harmony that she had learnt to love.

'Do you crave pleasure?'

'Oh yes, mistress.' Lucy enthusiastically replied.

'What do you seek?'

'Something new. Always something new. I need to go further than ever before, mistress.'

'What have you done?'

'I started sleeping with my brother's friends at seventeen, mistress. I picked men up in nightclubs and seduced a lecturer at university. But that bores me now.'

'Men can be clumsy, Lucy. And no woman has ever taken you?'

'Never. Nothing more than a kiss, mistress.'

'Would you like me to expand your horizons?'

'Yes!' Lucy gasped.

Miss Barbusse pressed her mouth on Lucy's moist sex, lapping greedily between the soft lips and caressing the tiny clit with a fast flicking of her dextrous tongue. She heard Lucy's moans rise to a stifled crescendo, and the girl's writhing increased within her restraints. Miss Barbusse clutched the captive's hips and held them down, continuing with her tongue's lapping.

Lucy shouted as she came and every toned muscle strained within her young body. She pushed her soft and fragrant sex on to Miss Barbusse's face in one final determined surge before her body relaxed, wracked with sobs and hung in chains.

Miss Barbusse rose from between Lucy's thighs and smiled at the blindfold face. The flushed cheeks below the wet stocking were now tear stained.

'To think that I have only just begun ...' she whispered, close to the panting girl's ear.

Penny repeatedly glanced over her shoulder as she flitted between the oak trees lining the main driveway. The dark manor house was now eerily bathed in strong moonlight, becoming a spectral edifice among the flat and almost luminous lawns. The bedroom lights on the second floor, and in the male quarters on the first floor of the utility building, had been doused. At odd intervals, Penny spotted the tiny glowing ember from a smoking female student's cigarette on the solemn face of the main manor. On the ground floor, chinks of light peeked between the lecturers' heavy red drapes. Penny wondered what they were doing in the hour approaching midnight. Were they entertaining? she mused. Had they already taken lovers from the new student populace?

When she drew level with the tennis courts, the bright moon offered her little cover on the open ground. She peered across to the immaculate grass courts, her bright eyes sweeping about for Rupert's silhouette. The courts were surrounded by a privet hedge, rhododendrons, and neat lines of rose bushes, and Penny's eyes failed to detect any movement amongst the orderly foliage. She checked her wristwatch: 11.35. He was late.

Penny crept across the cool grass to take a closer look, trembling with vulnerability beneath the bright starlit sky, and wondering whether her shivers were caused by the cool breeze. Meeting a complete stranger in the dark was not something she would have even contemplated back in London, but at Whitehead the game was played by different rules.

She reached the dark rose bushes, her skin goose-pimpling beneath her blouse. Penny's heels sank into the cool grass. The shadows from the bushes obscured her view of where or what she was standing in. Penny bent down, straining her eyes to spot a gap in the shrubbery.

A hand clamped on to her mouth from behind. Penny tried to scream, struggling and fighting to pull away. She felt a firm body pressed into her back; the assailant's other hand gripped both of her wrists:

'Easy, tiger. It's me, Rupert,' a voice whispered from behind her.

Penny relaxed and he released her.

She spun round, her body electrified by shock. 'You bloody maniac! My heart nearly stopped!'

A smile broke across Rupert's handsome face and one eye glinted, unmasked by his floppy fringe. He put a finger up to his lips. 'Shh. Keep your voice down, you're far too conspicuous hovering by the hedge. Sometimes there are security patrols, and dogs tied out by the perimeter wall, in case of intruders. Follow me to the caretaker's hut, it's too bright around here. You never know who's watching from the manor, we're in full view on this side. Oh, and you look simply divine.'

Penny gripped his offered hand and followed his rangy shape into the shadows. She teetered behind him, skipping on the ultra-high heels and panting for breath as she recovered from her panic.

They reached a small wooden hut on the far side of the courts, their position now completely obscured by the wire-mesh fence and caretaker's outbuilding.

'I didn't think you would come. It was rather rude of me to just post a note, but if Kloster caught me on the second floor I would be sleeping on my front for a week.'

'You wish,' Penny teased, feeling more at ease.

Rupert frowned. 'What do you mean?'

'Nothing,' she replied, smiling naughtily.

Rupert bent over and fished around by the hut with his hands. He straightened his tall lean figure, clutching a bottle of champagne and a punnet of strawberries. 'Just like Wimbledon, Pen.'

Penny smiled: an attempt at seduction was on the cards, which caused something to rejoice inside her. She was still only too aware of what the morning with the doctor had done to her hormones. The longing had become almost unquenchable: she had gone beyond the point of merely contemplating sex with a stranger. She hardly recognised the intense appetite coursing through her body. She wanted to do something forbidden, and tingled with excitement at the thought of copying Amanda's sexual confidence.

'So who sent you to Whitehead?' he asked.

Penny paused and composed herself before replying, 'Polycorp. I'm in creative development.'

'What a coincidence, so is my friend Hugh. Tall chap with a ponytail. Do you know him?'

Penny's throat closed. She began to stammer, 'No, I'm a new girl –'

'You must be. Hugh would have told me about pretty Penny.'

Penny felt her cheeks blush and, eager to evade Rupert's line of questioning changed the subject. 'What about you?'

'Hong Kong. Stocks and bonds, you know. I travelled for a couple of years after Cambridge before landing a job over there.'

'Something else that just fell on to your silver plate?' Penny queried sarcastically.

'Not at all. My dad is a carpenter, my beginnings are entirely humble. I was born with a wooden spoon in my mouth.'

Penny giggled and pushed him closer to what she had in mind. 'So, Rupert, what do you make of Whitehead?'

Rupert rolled his eyes. 'Where do I start? We have to dress like Cary Grant, be in bed by eleven, keep away from you girls, in those delightful costumes, and are punished for the slightest degree of tardiness. But it's not all bad, the food is marvellous and the training with Mr Klima is fascinating. We are studying the parallels between Samurai military tactics and market strategies. It's funny, there are actually similarities. The most bizarre lessons, though, are taken by the female staff. The Celeste twins take us for physical education, Miss Barbusse teaches seduction, while Kloster lectures discipline and motivation. It's all a little crazy at first and the discipline is harsh, very tough, but I suppose we are too scared to fail.'

'Mr Klima. Is he the arrogant one?' Penny queried, unable to completely relinquish her journalistic discipline.

'Yes. A Russian. A descendant of the royal family, apparently. He used to work in a similar academy in Prague, during the Cold War. Imagine what that was like.'

Penny raised her eyebrows thoughtfully. She saw another angle: international espionage perhaps, or the sinister history behind an Eastern European refugee of noble origins. Her mind spun. She wanted everything, the complete picture. She decided, almost reluctantly, that it would soon be time to begin her surveillance in earnest, to acquire the real evidence. For now, however, Penny wanted to erase the thoughts of sneaking and double-guessing from her mind and concentrate on the young lad before her.

Rupert unfolded a tartan blanket on the grass and beckoned for Penny to sit beside him, offering the bottle of champagne and making grinning apologies: 'Sorry, no glasses. But Roberto assures me that it is an excellent vintage.'

Penny smiled, relishing the moonlight, the danger, and the pleasing company. For effect, she remained standing, casually pushing her breasts out and allowing her face to adopt a playful expression.

'Thought you would get me drunk, eh?' she teased. 'Get some action, break the segregation rule?'

'No, not at all, I –' Rupert stammered.

'With the girls out of bounds, you guys must be desperate. All those high heels strutting around beneath pert breasts. Is that why they make you start school two days before the girls, to destroy any alternative ideas you may have about sleeping arrangements?'

'Must be,' Rupert answered, his voice vague and barely a whisper.

Penny watched his eyes transfixed by the sight of her unrestrained breasts quivering above. She could almost feel his eyes pressing against the silky fabric of her thin blouse. She pouted and licked her lips slowly, unable to prevent herself flirting. Penny winked at Rupert's startled eyes and began to trace a finger around a hard nipple, astounded by her new confidence.

'Please, Penny, sit down before I faint,' he gasped.

Penny reclined alongside him and stretched her long legs out across the blanket, determined to entice him further. 'Tell me, young Rupert, what do you think of the sexual theme to the place? Does it excite you? I mean, all of these uniforms and cold dominant women? I hear guys like that. It must be awful watching us from across the dining room and knowing that you cannot touch.'

Penny leant a little closer to Rupert's quickly rising chest, allowing her breath to deliberately brush his tanned neck and her lips to glisten only a few inches from his own.

'It's murder,' he replied, shaking. 'I think they do it on purpose – subject us to so many subtle arousals. You know, keep us on the boil for their own designs. And it bloody works.'

Penny had to agree. She took another slug from the champagne bottle, holding it aloft with both delicate hands, making sure her body pressed against his as she drank. She saw Rupert stretch out one hand in the dark to trace a finger along her jawline and tuck a loose strand of hair behind her ear. Penny shivered, enjoying the little explosions along her spine. She lowered the bottle and closed her eyes, leaning backwards and baring her throat to the lad beside her.

In the dark she felt Rupert's breath, a soft panting, fragrant with wine, tickling her neck. The delicate tip of his tongue flicked across her ear and Penny squeezed her thighs together, experiencing a warm moistening in her sex.

Her lips found his in the dark. His kisses were gentle and almost unsure, but Penny's mouth was not lacking in confidence as she slipped her tongue deep into Rupert's mouth. He responded by sucking on it greedily, and Penny's body surged with a keen hunger – a hunger to be filled. Her nipples tingled with a need for firm caresses. She grasped the rear of Rupert's head and entwined her fingers through his soft hair, clenching her hand before forcefully pulling him on to her face. She kissed his mouth passionately, stealing his frantic breath and tongued the inside of his mouth, wanting to drive Rupert away from courtship and into something more aggressive.

Penny sensed his body tensing as his arms encircled her tiny waist and lowered her on to the blanket. His hard body gently moved on top of hers and immediately she could feel his cast-iron erection pressing through her skirt. He rotated his hips, stimulating his cock against her corseted softness. Penny tucked one hand under his stomach and fingered the length of his thick shaft. Rupert's mouth left hers; he groaned and rose above her in a press-up position. Penny unbelted his slacks and freed his cock with her determined fingers, getting his hard penis out to pulse in the palm of her hand. She wanted to taste it, smear it across her face, swallow him and shove it inside her sex all at the same time.

Penny stroked his cock and tickled the moist tip with one finger. Rupert shut his eyes above her and she listened to his little, almost childlike, moans.

'Don't you dare come. I want that inside me,' she whispered.

Penny saw Rupert's body tense above her, desperate for her, clutching inside of himself to prevent the eager eruption. She immediately released his cock, delaying the ejaculation.

Rupert's eyes fluttered open and he moved to sit astride Penny, gripping the lapels of her blouse. Penny heard the rip and watched two buttons disappear into the dark before Rupert's face fell between her breasts in a frenzy. The rough palms of his hands massaged her sensitive fleshy orbs, while his teeth and tongue latched on to her nipples, devouring them, making her writhe and squeal under the brutal feasting.

Whenever a man progressed far enough to put his hands on her naked breasts, Penny knew her greatest weakness had been exposed: only then was she truly his. She had often fantasised about a stranger grasping her buxom delights in the dark; ensuring her instant surrender.

Unable to restrain herself, Penny moaned and clawed at the cool grass, digging her heels into the soft turf, raising her chest to press her flesh into his teeth and squeezing hands. Rupert's hair tickled the delicate skin above her breasts and his mouth engulfed her nipples, smearing them until they glistened in the moonlight. When he pinched her nipples between his fingers, Penny slapped her hands on to his back, clawing at his shoulders, marking the tanned skin. 'Take me now, Rupert,' Penny gasped.

She relaxed between his strong arms, enabling him to flip her over on to her stomach. She felt him unzipping her skirt and sliding it down her legs and off her high-heeled feet. Penny rolled on to her back and watched Rupert's face, which was mesmerised by sheer black nylons and high heels. He began massaging and stroking her warm legs, lifting them up in the air and sucking at the delicate seam on the rear of her shapely ankles. She saw him peer down and spot her knickerless sex beneath the black girdle.

Rupert slid his hands down the outside of her legs and his face descended on to her quim. Penny immediately wrapped her shiny thighs about Rupert's neck and imprisoned his lapping face on her impatient sex. His mouth delighted her, burrowing through her lips, his tongue lapping at her little clit before slipping down and into a tight vagina. Penny lost herself to a powerful arousal, the one that had been brewing inside her all day, hampering her efforts at concentration. At last her sex had been freed and ruthlessly eaten, mauled by a nuzzling mouth with its biting teeth and probing tongue.

Rupert slipped two and then three fingers inside her vagina, stretching them wide to part her clinging inner walls. The sensation was overwhelming: Penny wanted to scream and bite his neck. He began tickling the walls of her vagina as if by instinct, somehow guessing at how much she adored being played with. Penny began thrusting her groin forward, sliding her sex up and down the bones on Rupert's hand, smearing it with honey, attempting to swallow even the wrist inside of her.

'Your cock, Rupert. I want your cock in my mouth!'

Rupert gasped and withdrew his fingers from Penny's sex. He swivelled round and straddled her face. She looked up at the long and trembling tool above her. Penny stretched her tongue out and lashed the dewy nib of his circumcised phallus. It looked huge and purple and veiny, almost menacing in the dark. It was a menace that Penny now craved.

Her mouth ran away with itself: 'In my mouth. Shove it in my mouth, make me –'

Penny felt the thick shaft widen her glossy lips and fill her mouth. She sucked and pumped her head up and down on the hard penis. His thick tool was wrapped luxuriously in velvety skin and she relished the salty taste. She heard Rupert groaning before he dropped a sticky face between her legs once more.

Penny lost herself in the writhing and rolling embrace. Time and situation no longer mattered as Rupert lapped at her sex, sucking her little clit towards a crescendo. She breathed heavily through her little snub nose and greedily devoured his delicious erection.

Penny felt herself approach orgasm. She pulled his penis from her mouth and began massaging the thick shaft above her face. Rupert concerted his oral efforts in one final lashing on her sopping sex.

Penny gasped, overwhelmed by the sudden tidal wave of pleasure rushing through her body and across her mind.

Rupert groaned loudly, his body tensing as his hips pumped the stiff organ through Penny's hand. It began to pulse between her fingers and the first spurt of white dew splattered on to her wet lips, its pungent aroma filling her nostrils.

She yanked at the solid shaft in her frenzy, determined to milk his lovely balls dry. Penny stuffed the cock back into her mouth and gulped at every creamy dollop it had to offer. The thick splashes pumped on to her tongue and ran down her hastily swallowing throat.

Rupert's lean shape collapsed on top of her. Penny swallowed the last drop and sucked the head of his phallus clean. Rupert's flushed face lay on her soft girdle and his hands stretched out to grip her slippery ankles.

'Oh, Penny, that was fantastic,' he stammered. 'You have such a wonderful mouth.'

'You can talk, sweetie, my legs are still trembling.'

He shuffled up the blanket to lie beside her. She raised her tousled head and let it rest on his chest. They lay together quietly, damp with sweat beneath their dishevelled clothes, and watched the stars. In the distance Penny heard a dog bark.

'Rupert, are you sure we are safe here?'

'Yes. No one can see us or disturb us.'

'Then you would not mind satisfying a very serious craving I have?'

'What sort of craving?'

'I need to be fucked. This place is driving me nuts. I want you inside me. I want you to make me come again.'

'On one condition.'

Penny rolled on to her front and frowned at Rupert's smiling face. She mimicked Doctor Kloster's haughty Prussian tone: 'You are in no position to start making conditions, young man.'

Rupert laughed and cupped Penny's flushed face with his hands, whispering to her, 'I have a similar craving. I am anxious to fuck a naughty little temptress on all fours.'

'Be my guest,' Penny replied, already imagining his hands on her hips and his thick organ pulsing inside her eager sex.

Penny assumed the position, wiggling her soft behind at Rupert, tempting him as he manoeuvred behind her. She looked back over her shoulder and watched the eager face; he pursed his lips, surveying her curvaceous shape. Penny felt him stretching his hard chest over her back as he reached beneath her, resting on his knees. She felt the fingers of his left hand pinch her nipples. Penny closed her eyes and began drifting back towards that hot and desperate mode. His other hand nestled between her legs to begin a slow rubbing against her clit. She felt his hardening cock pressed vertically against his stomach. He shoved it between her cool buttocks and it grew and solidified against her. Penny delighted in the submissive position she had taken on the grass – she felt bestial, on all fours, about to be mounted beneath a night sky.

'Come on, Rupert. Don't tease me. Get that cock inside my little pussy.'

Rupert denied her demand and continued to rub her sticky clit and hard nipples. Penny moaned and pushed her backside against Rupert's penis. 'Please slip it into my little pussy. It is so tight and wet. If you do, I may offer you my arse a little later.'

Rupert slapped her backside before stuffing his shaft between her legs and into the tight entrance of her sex.

Penny closed her eyes and savoured the slow penetration as the cock inched through her vagina. He pushed into her sex, deeper and deeper, gradually filling her.

As Rupert developed his rhythm, increasing the pace of his thrusts, Penny clenched her fists on the grass and dipped her head down between her shoulders. He began to pull his cock almost entirely out of her before plunging the thick tool up and into the depths of her sex.

The sensation intoxicated Penny. She had never let anyone screw her backwards before, having always preferred to be on top. The secret moonlit liaison and the breaking of rules had unleashed something inside of her again. She found her old limits disappearing and her imagination expanding. The submerged yearning for being taken, for being used by another's passion, had begun to explode through her. Penny found herself desperately wanting a faster action from Rupert's shaft; she wanted to feel his balls slapping against her thighs; she wanted to shake and scream with ecstasy.

'Fuck me, Rupert. Fuck me hard. Just take me. I need it. Do it!'

Penny heard him groan in approval and felt his body explode with fresh vigour behind her. She gasped and shuddered as he began ramming his penis right up and inside her at a savage pace. Her breasts swung beneath her from the force of his noisy thrusts and she could feel the bones of his pelvis grinding into her soft cheeks. He clamped his hands on to her hips and began pulling her backwards to meet the powerful thrusts. Penny felt her body shake like a rag doll and bit her lips to prevent herself screaming.

It was not just the fast passage of Rupert's thick cock inside her, it was the thought and the thrill of being held firmly and rutted ruthlessly. It was animal and she felt depraved – to be on all fours at midnight with a man she had only just met, her back arching beneath the moon as he rammed a strange penis inside her. Penny felt exalted by the primal activity and sobbed with delight. She became lost to the night and thought of Doctor Kloster's spanking hands.

Her mind and body teetered above a precipice of complete delight and her mouth spouted pure and delicious filth. 'Up my arse, Rupert! Fuck me properly! Where I need it! Spank me, you bastard!'

Penny could hardly believe that those words had fallen from her mouth. It was as if something else was taking over her body, dashing her calculating mind and careful nature to the four winds.

She felt Rupert's shaft rip itself from her vagina. The head of his phallus began to nudge upward and to press against her tiny puckered anus.

Pain mingled with pleasure and Penny screamed with delight, grinding her teeth together. Her whole trembling body seemed to welcome the slow passage of Rupert's slippery cock up her tight and virgin rectum.

Penny thought her heart would explode; the sensation was both excruciating and exhilarating. She screamed 'Yes' into the night. She felt Rupert's hands slapping her soft backside and sobbed from the glorious feeling of another two inches easing into her rectum. Penny reached beneath herself and began vigorously rubbing her clit.

'More, more,' she heard her own mouth sob.

'It's so tight, Penny. I'm going to come. It feels so good.'

The thought of hot come in her back passage pushed Penny over the edge. She slipped her backside on to another inch of Rupert's penis, feeling his hands immediately slap on to her backside. She bucked and moaned, going further than ever before, while his fingers shot up and gripped her girdle to hold her steady, to hold her down. She came.

She felt the pumping muscles in Rupert's thick shaft through her shrieking haze. She felt the hot come spilling out inside her and cooling in her widened rectum. Penny felt faint; never had she known such pleasure. She collapsed on to the grass, taking Rupert's panting body with her. She could feel his cock softening inside the clinging walls of her deflowered anus and his hot breath washing over her neck and shoulders.

When the two flashlights licked across their perspiring bodies, Penny felt Rupert's weight suddenly rise off her back. Sensing danger, she curled into a ball, her postcoital calm shattered by the intrusion. Through the blinding lights her eyes flashed across two peaked leather caps as the Celeste twins sprang into action. Penny watched Rupert's hapless, half-dressed body being pulled across the grass. A pair of cuffs glinted against the sky.

Penny stretched out to grasp her skirt and blouse, desperate to cover herself. She found herself staring up a tight leather thigh-high boot to the severe but beautiful face that grinned down at her. A torch wandered over her scantily clad body, forcing her to recoil with embarrassment and panic.

Somewhere behind her, Penny heard a voice. It turned her blood to ice.

'Bring the slut to me!'

Three

With her hands cuffed tightly behind her back, Penny was dragged across a lawn and along a path in nothing more than her heels and hosiery. The Celeste twin, shod in shiny thigh-high platform boots and a knee-length leather coat, had hooked her arm inside Penny's and frogmarched her behind the enraged Kloster. The doctor strode out in front, her chin held high, her voice drifting back in spasms of gasping rage: 'Ignorant, libidinous fools. Fucking on the grass. No sense of decorum.'

Penny, and Rupert behind her, were each led by a twin to the outer boundary of the playing field, where a large stone cottage stood gaunt and sepulchral beneath the moon. The door had been heavily reinforced and the windows were shuttered, as if to keep someone out or something in.

Despite her embarrassment, Penny's wildcat petulance and sense of injustice kicked in. 'What the hell do you think you are doing? You cannot treat us like this. It is unlawful behaviour! I am not your prisoner! OK, so we bent a rule, but so what? You couldn't wait to get Amanda's knickers down this morning –'

Doctor Kloster swivelled on the heels of her tight riding boots and cut Penny short with a petrifying glare and spite-filled riposte: 'Little slut! What do you think this is? A holiday camp! You English have always been the same when away from home for a few days. Gag her immediately!'

Penny had little leverage to struggle and the gigantic twin's arms were too strong: they clamped around her naked chest and secured a leather strap between Penny's teeth. Penny shook her head and her eyes performed the scream that her mouth was incapable of uttering.

The twin slipped a hand between her soft knickerless cheeks and tickled her still-wet sex from behind, thrilling Penny but forcing her to kick out. One of her heels struck the glistening shin of her captor and the twin released a cry of surprise and pain.

A hand gripped the rear of Penny's neck and forced her torso down, snapping her body over in the middle. Staring at the grass with a gag between her teeth and her hands chained together, Penny had no defence against the stream of assertive smacks that slapped her naked backside.

'Little tramp, I'll give you a damn good hiding!' the twin shrieked, pushing Penny on to her knees and belabouring her soft buttocks with the palm of a leather-clad hand.

Rupert strained on his leash behind, tugging towards Penny as if to offer some manner of assistance. His captor tripped him up expertly and unleashed a riding crop from the confines of her jacket. Penny heard his yelps and the swish of the braided leather that flexed and snapped at the crop's tip before skipping off his thighs and backside.

Penny's attention was torn from Rupert when she felt the twin take up an ominous position, on all fours, behind her. She peered over her shoulder and watched the captor's coat fall open. The glossy leather of a tight basque, permeated by several studs, glinted back at Penny. The twin's beautiful face had set fast into a snarl and her eyes blazed with a zest for a thrusting pillage. Penny quivered and moaned over her gag as the long and thick appendage, fastened between the twin's legs, slipped against her outer labia and prodded at her vagina.

'Enough!' the doctor yelled. 'Leave her be, she has been loosened enough for one night. The slut will only thrive on such a deep and ruthless penetration.'

The dildo was withdrawn from Penny's tingling ecstatic sex and she was hoisted back on to her feet in one swift motion by the twin's sinewy arm.

'Another time, my sweet,' the twin whispered into Penny's ear before biting her lobe with two sharp front teeth.

The other twin had successfully subdued Rupert and ceased the flogging. She pulled him back on to his bare feet by his hair and licked one side of his handsome but perspiring face with her long pink tongue.

Kloster knocked on the cottage door three times with a drill sergeant's baton and stood back to await a response.

The sound of heavy bolts snapping back inside the cottage filled Penny with a new dread. Were they to be imprisoned? Or executed? Was this the fate of her colleague Sebastian? A lump formed in her throat, choking her with anxiety as the heavy door creaked open.

Warm yellow light flooded the patio in front of the cottage, illuminating the five figures outside: three proud and leather clad and the two half-naked and dishevelled wrecks awaiting some malign sentence.

Penny, however, was amazed to see a kind and handsome female face beaming back from the doorway. The woman in the black iron wheelchair had dressed in a long, dark woollen gown and her hair had been stylishly curled into a bun on top of her head. There was something of the school mistress about her, or the homely matron of some charity or refuge for orphans. She seemed to glow from the wheelchair, filling the surrounding air with melody and warmth. Penny had not expected to find a disabled and compassionate soul behind any barred door on the Whitehead estate and struggled to conceal her obvious shock.

'Well, what a pleasant surprise, doctor,' the woman cried, her voice honey rich and oozing with benevolence. 'We were all just about to turn in for the night. All the boys and girls will be so pleased to see you and the twins! Oh, what a lovely pair of girls. And who are our new friends? We always welcome new friends at the cottage.'

'Evening, Madam Skinner,' the doctor replied, bowing graciously. 'I apologise for the late visit but I am operating under the dean's strict instruction. These two reprobates may end up spending a great deal of time with you. The doctor paused to glance spitefully at Penny and Rupert. 'That is, if their behaviour tonight sets any precedents for future activity.'

'Oh,' the woman replied, laughing. 'Have they been up to no good, doctor?'

'Yes, madam,' Kloster answered abruptly, glaring at Penny and Rupert. 'They have repeatedly defied the regulations since their arrival. We believe a visit to the cottage may curb their appetites.'

The rosy-cheeked woman clapped her hands with joy. 'Come in, all of you, out of the night chill. The poor girl has barely a stitch on.'

Penny blushed: she suddenly felt foolish before this ordinary lady's blasé reaction. If she had been able, Penny would have kicked herself. Jeopardising her investigation, putting herself under suspicion and thoroughly humiliating herself within two days, when discretion and investigative guile had been her aim ... What has got into me? she thought, grateful for the crimson robe Madam Skinner draped around her quaking shoulders as the party entered a cosy and thickly carpeted reception.

The twins removed their coats and stood resplendent in matching boots and shiny corsetry. To Penny's surprise they removed her gag and uncuffed both her and Rupert. They were obviously certain, she mused, of

71

their superior power in catching and restraining any wayward Academy undergraduate. But where could they run to? The cottage door had been shut and latched. Penny and Rupert had no other option besides following the housekeeper's whirring chair through a door and into a large communal area.

Besides the Tudor-beamed walls and fireplace, there was nothing ordinary about the room they had entered. A rack had been fastened on the far wall, strung with every manner of correctional implement devised since the Middle Ages. From the central ceiling beam, two leather gibbets hung empty and forlorn, swaying in the warm cottage currents as if awaiting an unsuspecting man-sized meal to enter their soft traps. Other than this, the room contained nothing in the way of furniture or decoration.

Madam Skinner spun around in her antiquated chair to face the party. She raised her hands above her head and clapped them twice in quick succession. In a friendly but commanding tone, she shouted, 'Furniture!'

Within seconds, two figures clad completely in skin-tight rubber suits, with only the face cut away, erupted from the fireplace and raced into position on all fours before their mistress. The two creatures, in well-practised unison, dropped to their hands and knees, raising their behinds to create a shallow hollow at the base of each of their spines.

Penny's eyes blinked with shock and her vision blurred for a moment. When she recovered enough to scrutinise the rubber-coated human beings, she noticed that they were young men, with completely impassive faces and lowered eyelids.

'Have a seat, my young dears,' Madam Skinner offered, stretching her arms outward to point at the improvised furniture.

Penny and Rupert looked at each other with drawn and weary faces, each young throat barely concealing its involuntary gulps. Penny had no time to argue or refuse the hospitality: Kloster jabbed at her and Rupert with her baton. 'Do as you are bid! Sit!'

Penny shuffled forward, breathing deeply to clear her head, and took a seat on one of the rubber-encased men. Her soft behind nuzzled into the shiny base of the man's lower spine and his knees gave way just enough to welcome his perfumed load. Rupert followed suit and sat uneasily on the other human chair.

Madam Skinner never stopped beaming at Penny and Rupert from her own iron carriage. She clapped her hands again and shouted, 'Stool!'

From a rear door, beneath the impressive but hideous equipment rack, another figure appeared. This man was of mature age and completely naked save a black leather choker and a series of thin chains that circled his loins. Penny gasped when she noticed how the chains were fastened to his body: his penis and scrotum had been delicately pierced with tiny silver hoops that served as runners and supports for his groin necklace.

The grey-haired and distinguished-looking man skipped gleefully towards the seated guests before dropping, face upwards, to the floor at their feet.

'Go on, don't be shy, put your feet up. Make yourselves at home,' Madam Skinner invited. 'Harold won't bite, not any more, since he left that nasty bank. Imagine being responsible for all that money and all those people all over the world. You are far better off with Auntie Skinner, aren't you, Harold?'

Harold smiled and nodded his assent towards Penny.

'Young lady, Harold likes hot tired feet on his face and it is really very soothing, you will see. Go on, dear, put your feet up.'

In a trance of complete and unshakeable disbelief, Penny slipped her Cuban heels off and dropped her stocking-clad feet on to Harold's upturned face. His eyes immediately gleamed with a curious pleasure and a sigh of satisfaction escaped from his lips. From the corner of her eye she saw Rupert follow her lead and select the man's belly as a foot rest.

'There now, that's much better. Harold is a wizard with the Academy's accounts, and a true luxury for aching feet,' Madam Skinner said, laughing a little and folding her hands in her lap.

'Welcome to the cottage,' she continued. 'I am sure you have lots of questions and are both very confused as to why you have been brought to me. What you will see tonight will answer your curiosity. You are both young and free, away from home and surrounded by temptation. You have been a little naughty and I am sure you do not want to miss out on all the kind things that Miss Barbusse has in store for you.'

Penny shook her head in disbelief: there was not even a hint of irony in the woman's voice. Her handsome mouth just glistened and smiled with a mother's pride, while her buxom figure sighed and heaved with contentment in the chair.

'But the cottage,' Madam Skinner continued, 'so graciously provided by our generous benefactor, is a special place for special people. A sort of retreat from the pressures and tedium of the outside world. We all learn to earn our keep in other ways by fulfilling roles we could only ever have previously dreamt of. They may seem peculiar to you, but by the end of your stay at Whitehead I am sure you will understand the treasures we have here at the cottage.' Madam Skinner's voice lowered, and with it the temperature of the room fell perceptibly. 'But be warned. The cottage is a final resort and there is no way out.'

In a flash Madam Skinner's face animated once more with a broad and welcoming smile. She twirled around in her wheelchair and headed back to the reception. 'Follow me,' she said gaily. 'We haven't much time. My pets need their rest.'

74

Penny shuddered. Was this right? The 'pets', as she had called them, were disembodied, no longer human. It would be hard, Penny thought, when her feature was eventually published, for the world to comprehend this secret society of perversion, this annexe of the extremes of addiction and fetishistic submission. Was there really a meaning to grasp?

Penny followed the wheelchair, this time without a prompt from Kloster. Curiosity now compelled her to take in every sight the cottage had to offer, no matter how bizarre.

'Now, my dears,' Madam Skinner warned. 'Keep your voices down in the nursery. It took an age to put the babies to bed and I don't want them getting all excited again.'

Penny's face blanched and her stomach tightened. A wave of nausea passed through her. They had children at Whitehead? The thought appalled.

Madam Skinner had not lied: the cottage had indeed been equipped with a nursery. But this ground-floor chamber housed a particular brand of infant. The two figures who rose groggily from the massive cots were both male and well on their way to fifty years of age.

Kloster turned the main light on to reveal the spectacle in its every detail: gigantic coloured mobiles hung and spun from the ceiling above the timber-framed cots; the adult babies were surrounded by bears, dolls, dummies and blue plastic ducks filled with rattling beads; the base of each cot had been filled by a vinyl-covered floral mattress, upon which the occupants mewled and sprawled.

Penny covered her mouth at the sight of the two completely hairless bodies, which were rustling in the cots, naked save for the large white towelling nappies fixed around the waist by giant plastic safety pins.

Behind her, Penny heard Rupert whisper, 'Good lord . . .'

Madam Skinner wheeled her chair across to the cots and both adult babies leapt up to the wooden bars, gripping them with pink hands in an uncontainable excitement. The moment Madam Skinner unbuttoned her dress and released two massive breasts, Penny turned away and stared at the smiling Celeste twins. Despite looking away from the scene, Penny was still aware of the sounds as two mature infants suckled and fed.

After several minutes, Penny heard Madam Skinner soothing the cot creatures and kissing them good night. The wheelchair appeared between her and Rupert and Madam Skinner spoke, re-adjusting her dress, 'Michael used to be an airline pilot, one of the best they say, and Justin won two political campaigns in America with his press and advertising. But, when all is said and done, what they really needed was right here. Never mind fancy suits and big lunches. Poor darlings were pushed by unfeeling parents from an early age and all they wanted was a hug. When free from the nursery they are responsible for the lovely grounds here at Whitehead.'

Penny teetered behind the wheelchair, bereft of anything to say in response, as Madam Skinner continued on her guided tour of the cottage.

'Now, ever wonder where all that dirty washing goes? Hygiene is very important at Whitehead and your underwear is changed every day. It is expensive and very delicate, so it is only natural that the dean wants it cleansed by the very best hands. Let me introduce you to Serbio,' Madam Skinner whispered, her eyes wide with pride. 'He owns every coin laundry in the Antipodes.'

She opened another door at the end of the main reception. The dark room must once have served as a giant farmhouse kitchen at the cottage. The fixtures and fittings for food preparation had been removed and replaced by a bank of washers, dryers and large tin scrubbing baths.

Madam Skinner did not turn the lights on and made her way, by the glow of the reception light, to a huge linen basket in the centre of the laundry. She turned her head and grinned back at Penny and Rupert. 'Come closer, but be quiet. Serbio is sleeping, he has a long day ahead of him tomorrow. Hand washing two days' worth of soiled lingerie is enough to wear anybody out.'

No. Oh no. Surely not, Penny thought, as she made her way in a stagger rather than a walk towards the huge woven basket.

Madam Skinner raised the creaking basket lid a fraction and peered inside. Penny and Rupert gathered on either side of the wheelchair and took a peek. In the middle of an ocean of wrinkled nylon, lace, satin and the general wispy nothingness that the girls at Whitehead wore each day, a plump Hispanic man slept. His large body was half concealed by a spray of damp and limp underthings – all fragrant and in need of detergent.

Rupert touched Penny's elbow and steered her away from the vat and Serbio's strangely perfumed slumber. It was too much to grasp, too much to take in. Penny was rarely shocked by the crime and corruption that she faced each day in the *Inquisitor*'s reports, but Whitehead had topped them all. Penny was unable to make sense of her spinning thoughts. Her automatic reaction varied between shock and repulsion, but something else, deeper inside, purred with a strange comprehension and understanding.

'Want to go upstairs?' Madam Skinner asked, looking at each statuesque twin.

'Ooh, yes,' they purred in unison.

'Felicity plays upstairs. She and the twins have a unique bond,' Madam Skinner explained.

Penny drifted up the stairs beside the hydraulic chair lift that hoisted Madam Skinner to the first floor. Madam detached herself from the lift, with Kloster's assistance, and spun down a dimly lit corridor to the second door on the right. She unlocked the door and rolled soundlessly into the dark room. The twins overtook Penny and Rupert, pushing them to one side in their haste to reach Felicity's room first. The ever watchful Kloster took up the rear and prodded Penny forward and through the door.

The redheaded girl from the introductory film hung in a giant harness from the ceiling. The twins were already busy, rousing the groggy beauty from her rest by caressing her white nakedness through the thick leather straps. The girl began to moan and writhe softly inside the giant leather web, thrilled by the twins' roaming hands, which were immediately at work between her legs and over her large pink nipples.

'Who was she?' Penny murmured to Madam Skinner, her voice seeming to float from a numb mouth that had been incapable of speech for far too long.

'Felicity's identity is a secret, even to me. She came here two years ago and vowed never to leave. When released from the cottage she is responsible for the exquisite food that you eat in the dining room. The dean says she has riches vaster than an average oil baron waiting for her on the outside. But money cannot buy the pleasures she endures at the cottage. That is for sure,' she said, as one twin fiercely sucked at the girl's sex through an aperture in the leather harness.

The twin rose from between the girl's legs and encircled the harness with her arms, pressing her long body against it and her face upwards. The girl inside pushed her face down through a wide diamond-shaped slit and their mouths embraced noisily. Each pretty mouth lapped and bit at the other; each pair of delicately painted eyes lowered and fluttered in desire.

Penny watched the long tongues slipping about and smearing each other's face in a rapture of passion. The girls moaned, and soothed each other with a muffled communication of strange feline sounds. The other twin was absorbed with the redhead's alabaster backside, nuzzling her lips and teeth between the creamy ravine of cheeks to find a taut pink gem.

Penny watched Madam Skinner's rapt and attentive face, pleased with the twins' ministrations on her caged pet. Madam Skinner pulled the hem of her woollen smock up to her mid-thigh and fluttered it gently as if to cool a hidden fire. Her long motionless legs had been enhanced by sheer black stockings and her feet were tightly hobbled in patent Edwardian ankle boots. Penny wondered how she had come to be here as guardian and protector of the Academy's hidden inmates – individuals unable to escape the flood of sensuality unlocked by Barbusse's regime.

A gentle smacking sound emerged from the trio of shapely girls busy with each other on centre stage. The twin who had fed on the captive's curvaceous backside had begun to gently slap and then rub the girl's behind. Her playful whacks increased gradually in force and Madam Skinner began to sigh. The other twin held the girl's face steady with leather-gloved hands and sucked at her cheeks, eyes and chin, smearing her face with lipstick and saliva.

Penny felt Madam Skinner's hand touch her own and stroke it gently. Penny froze, unsure of how to react.

'Let us leave them. I feel they may take some time with Felicity. The twins are unable to leave the girl alone.'

Penny caught Rupert's glazed, aroused and confused eyes for a moment, before following the wheelchair out of the room. Penny turned her back on the slapping sounds and steadily rising groans, her mind pondering on the twins' dominant lesbian tastes and how she too might suffer and delight at their touch.

'There is only the stable left, but the pony is sleeping,' Madam Skinner called from her chair, her voice trailing behind the speeding passage of the iron carriage down the corridor. 'I am afraid I wore him out earlier this evening, so a tour of the stables will have to wait until a more convenient time.'

The revelation about a human pony and his stable did not surprise Penny. Her mind had already exhausted itself on a kaleidoscope of shock and enlightenment.

Madam Skinner led her guests back down the stairs and to the front door. In the hallway she stopped and whispered in Kloster's ear. The German doctor frowned and then began smiling, nodding her head in approval. Penny was only able to make out one or two key words: 'Please . . . the boy . . . I wish . . . taste . . . him.'

Penny looked across at the bemused Rupert and said good night, realising that he would not accompany her and the doctor back to the manor.

'You will stay here!' Kloster barked, pointing at Rupert with her baton.

Rupert danced from foot to foot, his eyes flicking about with fear. Madam Skinner's chair glided across to his quaking body and caressed the side of his naked ribs. She soothed him with words, and winked one big maternal eye at a face suddenly stricken with a shower of perspiration.

Penny left the cottage with the striding doctor, only turning back once to look at the two silhouettes holding hands in the doorway of the gamekeeper's dwelling.

'I hope tonight serves as a lesson, young lady,' Doctor Kloster barked, without turning her immaculate bobbed head to look at Penny. 'If you are caught once more I will allow the twins to indulge themselves with you for at least two days, before your disgraceful expulsion.'

Penny flopped down on to her soft bed, kicking her shoes off in the dark. It was past one in the morning and the evening had worn her out. The muscles in the backs of her legs screamed after so much high-heel punishment; her sex felt pleasantly bruised and her rectum still throbbed from Rupert's merciless pounding.

Penny's mind swirled with a host of images in the dark, all jostling for pole position and a possible explanation. She saw the pudgy babies busy in Madam Skinner's voluminous cleavage, and young Felicity writhing beneath the lash and the Celeste twins' skilful tongues. Penny rubbed the insides of her smooth stocking-clad thighs and pondered on the eventual destination of her hosiery and stained panties: to be wrapped, perhaps, around Serbio's face in a few days' time. How could she cope with the idea of human furniture and pony transport, not more than a few hundred metres from where she slept?

Across the darkened room, the white flesh of the girl in furs shone eerily back to Penny from the exquisite oil portrait. Penny slipped her fingers into her punished and still-wet sex, and moaned beneath the velvet canopy protecting her solitary rapture. Whoever the girl had been, she was in Penny and probably submerged in every other female pupil at the Academy. The girl embodied the desire in some universal woman, imprisoned by convention in every soul. At Whitehead, Penny knew, a woman could become anything: she could discover her true passion, no matter how obscene or excessive. In some curious paradox, she could be lashed and bound, fucked mercilessly, but rise fearsome and dominant from the ashes of the acceptable. In two days Penny had enjoyed sex with two strangers; she had been spanked and loved it. Would it be as easy to roll off the life raft of rent and routine and float into the gamekeeper's world of continual solace in pleasure, an endless cycle of exploration and deviant peaks of lust?

Penny drifted off into a haunted slumber where legs entwined around supple necks and thick cocks speared pink fleshy cavities.

Four

Penny and Rupert had not been the only students caught misbehaving the night before. At breakfast, Roberto and a svelte blonde girl served cereal and toast to the Academy populace in their underwear. The girl seemed ready to faint with embarrassment as she teetered between rows of giggling students in her girdle, seamed stockings and heels. Both Celeste twins were at the ready with large black canes to prompt her if the service should flag. Her firm little breasts, though, still managed to stick out in sulky defiance, and her curvy backside wriggled provocatively near the dining men.

Roberto poured coffee up on the lecturers' dais wearing nothing besides his boxer shorts, and threw warning glances down at the other, smiling, male diners.

Penny had to suppress a giggle herself, remembering a line from Rupert's letter: *A friend and I have managed to bend several rules without detection.* Their levity and guile, it seemed, had come unstuck in a dramatic manner. Perhaps, Penny mused, that is why they had been caught by the tennis courts – Rupert and Roberto may have been under surveillance, both becoming trapped like salacious rats when out on nocturnal female hunts. And where was Rupert now? His conspicuous absence from the refectory shot a little thrill up Penny's spine when she thought about what treats Madam Skinner had in mind for the firm young man.

'You look dreadful!' Amanda fired from across the table at Penny.

'Thanks, mate,' Penny replied.

Amanda laughed out loud and only hushed her mirth when Kloster's ashen face turned towards the girls.

'I had a late night,' Penny whispered back across the silver tureen filled with steaming bacon. The previous evening's visit to the cottage seemed like a bad dream. Her reason still chased her imagination and tried to comprehend the nightmarish world she had glimpsed in Madam Skinner's private annexe.

'Oh. Someone you should introduce me to?' Amanda asked.

'No,' Penny answered, giggling. 'There will not be a repeat performance after what I saw last night.'

'Don't you start holding out on me, Penny, we have a long and beautiful friendship ahead of us,' Amanda hissed back in mock fury.

'I won't, darling, but we have to be careful, really careful –' Penny stopped herself when she became aware of Lucy Harrington's obvious interest in their conversation. The girl smirked and turned back to nibbling at a crust of toast with her delicate mouth.

'Go on,' Amanda prompted. 'Ignore the teacher's pet. Tell me, what's up?'

'Later, Amanda, not now –' Penny tried to reply.

'Teacher's pet!' Lucy hissed. 'I advise you two slags to keep it shut.'

'Ooh, so classy,' Amanda taunted. 'Your airs and titles don't fool me. You're just a cockney scrubber with a bit of Daddy's dough in your hip pocket.'

Lucy's face boiled white with rage and her long fingers dug into the linen tablecloth. She pushed her chair away from the table and stormed off from the dining room, her every quick step watched by Miss Barbusse's cold eyes.

'Amanda!' Penny exclaimed. 'For God's sake don't

make an enemy of her. She's tight with the dean. Barbusse never takes her eyes off the girl. You saw her obvious favouritism in yesterday's lessons. I am in enough hot water without that brat running her mouth off to icicle tits up there on stage.'

Amanda giggled.

'Yeah,' the plump Bessy chirped in. 'And I saw her coming out of the dean's room last night, all messed up, with lipstick on her collar.'

'You're joking!'

'Never!'

'She didn't!'

A chorus of girls squealed along the bench, their pale necks leaning forward to immerse themselves in the morning gossip.

'Silence!' Kloster bellowed from the staff table, glaring at the girls. 'You will eat in silence!'

Every head dropped back to the business of eating or moving food around their plates. No girl, it seemed, wanted to perform the long walk down to Kloster's study that Penny and Amanda had undertaken on the previous day.

It is just like school, Penny thought, with everybody regressing back to churlish behaviour beneath an authoritarian regime – gossiping and squabbling, sneaking about and breaking petty rules. Amanda and she were already gaining some sort of kudos for being the bravest and most rebellious students. It seemed like such a contradiction: everybody had paid so much money to attend Whitehead and yet they just automatically put up with the system. She wondered if it was the same for the boys: were they terrified of Klima in the same way that the girls jumped at Barbusse and Kloster's shadows?

She would soon gain an insight into the male tutor's style and character – the girls were timetabled for their first lesson with Mr Klima after breakfast.

* * *

'You are all the most beautiful women in the world,' Mr Klima announced as he walked slowly and carefully amongst the seated class of girls. 'You are irresistible. Every part of your soft bodies will appeal to a man. Your breasts, your legs, your feet, your eyes, hair, shoulders, necks, lips and hands, every single part of you is a loaded gun. But it is a weapon that must be armed skilfully and aimed with precision.'

The girls sat rapt and attentive, watching or sensing the steady passage of the handsome Russian behind their seats and between their shoulders. His voice travelled from all corners of the classroom, caressing their ears and soothing their initial anxieties away. There was nothing curt or sharp in that voice; it could purr with a deep brogue or dance playfully inside a girl's head.

His lean and rangy limbs moved with ease and occasionally tensed with an acrobat's steel beneath his soft slacks and white linen shirt. The latter emphasised his tanned skin, which stretched taut over angular facial features.

'There are influential clients and treacherous rivals, there are dirt digging journalists and potential fortunes all around you. It is a war and a woman needs ammunition of the highest calibre. The way you cross your legs in a meeting, or carelessly drop a piece of paper in an embassy can be the difference between a million dollars and a fool. Nothing can be accidental or left to chance. In a world that men call their own, a girl must be devious and courageous. Whether behind the scenes or leading a charge across a minefield of bonds and investments, she must be fast and in control. I will show you how.'

Klima stood before Penny and looked into her eyes. She detected an innate sense of superiority, but also a wisdom acquired from experience and adventures that she could only guess at.

85

'Who am I?' He seemed to address the question to her personally. 'What do I know?'

Penny's mouth fell open; she struggled to say something apt or even clever, but no sound was forthcoming.

Klima answered his own question: 'The actual details, individuals and events of my past are irrelevant, but I once worked for an agency that reduced body language to a specific technique. We utilised all we had, our lives depended upon it.'

Penny sensed the atmosphere in the classroom – the girls were hanging on to his every word. The sound of his voice had become a hypnotic melody to their ears.

Klima moved away from Penny and sat leisurely on the desk before his class, looking at each girl in turn. He gave everyone a warm and comforting smile before making his next move. 'Each of you will seduce me.'

There was a sharp communal intake of breath from all around Penny. Every girl began to shift uncomfortably on her chair, coughing for composure.

Mr Klima laughed and slapped his hands on his hard thighs. The girls all laughed too, nervous and desperate to reduce the tension.

'By the time you leave Whitehead,' he continued, 'you will be the tutors and I will be on my knees, amazed at how much you have taught me in our time together. You see, every woman is unique and her individual graces will introduce new and subtle methods into the equation, which will be capable of surprising any man who thinks he knows it all. When your qualifications and commercial experience in the outside world incite envy or indifference, my techniques will shift the balance. Your intelligence and beauty will combine like a work of art to stun the onlooker. My treasures, let us begin.'

Amber from New York was chosen first. He instructed her to walk to a chair in front of the class, to sit down opposite him and to present a mock business pitch which each girl had been asked to study.

Wrong choice, Penny thought: the girl was so obviously nervous, finding her adjustment to Whitehead harder than any other pupil. She had done nothing but sob since her arrival; her swollen eyes that morning attested to night-time misery endured alone.

Amber tripped and stumbled towards the chair. She sat down with an exaggerated attempt at elegance and spoke in a high-pitched and fluting voice, each word stricken with terror. Her every move and mumbled sentence made the class aware that this girl hated being the centre of attention.

When she finished her proposal, Klima just stared back at her without speaking. The silence roared around the classroom, every girl throbbing with pity and anxiety, knowing that they too must take a turn under Klima's interrogation.

When the lecturer finally spoke, Penny clamped her hand over her mouth to stifle an outcry. 'Will you fuck me, Amber?' Klima asked with a sardonic air. 'I have a hotel room upstairs. If you come up for a drink and suck me off I might consider your deal. But you better be good, or I will never see you again. And you better give it up to all of my friends too. You seem weak and susceptible and you know how men just love to fuck a girl like that.'

Amber burst into tears and someone near Penny whispered 'bastard' under her breath.

Klima leant forward and offered Amber his handkerchief. He kissed her forehead gently and smoothed her silky hair with one hand. He stood up and walked across to the class.

'A bastard, you say.'

'I – I mean –' a girl spluttered behind Penny.

'You are quite right, my dear,' he said to the class. 'I behaved like a bastard. I am glad you pointed it out and you were correct to do so. It is commendable that you spotted my attitude, even though it was obviously dramatic, because that is what the managing director or envoy for foreign sales is thinking, when you sit in his office or across a business luncheon table. He has the cash and you want it, so why not have a little fun with the girls and shop around for a better deal. What is stopping him?'

Amber stopped crying and turned to listen to Klima.

'But, my girls, why not take the initiative and ambush the self-important fool from the moment you wake up and spray perfume against your delicate throats?'

The blonde girl, called Jade, took her turn on the chair next. She was last seen serving breakfast in her panty girdle but, despite her nocturnal digression, had obviously listened carefully to Klima.

Jade teetered carefully towards the chair and offered a delicate hand in greeting to Klima. Her eyelids fluttered softly and her measured gaze leapt across his chest and crotch as if in admiration of the man before her. She crossed her black-stocking-clad legs slowly and rotated her front foot. She pinched the hem of her skirt with red-painted fingertips and lifted it enough to afford Klima a glance along her thigh. Her voice was carefully balanced and husky. Jade laughed deliriously at each of Klima's deliberately coarse jokes and suggestive comments, always hinting at and half promising some future tryst with the lecturer.

When her performance had concluded, Klima smiled broadly. The class applauded the blushing Jade as she returned to her seat.

'Good, a very promising start but, if you will allow me to suggest, a trifle too deliberate, Jade. I have no doubt, however, that after this term my heart and cheque book will be in your hands. Just a whiff of your perfume will empty my company bank account.'

The girls laughed and Penny found herself nodding

with admiration. He was actually teaching them to defend and counter attack in a secret guerrilla war. Every career girl in Britain was aware of the sexual contest, but at Whitehead they had the opportunity to take a PhD in manipulation.

Lucy Harrington took up the challenge next. Despite her instantaneous distrust of the girl, Penny had to marvel at the young heir's skill. Lucy even moved her chair closer to Klima and, within minutes, had pulled his stare from her glossy lips, to her breasts and on to her shiny legs. For several seconds the toe of her stiletto even brushed the lecturer's shin and forced a noticeable ripple of emotion to pass across his face.

When Amanda took her turn, it became obvious to Penny that she wanted to outdo Lucy more than anything else.

Amanda feigned tipsiness like an actress and drifted away from the script: 'I know what you are expecting. You think that after a little business chat and a glass of Chardonnay I am going to fuck you senseless.'

'I do?' Klima exclaimed.

'But I don't mix business with pleasure. I made that mistake once, as a junior in a firm. I did something that I am not very proud of to get a head start on the other potential partners.'

'What? Tell me. I must say this approach is most unexpected, if not unprofessional, but all the same I am intrigued.'

'Between you and me,' Amanda threw out casually, 'I wanked the boss during a boardroom meeting with thirty executives in attendance.'

'You did?' Klima rasped.

'Oh yes,' Amanda whispered, leaning forward and stroking the lecturer's knee. 'He could not react, everyone was listening to his speech. He stumbled a little but put on a good show. He was respectable and had a status to maintain but became unable to shake my long fingers off – working on him under the table in his lap. Nice cock too, really thick. When he came, it was fortunate that someone else was speaking. Some guy was wittering on about why he had blown a deal and I had wrapped one of my silky black stockings around the guy's cock for an extra thrill. The boss did not hear a word: he kept groaning into his handkerchief and then out it came, shooting all over my feet. I got some strange looks walking out of that meeting wearing only one stocking.'

Klima and Amanda both laughed, while Penny wondered, with a wry smile on her face, about how fictional the experience really was.

Amanda, under the cover of irrepressible giggles, allowed her hand to tickle the lecturer's inner thigh as she struggled to speak. 'So, do we have a deal? Or do I have to get your pecker out to prove what a good investment I am?'

The class laughed along with Klima as Amanda waltzed back to her seat, throwing an arrogant look over at the sneering Lucy Harrington.

Klima's eyes smiled as he said, 'Well, it may not work for everyone, but I am pleased to see someone using their wits and taking an outrageous leap of faith. I think Amanda could close a deal and make a man feel as if he had been in bed with her for a week, without her even doing anything more than shaking his . . . um . . . hand.'

More mirth followed and Penny relaxed into the spirit of the training session, already imagining the insertion of these techniques into her future interviews.

'You see,' Klima said, 'we are not asking you to sleep with a potential client. We are asking you to project the image of already having done that, to drive him wild for more, so he feels as if he could not spend another night without you. Or, alternatively, maybe promising to do that in a manner so convincing that he will be a puppet dangling beneath your strings.'

The girls were all given three attempts at working on Klima in the first lesson, and Penny was pleased to see his discreet encouragement of the shrinking Amber. He rewarded her, without condescension, in the form of gentle praises, and Amber responded – her third attempt at the proposal raising a noticeable erection beneath Klima's loose-fitting trousers.

The pace was lifted and the obstacles were raised in the next seminar. Klima played the part of a pompous, boisterous and outspoken business man. His every word was carefully loaded with contempt and sexist jibing. This character held strong views, dominating every interview with a frightening voice and an intimidating presence.

Every girl struggled with Klima; even Lucy Harrington perspired and garbled her answers back to the explosive bigot. Every hope seemed to have been lost, and Penny doubted whether any girl in that room would ever find a weakness in the true-to-life persona that Klima had adopted. This was, however, until plump Bessy from the mining corporation took to the stage.

'I asked to see the manager. I want the organ grinder and not the monkey!' Klima began. 'I don't trust women with money, not if my ex-wife's performance was anything to go on.'

'I am the manager,' Bessy replied curtly in her broad northern accent.

'Oh!' Klima retorted. 'Positive discrimination. Is no industry safe from political correctness? You'll be telling me you're a lesbian next.' Klima chuckled to himself, playing the role with an expert's ease.

Bessy did not even flinch. She walked around his chair, her plump corseted curves whispering around the lecturer's face. A flicker of mischief played across her eyes and Klima seemed genuinely perplexed as to her movements.

Bessy upended the lecturer from the chair with her

powerful arms. The girls all gasped as Klima's body sprawled unceremoniously on the floor beneath Bessy's heels. Penny expected him to leap up and send the girl to Kloster in a storm of shouts and curses. He did not; his body remained on the floor. Bessy stood over his face, her hands on her hips, her massive chest pushed out with pride.

'When you come into my office, you enter with respect or you leave on your knees,' she warned.

Klima tried to lift himself from the polished floor but Bessy pushed him down, placing one heel in the centre of his broad chest.

'Did I say you could rise, worm?' she asked matter-of-factly, her face betraying nothing save contempt.

Klima shook his head, his face a whirlpool of confusion. Bessy pulled up a chair and sat next to Klima before speaking again in that commanding tone: 'Before I allow you the dignity of a chair, you will ingratiate yourself by soothing my feet. A man like you is fit for little besides licking a woman's feet. You are a silly, big-mouthed, small-minded prat!'

Klima tried to sit up again, but Bessy was quicker: she kicked a shoe off and pushed her stocking-clad foot on to the lecturer's face, forcing his head back down to the boards.

'Hold my foot, fool, and do as I say!' Bessy bellowed, her voice ringing around the room.

Klima's hands scrabbled for the foot and began caressing its silky shape in the palm of his hands.

Bessy continued to surprise everyone present in the room. She slowly unbuttoned her blouse and allowed her pendulous chest access to the air. Her black bra offered little support to the mass of soft white flesh that rose above the half-cups. Her breasts were large, powerful and surprisingly firm; the two large saucer-shaped nipples had risen to hard nuggets and caught

Klima's eyes instantly. He just gaped and stared at the glorious mountain range above him.

'Did you think that a woman has no other purpose than to bear children and clean up after your dirty stinking habits? Has your wife ever told you what a prick you really are? I guess not. Before you do business with my company – because you will meet my demands – you will write a long apology to me and attend dinner tonight with not so much as a stitch on beneath your trousers. If I have to whip your tiny cock in a crowded restaurant, I want no impediment. Under your shirt there will be a collar to fit my leash, and after desert I will show you exactly who calls the shots in business. I will train you like a dog. Now, little boy, are you going to be my dog?'

Klima nodded his ascent and Penny became unsure as to whether his show of fear was something more than just an act. Bessy reclaimed her shoe, still straight-faced, and hauled Klima to his feet with one mighty arm.

'Wonderful,' Klima whispered, his face a portrait of astonishment. 'Marvellous.'

The girls applauded and Bessy strode back to her seat, her wide rosy face beaming.

Klima said, while straightening his clothes, 'Bessy, how did you know? How did you know how to react?'

'I have come across that attitude a number of times, sir. The primary industry can sometimes be a breeding ground for that kind of man. I just reverse the roles, because men like that have waited their whole lives for a woman to take charge of them. A big, strong and powerful girl. They love to feel small, like little toys, being crushed beneath high heels. I guess it works for me.'

Klima smiled and held out his hands in admiration. 'I pity the man, Bessy, who ever makes the mistake of underestimating you. Girls –' he turned to address the class '– I think we can all follow Bessy's lead. She can be an icon of femininity and sensuality, but a demon in a D cup in the twinkle of an eye. Congratulations, Bessy.'

'Stephen, you could not seduce a mouse out of a paper bag if you were made of cheese. Go and sit down!' Miss Barbusse volleyed at the lad's lack-lustre attempt at flattering her to extract information.

The male students were always a handful at the start of any term, Miss Barbusse mused. They were too afraid of really opening up and trying, too embarrassed about what the others might say when they were asked to assume romantic postures in specially prepared conditions.

She sat at a candlelit table, looking serene though formidable, sipping mineral water from a wine glass. The male students all sat before the table on a row of chairs. Each in turn had been instructed to approach Miss Barbusse, as if to fulfil an important dinner obligation, and to woo her with all their might.

Roberto had volunteered to start the lesson, convinced that a noble Sicilian ancestry endowed him with superhuman powers as a female magnet. He was wrong, and far too confident and arrogant for the dean's taste. When Roberto tried to hold her hand within a minute of taking his seat, Miss Barbusse had thrown her glass of water in his face. When he mentioned that she had 'a body created for sin', the dean had slapped his still-dripping face. The blow had shot out quickly and left his cheek smarting long after his sudden exit from the table in disgrace.

The next two had rambled as the dean yawned unsympathetically before their clumsy attempts at creating the right impression; boasts of wealth, rugby heroics, computer genius, and alcoholic excess had left Barbusse cold.

'What am I? A tart?' she had exclaimed in horror.

94

'No! I am a wealthy potential client, looking to make a good investment. I want charm and manners, good conversation and, most of all, I want to feel special. My money is of no real importance; it is my graceful presence that you crave. I want to be elevated and adored, not drooled over or told bawdy locker-room stories. You are all hopeless! Next!'

A slight and willowy man called Paris made his way slowly to the table. He worked for a leading international publisher. Miss Barbusse recalled that he was being groomed for the position of a leading editor. He would have to learn to sell his company through himself, perhaps, in order to clinch a publishing deal ahead of eager rivals. How will he fare? she wondered, with low expectations.

Paris was a quiet twenty-something, and the most solitary of all her male pupils. His performance in PE with the Celeste twins had been unremarkable, and he rarely smiled, possessing a brooding and too thoughtful temperament. Mr Klima, however, had noted his perceptive character and natural flair for stategy. Another drab bookworm, Miss Barbusse presumed, amazed that his firm had not sent an individual with more style and noticeable vigour.

Paris approached the table and bowed to Miss Barbusse. Old fashioned but quaint, she thought.

He pulled out his chair and smiled sweetly before beginning his ploy. 'You know, when I walked through that door, I kept imagining that this was a blind date. When I looked around the room there was only one table that I wanted to sit down at. When I told the waiter about my appointment and he pointed you out to me, my stomach did a little loop: it was that table, the one I had seen and felt curiously attracted to from the reception.'

A novel opening and he looks as if he means it, she thought.

95

Paris filled Miss Barbusse's glass. He smiled and said, 'Forgive me if, at any point during dinner, I am clumsy enough to tuck the tablecloth into my belt. I have done it before and carried a ton of cutlery with me to the gents'. A slapstick moment could be very amusing but awful for creating the right ambience. You know, I am stricken with a perpetual shaking when confronted by . . . by a beautiful woman.'

The boys all roared with laughter, but the dean scrutinised the boy a little more closely. A nice touch. Every girl likes to laugh, and that facade of vulnerability is very appealing on a young man. His mouth . . . something there interests me, she thought.

'You look so very chic this evening, Miss Barbusse,' Paris almost whispered – his final mention of her name a little hushed.

'Thank you, Paris. I bought the dress in Prague.'

'*Dva cherrni pivo prism*,' Paris aired stridently.

'What?' Miss Barbusse queried.

'It's Czech. Roughly translated it means: a strength in elegance,' he answered, raising his glass in a toast to her.

Miss Barbusse smiled and did her best to suppress a laugh. She knew Czech and his phrase, under the scrutiny of an accurate translation, asked for 'two dark beers, please'. He was trying. Half buffoon and half darling. Miss Barbusse felt her tightly corseted body warming to the young man. He had listened to her and studied her suggestions. She decided to encourage him in a manner that she had not attempted for years.

Under the table, without detection from the other boys, Miss Barbusse stretched out her long and exquisitely stocking-clad leg. While continuing to laugh at his quips and bask in his flattery, she stroked his calf muscle with the top of her slippery foot and let her mouth suck on a breadstick.

Her snaking foot beneath the table climbed gracefully up his leg and placed itself on his lap. Paris blushed but seemed encouraged by the illicit contact. The dean liked the way he looked into her eyes, fascinated by her dialogue, asking her questions with a genuine interest – attentive to perfection.

His cock had become quite solid beneath his trousers. She caressed its length with her pointed toes and watched him surreptitiously glance down to see her pretty pink toenails, just visible beneath sheer black nylon, stroking the outline of his now throbbing penis. She began to imagine his velvety shaft, thick and topped by a fragrant dew at the tip. She imagined his pale-pink glans, and the pouch holding two silken balls between his slim legs – they always seemed at their best, aesthetically, when gently cradled in painted fingernails.

Miss Barbusse began to feel truly inspired as the conversation continued, her predatory instincts rising. A wave of assertive desire pulsed through her and she knew that, if this engagement had been in the outside world, then young Paris would have discovered an unrivalled pleasure within her hands. It was a shame that she intended to continue with Lucy's training that evening: a young and healthy cock would have satisfied a certain proportion of her cravings.

'Do you have a girlfriend?' Miss Barbusse asked, only half in role.

'No, I am afraid a life of solitude and contemplation seems to be my lot. But, it really is refreshing to enjoy a stimulating evening with a woman. I mean that,' he whispered.

I bet you do, she thought. The dean continued with her rubbing ministrations in the lad's lap, pushing his cock flat against his groin and rubbing the base of his shaft quickly with the ball of her foot, increasing the friction and his pleasure.

The dean shielded her stunning eyes with her heavy lashes and purred across the table at Paris, 'I wonder if you would like to enjoy a coffee with me after dinner.

My husband is away playing golf for the weekend, so I have no other plans. I am staying at the Havana where they serve an excellent Brazilian roast, through room service.'

The other students leant forward, sighing with amazement and envy. Miss Barbusse could see their faces over Paris's shoulder; a dozen young men were desiring her, wanting to swap places with the triumphant Paris. The thought appealed to her and it seemed a guarantee of their absolute attention in future.

'I would be honoured,' Paris replied, his eyes and heart lost to her charms.

To celebrate and seal the breakthrough, the dean rose from the table and approached Paris. She smiled at the young man and stroked his floppy blond hair with her manicured hand. The other men gasped and stared at each other, double-taking in disbelief, finding it hard to comprehend this change in their principal and tutor.

Paris, as if under a spell, turned his chair and faced Miss Barbusse. She lowered herself between his legs. It was almost too much to believe when the sound of a descending zipper broke the silence.

In full view of every man in the room, the dean took Paris's fully erect cock in her slender fingers and massaged it gently from base to tip. Several legs crossed in the room and every pair of eyes was unable to blink or remove its gaze from the unexpected scenario unfolding before it.

Her mouth met the tip of the cock, her glistening red lips rotating without closing around the swollen head. A little pink tongue appeared from between perfect white teeth and began a quick flurry of lashes across the tip of the penis. Paris groaned and closed his eyes, automatically attempting to raise his backside from the chair.

The phallus slipped between the dean's slick lips and her cheeks hollowed as her mouth began to suck. His entire body trembled, while his face darkened and moistened with the blood and sweat of an intense arousal. The sleek head of the dean slowly moved up and down the hard cock, while her hand found his full and bloated pouch and tickled it with dagger-like nails. She began to hum through her nose, the sound of her arousal delighting the captive audience.

Paris moaned in time with her sucking rhythm. She smeared his long cock with lipstick and glistening, priceless saliva. The dean enjoyed the thick shape, which expanded her cheeks, stretched her jaw wide and slipped across her undulating tongue. Her student's body tensed; she sensed every tendon and sinew stretching tight throughout his lean physique.

The dean increased the speed of her soft red mouth up and down the spasming cock. Her head leapt up and down his penis at an astonishing speed and Paris rasped the word 'Yes!' out of his trembling mouth.

The dean removed her mouth for a moment so that the other pupils could watch the thick clots of cream shooting across a narrow chasm and into her eager mouth. As she turned to face the class, she swallowed the frothing load on her tongue and purred her approval at them all.

There was a long period of silence before the dean explained the next scenario and lesson to them.

For the remaining period before luncheon, Miss Barbusse became amazed at the efforts and passion her pupils invested in the mock phone conversations she had devised. It was as if every student had raised his performance in order to achieve the next reward.

'Who's going to fuck him first?' Amanda casually asked the group of relaxing girls.

'My name's down!' Bessy giggled, slapping the cool grass with her hands.

'Do I sense a bit of competition here?' Penny asked.

'You bet,' Amber piped in, already evolving beyond the shrinking violet after one morning with Klima.

He had released them ten minutes early after a morning he described as 'thoroughly promising', and the girls now relaxed on the lawn outside the refectory.

Lucy Harrington sat off to one side with Jade, the only girl she seemed even vaguely friendly with. The two blondes watched the other girls. Jade studied Lucy's face, following her new friend's every move and opinion like a sheep.

'I put my money on little miss hot pants, Penny Chambers,' Lucy quipped sarcastically. 'She will want to practise her creative development on him: she's been through half the students already.'

Lucy began to laugh and Jade joined in; the other girls fell silent around Penny. Only Amanda seemed unperturbed by the young heir, whispering, 'That's it,' and attempting to rise to her feet in response. Penny blushed but grabbed Amanda's arm and made her resume her seat, determined to fight her own battles.

'People in glass houses, Lucy,' Penny replied, staring daggers at the beautiful young debutante. 'From what I hear, you go straight to the top, all the way with the dean.' Penny was unable to stop. 'But, tell us, who goes on top?'

Lucy Harrington spat, 'Bitch,' and leapt quickly to her high-heeled feet.

Penny rose to the challenge, half from pride and half from anger. She screwed her hands up into fists and walked towards Lucy Harrington. The other girls fell silent and looked at their neighbours, searching wide eyes for a peaceful suggestion. Amanda followed behind Penny, backing her friend up and keeping an eye on the skulking Jade.

'Tough girl, huh?' Lucy hissed into Penny's face.

This is stupid, Penny thought. I have not had a spat with a girl since the third year at senior school. All she could remember about that was a blur of pinching, kicking and hair-pulling before the geography teacher waded in. The *Inquisitor*, however, had run stories on the streams of victims that Lucy had left behind her on the binges she favoured around the exclusive clubs and resorts of Europe. She had trashed a number of high-profile hotel rooms and blackened a rock star's eye in Monte Carlo – the girl loved to ruck.

The dinner gong sounded and rippled across the lawns.

'Saved by the bell, slut!' Lucy mocked.

'Any time, Harrington. As you can see, I am just wetting myself with fear,' Penny threw back.

As Lucy quivered with a fresh rage and prepared to fling herself at Penny, Miss Barbusse appeared from a side quadrangle with the men in tow, all of them laughing at something she must have said, crowding her and delighting in her very presence. When Lucy saw the dean she dropped her front quickly, bowed her head and scurried off towards the dining room.

Penny shook her head and watched Lucy teeter off with Jade, her intuition lighting warning flares across her mind.

'She's all mouth. You stared her down and now she knows who's boss,' Penny heard Amanda whisper. Amanda stood beside her and tickled the outside of her hand in support.

'I don't know. That girl is trouble and she's not stupid either. I'm going to keep an eye on her,' Penny answered, even more determined to get her research under way after the conflict. Kloster had warned of an expulsion and there was always the outside chance that Lucy knew her from London. This latter thought filled Penny with panic: if Lucy placed her with the press then anything could happen. She might even just disappear, like her colleague Sebastian. Amanda would stand by her and that was touching, but against the power of the dean, Kloster and the Celeste twins it was a barricade made from straw. Even if Lucy became nothing more than an agitator, Penny knew that her life at Whitehead could be hellish and she needed space to breathe and move, to collate information, open doors, ask questions. Round the clock suspicion and surveillance was tantamount to an expulsion. This was her first assignment and Penny felt as if she had already blown it, and that hurt more than anything else.

Penny sat before her mirror after the evening meal, stripped down to her antique underwear, and scratched a few more names and details into her notepad. Looking at herself in the mirror had become a pleasant pastime: pouting her lips, repeatedly crossing her nylon slippery legs, playing with her perpetually hard nipples and feeling fifteen in her big sister's clothes all over again.

She only had to rub her thighs together or tickle a nipple and thoughts of Rupert, Amanda and now Klima would pour back into her mind. It was a continual state of arousal, reinforcing her feelings of having 'missed out' for so many years as a career girl. Not any more, she promised herself: From now on I refuse to neglect my emotional side because, when I do, I'm dangerous.

Penny giggled to herself and gave the mirror another pout.

Someone rapped on the door of her room. It was a playful, singsong little knock. Must be Amanda, Penny assumed, and dashed towards the door without even bothering to stop for a nightgown.

Penny swung the door wide open, her face beaming and then suddenly dropping as Lucy Harrington chilled her room with an evil smile.

'Stripped for action and it's barely seven o'clock.'

'What the hell do you want?' Penny lashed back, throwing one arm across her half-cupped breasts.

'I have come to bury the hatchet – in your head!' Lucy hissed and pounced on Penny.

A maelstrom of fear and panic surged across Penny's

mind as she lost her footing and crashed on to a thick rug. Lucy was on top of her in a flash, pinning her arms to the floor and squashing her hips into the rug.

Jade raced into the room and closed the door behind her, locking it shut.

Penny's throat closed with fear, her breath coming rapidly in spasms through her nose.

'Not such a smart mouth now! You can't hide behind that lanky bitch any more!' Lucy gasped with a cruel satisfaction. She seemed to have passed beyond sanity – the look in her dazzling eyes frightened Penny to the very marrow of her bones.

'Get off me!' Penny spat, but Lucy just clutched her hips in an even tighter grip with her long thighs.

'You have been asking for this since day one,' Lucy accused. 'You're just a cock-hungry tart and I am the real thing. I know you, I've seen you around the clubs at home!'

Penny froze; her face must have been plastered, she thought, with the guilt of one about to confess, beg and plead for mercy.

'I've seen you with that cow from the dailies, who writes that science fiction about my love life,' Lucy continued, her rage building with every second. 'You know the one I mean, and don't try and deny it – Mel Katura, a friend of yours. Well, I hate her and any friend of hers is an enemy of mine.'

Penny hovered between terror and relief. Lucy must have seen her with Mel Katura, an acquaintance from the tabloid crowd, in a club. She could only hope that Lucy did not assume that birds of a feather always flock together.

'I hardly know her,' Penny gasped in her defence. 'I've only met her once. Now get off me!'

'Sure, sure,' Lucy mocked, before turning back towards Jade to issue a command. 'Give me the stockings and pull that stool over.'

Jade jumped into action, pulling the red velvet footstool into the centre of the room. She positioned it square to the four-poster bed and unhooked a tangled web of black stockings from her skirt pocket – Whitehead regulation-issue nylons but destined, Penny thought, for an unofficial purpose.

It seemed to be a well-practised wrestling move that Lucy used when Penny found herself flipped effortlessly on to her stomach with one arm hoisted up behind her back.

'Get her arms!' Lucy ordered, and Jade immediately complied, pulling Penny's arms out straight before her. Lucy slipped down to Penny's ankles and the two girls lifted her, face downward, towards the footstool.

Jade and Lucy panted and gasped, tripping on their heels, but still managed to hold Penny aloft above the cushioned stool, like a sacrificial victim they intended to hurl into some terrible well.

'That's it, lower her, belly down, and over,' Lucy instructed.

Penny felt her naked stomach, above the sheer girdle, land gently on the footstool.

She kicked out with her feet, bending her knees and pushing backward in a furious defiance, but Lucy just passed the legs under her arm and squeezed them shut at the knee.

Lucy squatted behind Penny and dug her own knees, painfully, into the rear of Penny's thighs to hold them still, before lashing her legs to the footstool supports with a pair of stockings. The sheer fabric became a strangling and inflexible rope, when lashed behind Penny's knees and wrapped around the tiny squat feet of the stool.

Penny's arms, still held fast by Jade, draped over the other end of the stool and Lucy raced around to lash her wrists to the stool's other two legs.

In seconds Penny had been fastened securely, as if

over a barrel, to a harmless though sturdy item of bedroom furniture.

'Hog tied!' Lucy squealed and clapped her hands with satisfaction at her handiwork.

She and Jade giggled and pranced around Penny, giving each other high fives of approval.

'Untie me immediately. You have three seconds to comply or I will scream until everybody on the estate has formed a disorderly queue outside this room. Do you under –'

Penny was never allowed to finish: Lucy had whipped her own panties down and slipped the salty fabric between Penny's teeth to silence her.

Penny heard Jade flop down on to the bed, making way for her leader. 'What are you going to do?' Penny heard her ask Lucy.

'To start with, this bloody tight skirt will have to come off. I can't move in it,' Lucy answered.

Penny raised her head and watched the young heir slip out of her creased hobble skirt. Despite her position and a blood-hot sense of humiliation and injustice, Penny paused in her struggles to admire Lucy. The girl has great legs, Penny instinctively thought, eyeing the long nylon-encased limbs, shooting up from high heels to a knickerless sex.

Lucy caught Penny's stare. 'Want some?' she taunted. 'Like what you see? Want my pussy on your face?'

Penny continued to stare at the blonde-shrouded nest of moist flesh and silken folds between Lucy's legs.

'While I teach you a lesson about respect, I'll teach you how to eat pussy, too,' Lucy spat down at Penny.

It may have been the act of being unceremoniously tied down by two pretty blondes, or the beautiful glistening sex hovering above her face, but Penny sensed a large and spreading reaction between her own legs. Her panties were clammy and clung to her moist clit, while her breathing became shallow in a manner that had little to do with the gag. Penny even began to lick the gauzy panty fabric in her mouth: she liked the taste. After feasting on Amanda's sex, her tongue had acquired a penchant for that distinctive flavour of female arousal.

Lucy sat on the floor before Penny and shuffled her petite little backside across the rug, closer to the stool and her captive. She leant forward and put her lips on Penny's to whisper, 'God, I never knew this bondage gig with a girl could be so good. Know what I mean?'

Penny had to stop herself from hissing 'Yes' over the gag. Lucy now unfastened it from behind her head. Penny quickly decided that it was best to just play along, let Harrington think that this was an extreme of humiliation, foisted upon an unwilling enemy. Penny knew that she was aroused, deeply enough to frighten herself, and wanted the girl's juicy sex dripping out of her mouth.

Lucy licked Penny's open and smeared mouth with a little pink tongue and stroked her hair roughly. Penny had to summon an enormous exertion of willpower to stop herself from responding to the pretty mouth.

Her captor changed her own position, removing her lips and rocking back on to her buttocks. Lucy supported her own body with her arms and opened her legs, pushing her groin up and on to Penny's face with a graceful lunge.

The scent of the young heir's sex filled Penny's nose and her wet sex-lips pressed against Penny's open mouth. Lucy began to moan and rub her clit up and down on Penny's front teeth. She lifted her legs off the floor, one by one, and slipped them over Penny's naked shoulders.

Penny sucked at the wet vagina stuffed into her mouth and adored the long and slippery legs sliding over her back. Lucy squeezed her eyes shut and began making little squealing sounds from the back of her throat, increasing the rubbing on Penny's hungry mouth.

Behind them, Penny heard Jade begin to respond: 'Ooh, that's nice. Oh, Lucy, that must be good.'

'Oh, it is Jade. The slut has such a beautiful mouth. Ah, she's really doing me, her tongue is up inside me.'

Lucy had called her a slut, she had tied Penny to a stool and stuck a naked vagina on her face – Penny exploded, erupting with desire and not anger.

Penny lapped at Lucy's sex and moaned through her nose. She pushed her face deeper inside the sopping wet cushion of perfumed delight and made Lucy howl with a true passion.

'Spank her!' Lucy gasped, her whole body now bucking and shivering in orgasm, 'Spank the little slut, give it to her!'

Jade needed no further prompting; she ran across to the stool and fell to her knees. Penny could hear Jade panting behind her, overcome by the arousing sight of two blonde girls punishing each other with tongue and clit. Jade began to slap Penny's backside with all her might, her little hand spanking the transparent black panties and delectable creamy mounds before her.

The tiny sparks of pain thrilled Penny and brought on her own climax. No one had actually even touched her clit and yet Penny orgasmed with a blinding intensity: the sex on her face and the little slapping hand had been enough to drive her into paradise.

Her own wet sex, however, did not remain neglected for long. Jade slipped three fingers inside Penny's panties and thrust them up into her slit. The stool began to move and shake on the rug as Penny tried to push her sex down to meet the stuffing motion of Jade's hand. The fingers had become heavy with dew, almost immediately, and slipped with ease in and out of Penny.

Penny quaked and shuddered through another climax, but her lips refused to leave Lucy's sex, her mouth lapping and probing at the hot vagina for all it was worth. Lucy collapsed on to her back, responding to the vigorous mouth and its dynamic manoeuvres on her tingling clit. Her legs kicked out and raked the air, both of her heels flying off to crash in the corners of Penny's room.

Jade caught her friend's whipping legs and held them down against Penny's spine, refusing to allow Lucy any outlet of steam, attempting to contain every ounce of sexual energy at boiling point inside the beautiful heir's slender body.

Lucy gasped and croaked on the rug, her sex eventually falling away from Penny's red and glistening mouth. Jade sat back and stared at her friend, unable to really believe that she had taken such an active part in the submission of Penny.

Penny closed her eyes and savoured the taste of her enemy, still drying on her lips.

'Come on, Jade. Let's get out of here,' Lucy stammered, seemingly embarrassed at the turn of events. 'No, leave her!' she said to Jade, who had begun untying Penny's bonds. 'Let someone else bother with that. She knows when to keep her mouth shut and she understands that we might come back. Don't you, my little pet?'

Amanda drifted in through the unlocked door just after midnight, dressed only in a sheer, black, see-through gown that fell in a dark whispering smoke from her broad shoulders to her slender ankles. She stared at Penny for a long time, shaking her head in disbelief.

Penny raised her own head slowly, her neck having stiffened during the hours she had spent bound over the cushioned footstool. She smiled at Amanda to reassure her that she was all right.

'What? Who did this? When . . .' Amanda stammered, her hand clutched against her suddenly pale forehead.

108

'Get me off this thing and I will explain,' Penny replied, anxious to get the blood flowing again in her arms and legs.

Amanda went straight for a pair of nail scissors on Penny's dresser, and cut the nylon restraints off Penny's joints. She raced to the window and closed the curtains, before flicking the lights on.

Penny flopped on to the rug and stretched her legs out, while simultaneously waving her arms in circles to revive her aching limbs. She had slept fitfully for several hours after the exhausting rollercoaster of fear, panic and then ecstasy at Lucy's hands.

'How long have you been tied to this thing?' Amanda demanded, still incredulous at the sight of Penny bound and immobile in the centre of a rug at midnight.

'Since about seven,' Penny murmured. 'It wasn't so bad after the cramp passed away at ten. God, I am so tired I just want to sleep.'

'Damn sleep!' Amanda shrieked. 'How on earth did this happen? Tell me.'

Penny staggered to her feet and moaned as her knees cracked some more. She wandered over to the door, shut it tight and turned to face Amanda.

'Sit down on the bed. You are going to need a seat when I tell you what happened tonight,' Penny warned and took Amanda's shaking hand, leading her over to the bed.

'Kloster?' Amanda guessed.

'No, but someone just as ruthless and insane barged in here tonight and tied me down.'

Amanda realised in a flash. 'That bitch Lucy! She did this. She has to realise she's messing with the big girls now!'

Amanda leapt off the bed and made for the door, her face a mask of howling rage. Penny reached out and seized her by the arm, stopping her abruptly. 'Calm down, it really wasn't so bad. She just tried to scare me and I think she freaked herself.'

'But you could have frozen to death! What if I hadn't popped in to see you? What –'

'What were the chances,' Penny replied, smiling, 'of you not popping in to see me before bedtime? I was counting on it, because I know I can count on you. I have only just met you, Amanda, and I know that I trust you and can rely on you. That means a lot, but you have to stay out of this vendetta thing. We will all get into trouble and end up serving time as gimps over at that cottage.' She had to stay cool, Amanda had to stay cool and the surface of the girls' corridor must remain as flat as a mill pond.

'You cannot let her get away with tying you up,' Amanda insisted. 'To think of that cow's audacity. Where's your fight? We should be in her room right now giving her what for with a leather belt!'

'I know, I know,' Penny hushed her, stroking her face and kissing her chin and nose softly. 'But I will bide my time, and when things are right I'll get her back, you'll see. And when I need back-up, you are the first person I am going to call, but please don't do anything on my account. Promise me.' Penny kissed Amanda's mouth and smoothed her hands along the girl's shapely body, made even silkier by the transparent black gown.

'I promise,' Amanda whispered, caressing Penny's breasts over the top of her brassiere and responding to her kissing mouth with her own lips.

'Now, that's better,' Penny whispered, kissing Amanda's fragrant neck and squeezing her soft behind through the sheer gown. 'Just a little cuddle before bedtime and then you will have to go.'

'No,' Amanda squealed. 'I fell asleep after tea and woke up thinking about you. I want to nuzzle into bed with you. I don't like sleeping alone.'

'There is no way around it, sweetheart. After the debacle with Rupert last night, and then Kloster finding out about us two on the first night, it's going to be three

110

strikes and you're out for me. I need to keep a low profile until things have settled a bit. If I get sent home, how am I going to be able to kiss your entire body, day after day, and suck your pretty nipples and make you shiver between your legs?' Penny whispered and lulled Amanda's frown into a smile.

'I suppose so, but if you even hear a bump then scream for me and I'll come running.'

'OK,' Penny chuckled. 'And, by the way, I love the outfit. I would like you to wear that again, for me.'

Amanda kissed Penny passionately on the lips and moved one hand between her legs. Penny fell against Amanda, beginning to swoon for more, becoming desperate to take the tall girl to bed, to kiss those firm breasts enhanced by sheer black silk, and to bite her soft stomach with passion. Lucy and Jade had left her simmering for hours and the last thing she wanted was Amanda's departure, but for once she had to seriously consider the investigation.

'Go or I will disgrace myself between your legs,' Penny moaned, pushing Amanda towards the door.

'I want you soon, Penny Chambers. We better find the time. I need you,' Amanda crooned, before disappearing into the corridor.

Five

Penny had staked out Lucy's room following the Thursday-evening meal. She had hidden in the ladies' bathroom, at the end of her hall, and waited for the inevitable turning of a key in a lock. When Lucy emerged, quickly and without hesitation, Penny had followed the distant echo of her footsteps and the trails of exotic perfume the young girl had left behind in the corridor. It came as no surprise to Penny when the clues led her down to the dean's ground-floor study and chambers beside the grand Whitehead reception.

After Miss Barbusse's door had closed to seal the young beauty within, Penny had crept silently, in her stocking-clad feet, across the smooth marble floor and pressed her ear to the door. The other girls were all resting after an arduous day of PE with the Celeste twins, so the hall maintained a deep silence.

Penny, however, could detect no sound from within the study. There was, perhaps, a lonely strain of string music and the odd vibration of movement, but nothing as telltale as she had wished.

Penny dithered outside the dean's study, scratching for a solution: she wanted to see the dean in action and actually witness a true Whitehead liaison with Miss Barbusse directing affairs. Her story had to develop beyond circumstantial evidence and the diversions of secondary players, but where was the discreet access she craved? She needed a control over the investigation and not just the random strokes of luck that had allowed her access to the cottage and Kloster's study. She had seen the symptoms but where was the source?

Some time later, the sound of a second pair of footsteps approaching through the reception forced her to flee behind the large oak doors that opened out from the marbled foyer and into the staff corridor.

She held her breath and pushed her back to the wall when Paris appeared, walked past her and made a furtive approach to the dean's door.

The entrance of Paris, a third and unexpected player in the dean's nocturnal secrets, shocked Penny. The news of Miss Barbusse's expert fellatio, performed upon Paris before the entire male form, had spread across the Academy like a tidal wave, followed by a hush only broken by the odd gasp and whisper of disbelief. That act of passion had made each and every student reappraise their opinion of her. The girls had fallen into a mute and stunned admiration and the men had placed her upon a pedestal – a pedestal that they all now wished to mount.

The young man waited outside the door, never taking his eyes of his watch. Penny remained in shadow. Her body began to ache but she dared not move. She took shallow inhalations of warm air and pressed her back further into the wall. She was even deprived of a glimpse of Miss Barbusse when the door finally opened and Paris slipped through to the inner sanctum.

With no valid alternative to aid her search, Penny crept back to her chamber, angry, thwarted and disappointed. What could she learn through a shut door? Seduction seemed to be an impossible option, as the dean had already selected her distraction. You need bottle: start breaking and entering, Penny's mind screamed in rage.

When stamping back inside her own room, she noticed a small disturbance on the bed. Someone had let themselves into Penny's room and supplied a fresh batch of laundered clothing.

Penny approached the bundle of neatly folded and expertly pressed fabrics, determined to tidy them away as a method of keeping her hands occupied. Under a black skirt, in the laundered pile, Penny's eyes spotted an envelope. She picked it up with shaking fingers and neatly tore along the gummed flap. She held her breath as her long red nails pulled the note free of its cover.

In a large and feminine script three words had been written, intended for her: 'Look no further'.

Penny's blood froze. Someone at the Academy knew who she was. The note had been delivered as a warning, a final demand, perhaps, from an individual who knew of her purpose.

A dozen faces and names flashed through her mind. Who would warn her from afar without running straight to the dean? It was someone protecting her and yet attempting to kill her investigation.

Lucy? But never, Penny decided, would that girl consider her well-being; she had far too large a grudge with journalists to ever consider her safety. No one seemed to fit the role. At least, no one she had met.

Penny sighed, devastated and close to throwing in the towel. She wanted a drink, but the rules prohibited alcohol. If I try and steal a bottle I'll only get bloody caught, her conscience cried. Slumping into the lowest ebb in her investigation, Penny flitted to the window for a lungful of fresh air.

In the distance, to the far side of the playing fields, she spotted a figure running in the direction of the perverse cottage. She squinted her eyes and concentrated her focus on the fleeing silhouette. It was, perhaps, the young man's haste that revealed his identity. Before he passed behind the tennis courts, Penny had recognised the tall and floppy-haired Rupert scurrying eagerly back to Madam Skinner.

Penny threw her drained body back on to the bed, shaking her head with apparent disbelief, questioning everything: her surroundings, adventures, the people she had met and what the Academy was doing to all of them.

She needed a cup of hot and sweet coffee inside her, the only available stimulant, to restore the balance and sense of clarity that had fled only days ago when her body first tingled inside a Whitehead uniform.

Penny put her shoes back on and walked down to the kitchen area, where the girls were allowed to make themselves coffee or to pursue a shortbread biscuit. This area was on the ground floor – the staff and amenities floor – but at the other end of the rectangular building to the dean's room. The self-service kitchen, designed for snacks and insomniacs, stood beside the beautifully tiled washrooms that the girls showered or bathed in.

No sooner had Penny reached the foot of the staircase than a familiar sound danced into her ears. She shivered and felt every hair stand up on the rear of her neck.

It was a rhythmic female moaning, a stifled cry of passion, floating from the washrooms.

In the dean's bedroom, Lucy had slicked her blonde hair back from her face, making it appear darker. The colour of her hair matched the silk blindfold, which was pulled tightly across the bridge of her delicate nose to conceal the flickering candlelight from her entrancing eyes.

Miss Barbusse had decided that her protégé, on the fourth evening at Whitehead, should be blindfold for the next rite of initiation. Four silver candlesticks had been placed in the corners of her boudoir, topped with thick black candles whose flames danced in the faint drafts that crept like wayward spirits from behind the heavy drapes.

Lucy stood obediently on the centre of the dean's rug, with her pinched high-heeled feet at angles, as if in the first step of some elegant dance. Her skirt and blouse had been shed and she knew better than to present herself to the dean in a peephole affair. Instead, Lucy's breasts were covered by a beautiful plain-silk Academy bra and her hips had been contoured by a sheer Whitehead panty girdle. Only her hosiery deviated from the Academy standard. On Lucy's long and sculpted legs she wore high-sheen, flesh-tinted stockings, complemented by a thin black rear seam – a present from Miss Barbusse.

Lucy had raised her chin above a diamanté choker, and her crimson-coated lips betrayed no emotion. She stood silent and motionless, as she had been bid, with her delicate hands folded behind her back.

Miss Barbusse slowly walked around Lucy, admiring the girl's every curve and smooth hollow, smiling with appreciation at the fine and untarnished creation before her, only stopping occasionally to inhale her intoxicating aroma.

Miss Barbusse moved her shiny red lips close to Lucy's ear. 'Tonight is a test of faith, my dear, a trial to judge how far you will go for your mistress.'

She moved her soft hands to hover a hair's breadth away from the girl's slender lower back and flat silky navel, only resisting the desire to stroke with a practised act of will.

'There will be no shame in what I ask you to do, only pleasure, if you give yourself totally to my guidance.'

'Yes, mistress,' Lucy answered.

'I am, though, still unconvinced,' Miss Barbusse said, 'of your total celibacy beyond my door. I have seen the hunger in your eyes around Mr Klima and a certain flush beneath your skin when near a pretty girl.'

'No, mistress, I have done as you have instructed me, to save my inner self for our time together.'

The answer came too quickly, an immediate sign of guilt to the dean.

Something hot and ugly suddenly turned and rankled inside Miss Barbusse. She could imagine Lucy's immaculate flesh within another's hands and mouth – it seemed to sully their pact and bond. She had begun to think of the English rose in every spare moment of every day. She had no respite at night either: her dreams had been filled with Lucy's young face sneering with pleasure when mastered from behind or made crimson beneath the crop. Her own imagination had become an enemy, teasing her with images of the beauty heaving under another's passion with her legs kicking out and her mouth panting for more. The very thought of Lucy's infidelity lashed the dean's heart with a red-hot wire. She had to confess, though, the thought curiously excited her, too. When she thought of her young slave seeking satisfaction with strangers, the dean's chest would heave as if some choking and inexpressible lump of emotion had stuck fast beneath her breasts.

'You will be candid and you will answer me truthfully. Who have you . . . who have you fucked?' the dean rasped, her white body trembling beneath the tight corset and seamed black stockings.

'No one, my mistress. I . . . I have preserved my desires for you and you alone. I –'

The spindly, black, seasoned cane in the dean's hand lashed across the top of Lucy's suspendered thighs. Miss Barbusse knew a lie when she heard it and her feelings for the young minx had become volcanic.

Lucy gasped and stroked her stinging thighs with both hands.

The cane fell across her wrists and then flicked, expertly, across her soft buttocks – the gauzy panty girdle offering little protection from the lash.

'Liar!' Miss Barbusse practically screamed, her haunting beauty now distinctly spectral in the flickering candlelight. 'You come to me and you lie like a cheap watch.'

117

Miss Barbusse raised the cane once more.

'Jade and I explored the things you showed me,' Lucy blurted out, wincing in anticipation of the bamboo kiss from the cane she could not see.

'Jade! The pretty blonde slut who was caught by the doctor with a cock in her mouth. You defy me for her?' the dean cried.

'I could not help myself, mistress. You have started a fire inside me. It needs satisfaction or I will go mad,' Lucy panted, her cheeks flushed with excitement, her buttocks moving in tiny circles as if to prompt another lash.

It was not long in coming. The air sung with the soprano of discipline around the speeding passage of finely carved wood. The cane smacked thrice more against Lucy's soft lower buttocks, just beneath the hem of her girdle,

Lucy panted and stroked her velvety cheeks with desperate fingers, her blood-red nails leaving other ghostly trails across the finely lined skin.

Miss Barbusse slipped her hand between Lucy's legs and rotated her fingers in the fragrant honey that had gathered.

'I punish you and yet you weep with arousal. You seep because you crave a penetration, a thick and aggressive penetration that relieves your mind and heart of its load. Am I right?'

'Yes, mistress. At the Academy I need satisfaction like never before, but I want it from you, every minute of the day.'

'Liar!' the dean shrieked. 'You have danced on Klima's rigid treasure.'

'I have not!' Lucy squealed.

The dean had warned the other staff off Lucy – she was to be hers, and hers alone. She would be furious with Klima if he had sullied her treasure with his long and agonising lovemaking, which had been practised in the most powerful bedrooms across the world. He had mentioned Lucy's beauty in passing, on her first day, and that comment had rankled into life-size and hideous proportions in the dean's mind ever since.

'Has he had you?' Miss Barbusse pressed, her tight lips brushing Lucy's softly rouged cheekbone.

'No. I swear, mistress, you forbade me from taking a cock and I have obeyed. I mistakenly thought that pleasuring myself with girls would not hurt you.'

'Girls!' the dean hissed. 'The plural has sunk your treacherous vessel.'

The cane fell, lashing and whipping Lucy over to the bed, where she fell, still blindfold, and deeply aroused by the dean's jealous passion.

'There has only been one other. I swear, my mistress,' Lucy stammered.

'Her name!' Miss Barbusse demanded, swiping at the air a few inches from Lucy's shimmering thighs.

Lucy's words crept slowly from between glistening, pouting lips: 'Chambers, Penny Chambers. If you must know it all, then I will tell you, mistress. I took her and I punished her. I bound her, gagged her and I made her taste me.'

After the dean's sharp inhalation, a silence reigned in the bedchamber. Lucy had curled up on the bed, her exposed rear candy-striped from the cane and her beautiful blindfold face still haughty after the forced confession.

'Chambers,' Miss Barbusse said at last, in a staggered and hushed tone, her French accent more apparent under duress than ever before. 'Penny Chambers. You took her with your beautiful, sacred sex?'

'Yes, mistress, and she adored every bit of me,' Lucy teased, her voice loud and triumphant.

'You caressed her breasts, no doubt?' the dean asked, punishing and arousing herself.

'Yes, mistress, and I left my lipstick all over her sluttish face.'

The dean gasped, shocked by the confession, but feeling light-headed at the thought of her delicate pet's deviant excursions. She was so rare, so beautiful, so deadly and so like herself in years past.

'I have something for you, Lucy. I have a cure for your boundless promiscuity, girl, and I have an antidote for these wayward, disobedient and addictive desires.'

'I want it, mistress. I need it, mistress,' Lucy hissed at her trembling, older lover.

Miss Barbusse recognised the tone of voice: it slithered, serpentine and clotted with greed, through the vapours of her own memory. It was the voice with which she had taunted her own master, until he was driven by a wolfish blood lust to placate her so many years before.

'I will feed you with a cock, my dear,' Miss Barbusse promised with resolve. 'And I will flog every ounce of betrayal from even your most secret thoughts. I have created your appetites and I alone will feed their cries. Am I understood?'

'Yes, mistress. I promise, my mistress,' Lucy gushed from the bed.

When she had become convinced of Lucy's sincerity, Miss Barbusse opened the interconnecting door to her study and collected Paris.

He too had been blindfolded with black silk and tottered, unsure of every footfall, into the dean's rarely glimpsed bed chamber. She guided him by his elbow, walking backward on her four-inch heels, leading him to the canopy bed.

He had been told to utter no word and to follow her every instruction. The lad had agreed to her terms, instantly and completely, desperate for any time spent intimately with his chic principal.

Miss Barbusse seemed to glow with power, a strength and influence from within, matured over decades and wielded by few. She caressed Paris's face and hard shoulders; she kissed his open mouth and licked his throat, devouring his aftershave. He quivered and sighed, his breath becoming lost among her rustles and whispered entreaties. When her long white fingers peeled his shirt from his lean chest and scratched his stomach, the dean heard him whimper. When her hands unbelted his silk trousers and freed a pulsing shaft, she watched every muscle harden beneath the lightly tanned skin of his stomach.

Her thickly coated lips swallowed the thick strawberry head of his penis with little delay. She flicked her tongue around the salty morsel for the second time in two days, lavishing the softest parts of her mouth on his eager manhood.

Miss Barbusse tugged his trousers, sock and shoes off, while sucking on his length, delirious with her own pleasure and aware of Lucy's sniffing presence. The girl squirmed soundlessly on the thick bedspread, sliding her long legs about and tasting the air with a little pink tongue.

'What a beautiful cock,' Miss Barbusse purred, stroking the thick shaft with her hand and watching Lucy's growing excitement on the bed. 'A cock fit for a desperate little madam,' she sighed, shivering all over from the delicious anguish of sharing her jewel with another. 'A thick, pummelling tool. Young and vital and deprived of a soft cunt for far too long.'

Both Lucy and Paris seemed to jump at the word 'cunt', spoken with such emphasis from a cultured tongue. The language both surprised and delighted them – Lucy clawed the bed and Paris began to rotate his hips, pushing his penis towards the luxurious mouth that had coated it with a rare wine.

Miss Barbusse took it between her lips once more and cleansed it of preparatory dew. If she continued lapping the man's penis for much longer, she knew he would spray her face with a hot passion, and she wanted that seed pumped deeply inside herself and Lucy – to complete a triangle that no participant would ever forget.

He was ready and so was Lucy; Miss Barbusse stood in the narrow electric gap between them and made her final preparations. She pulled Lucy down the bed by her ankles and spread the long stocking-sheathed legs wide open; she manoeuvred Paris between the thighs he could not see and took hold of his penis with one hand. Miss Barbusse slipped behind Paris and gently pushed his tight buttocks forward. When the sensitised tip of his penis touched the heart of Lucy's sap-drenched flower, both lovers cried out in expectation.

'Take her!' the dean screamed, blasting the eerie silence into oblivion. 'Ream her! Fuck her with every ounce of your strength! Feed off your passion and anger and desire! Spear her and you shall have me also!'

Paris sank his penis right to the hilt in Lucy's sex with one quick and easy motion.

Lucy screamed with pleasure and raked the bed linen with her red claws. Paris reached out and instinctively found her slippery ankles. He slid his hands down to her knees and held her long legs firmly. He squeezed her stockings until they spider-webbed with ladders and tore. He began to pound his blond-haired groin into Lucy's own bush.

Miss Barbusse stepped back, away from the rutting couple, and listened to the gasps and slick squelches. The coupling was ferocious as the participants ground their hips together and mouthed obscenities into the candle-smoky air.

Without them seeing or being able to guess, Miss Barbusse collected a large onyx shaft from her dresser, a toy that was slick and smoothly phallic. She lay alongside Lucy on the bed, opened her own legs and stared at the exquisite young beasts who were mating in her secret den. She thrust the savage implement into her noble sex and bit her lip to muffle her cries. She began wrenching it out and stuffing it back in again, in time with every one of Paris's powerful and unbridled thrusts into Lucy. While the polished tool widened and stretched her drenched sex, she thought of the veiny erection slipping into her young lover, and knew that she too must have it banged hard and ruthlessly into her every cavity upon that very night. She took a man rarely, but this lad had stamina and style; he knew when to caress and when to thrust like a wild animal. Tonight, she decided, he would have the very best, the most unashamedly depraved and devious felines on campus.

'Fuck her!' Miss Barbusse cried, ramming the now slippery and dripping device in and out of herself, tipping herself over the hallowed precipice and into a shaking, screaming climax.

Lucy came as she stuffed the toe of her shoe into Paris's open mouth. Sweat ran off his shaven top lip and stained the polished patent leather of her shoe. Paris's penis pulsed inside Lucy three times before he pulled it free and massaged the last two spurts of fragrant semen on to her divine stomach.

Paris fell forward into Lucy's arms, his wet face finding comfort on the soft cushion of her chest. They clutched each other, anonymous lovers, their lips seeking out and finding a counterpart in the dark.

Miss Barbusse watched them, spellbound and still quaking from her paralysing climax. Her favoured tool could sink to the farthest reaches of her womanhood and caress any hidden grotto of pleasure. She rolled across the mattress and sank into the crevice that held Paris and Lucy.

Penny made a cautious approach to the washroom door, listening to her heart stampeding beneath her tightly bound breasts. She pushed the door open and slipped into the main washroom corridor. A row of

123

cedar doors, concealing the showers and hot tubs, faced her. The sounds were louder now and coming from beyond the first array of cubicles. Penny stumbled past them, removed her shoes, and arrived at the central court that held the washbasins and bright wall mirrors. Still no sign of life; the cries seemed to be emerging from further down, from out of a toilet stall in the far annexe.

All the doors were closed in this final corridor, and the lights had all been switched off save one. This solitary bulb threw an eerie glow over the shadowy passage, seeming to amplify the sounds.

Penny fell to her knees. She peered under the saloon doors and her eyes flashed along the tiles looking for life.

She almost cried out when confronted by the sight of so many legs entwined about each other in the centre stall, the only toilet cubicle lit from above. She saw six legs, from the knees down, crammed inside the tiny square space. Two pairs of feet had been coated in slick and extremely tight leather boots, while the last, pressed between the others, was without shoes and clad in sheer, seamed, nylon stockings.

Penny winced but her body flushed with excitement. Three women were making love in a dimly lit toilet cubicle, only feet away from her crouched position. Between the moans and whimpers, Penny's sharp ears discerned several words: 'Yes ... that's it ... up ... harder.'

The activity inside the enclosed space seemed to speed up. The bodies started to bang against the thin wooden walls and the feet started to lift, stamp, scuffle and kick with passion.

'Please ... more ... damn it ... more!' the voice cried out, louder and more distinct.

Penny stuffed her fingers in her mouth – she recognised the American accent. It was Amber in the cubicle with the two booted individuals: the shy and tear-prone girl from across the Atlantic was making love and demanding a harder service from her partners.

Penny scurried on her knees down the narrow tiled corridor to the neighbouring cubicle and crept quietly inside. She had to see Amber in the throes of release and abandon; she needed visual proof to actually believe her ears. The girl had become more confident and relaxed after the Klima lesson, but for Amber to take a female lover in a toilet stall? This was beyond Penny's imagination.

Penny lowered the toilet lid in her stall and watched the vibrating wall which separated her from the trio of noisy lovers. She could smell their perfume above the pine disinfectant and watched a high-heeled foot slip momentarily under her own stall as one determined lover lost her footing.

Penny silently climbed on to the toilet seat and raised her head. Not even daring to breathe, she slipped her head forward and peeped into the neighbouring stall.

Penny immediately steadied her body with both hands when confronted with the sight next door: the Celeste twins, naked except for black thigh-high boots, had handcuffed Amber to a pipe at the rear of the stall and fed upon her body with a desperate haste and virtual brutality.

Penny whipped her head back and closed her eyes, her memory instantly replaying that single glimpse: Amber's body had fallen back against the cold wall, her chained hands supporting the weight of her body. She had been stripped naked, save for her garter belt and stockings, her immaculate hair sticking to a smudged and perspiring face. The girl's mouth had twisted and snarled, deserting its humanity for these violent moments of excessive fulfilment. She had raised her solid muscular legs off the floor and wrapped them around a twin's slender waist. The twin proceeded to pound in and out of the American's stretched sex with a brutish force, the thick strap-on device between her legs seeming to be at least a foot long. Penny had become familiar with these devices at Whitehead but had never seen such a thick or unwieldy version. Her mind struggled to comprehend how the tool actually managed to fit within the confines of a vagina.

A thin silver chain had been strung between Amber's two nipples. A tiny clamp at each end had sealed the nipple within its painful embrace. It must have hurt and Penny shuddered at the thought, her own nipples and sex tingling in sympathy.

Amber seemed to adore the brutal treatment – she was screaming with pleasure and actually demanding a harder lunge from the Celeste twin between her thighs. The second twin's movements were indistinct and had been partially shielded when Penny took the solitary peek over the divider. She had seemed to be, however, contenting herself with pumping movements beneath Amber's raised buttocks. Penny even believed she had seen a suggestion of something silvery passing up and into the girl's rectum from out of her tormentor's hands.

'Do it! Do it!' Amber screamed, shocking Penny, as the commotion increased its ominous tempo. The cubicle even seemed in danger of being ripped from the toilet wall. Penny dropped down from the toilet lid and fled from her stall. She never looked back but Amber's shrieks followed her, past the sinks and showers and into the kitchen: 'Yes! I say, harder. Harder, damn it! Punish me! Punish me!'

Penny shut the kitchen door and collapsed on a long bench, beside a wooden table. She told herself that she never wanted to go that far, never wanted to fall into the hands of the inhumane but stunning dominatrix twins. 'Oh, what a lovely pair of girls,' Madam Skinner had said.

Kloster had threatened her with them. How close had her own young body been to rivalling Amber's –

released from all control and propriety beneath the curse of those tools and the expert hands that operated them. They frightened Penny but delighted her, squeezing her sanity with an icy terror but thrilling her mind with explicit visions. Penny squeezed her own nipples in response to what she had seen, and longed for something to engage itself with her own sex.

With her high heels tightly clasped between her fingers, Penny fled upstairs to Amanda's room – willing once more to risk anything for her desire.

Pachelbel's *Canon* swirled about Miss Barbusse's juddering bed. The music thickened the air and seemed to incite the three lovers to greater acts of stamina and contortion than ever before.

Lucy and Paris were still blindfold, but they had learnt to see with their hands. Paris gripped the dean's two naked breasts with his open palms as Miss Barbusse rode his groin with a deeply pressing motion of her slender hips. While her sex devoured Paris's rigid member, she kissed Lucy's beautiful gasping face. She pinched the girl's nipples and occasionally allowed a hand to stray down between the girl's legs, to aid the already present fingers with the rubbing and caressing of an engorged clit.

The three lovers had pressed themselves against each other for hours. Each woman took the stiff penis inside their mouth and hungry vagina in turn – only easing their ministrations when Paris began to whimper and warn of an explosive ejaculation. When the young man's desire to empty himself wilted, the women would begin again, administering lips, hands and deep cushioned sexes to his solid offering. They would also pause to kiss each other and caress their breasts, willing each other to climax again and again.

Miss Barbusse adored the writhing entangled mess of sinewy arms, clawing and scratching at each other on her bed. She loved the sight of Lucy's kicking stocking-clad legs when Paris clambered upon her to thrust deeply. The dean had even buried her own face in a pillow, after offering Paris her tight and rarely plundered anus. She had guided his thick sex into her hallowed ground and pressed back through the exquisite pain to milk his second ejaculation inside her own rectum. Lucy had not been able to see this profane act, but had sculpted her hands across their rutting arrangement and cried out with delight when she realised exactly where Paris had planted his thick penis.

But now, Miss Barbusse had decided that it was time to feel his penis throb and spit again, so she rode Paris and pushed his exquisite rigidity to the very roof of her sex.

'Smother his face, girl,' she panted, beginning to rise and fall on the penis with a faster rhythm.

'Let me see you, dean!' Paris cried out, breaking his vow of silence. 'I need to see your face when I come inside you.'

'No,' she answered, 'feeling the weight of my body on your cock is enough.'

Paris moaned as Lucy straddled his face with her sex, pressing herself down on to his lips and teeth, demanding her own satisfaction and muffling his cries.

'Suck me! Suck me hard,' Lucy shrieked as her little nose began to wrinkle and her lips parted to welcome another orgasm.

The dean gripped the young man's hips and thighs with her smoothly stockinged legs, finding a tighter purchase on his splayed body to aid her pounding. She reached out and tore at Lucy's hair, beginning to croak as the first ecstatic wave of pleasure rippled through her body.

She tugged Lucy's face down and on to her breasts, making the girl bite her nipples, squeezing every ounce of satisfaction from her two young lovers.

Paris began to shout from under Lucy's sex and pump his backside off the bed, intending to spear the dean's sex at an even deeper fathom.

Miss Barbusse screamed and banged on and off his slippery hip bones, forcing the entire bed frame to rattle.

Paris roared and his arms thrashed about. Lucy croaked and clawed his chest as she climaxed on the man's face.

He was ready. With an expert's precision and timing, the dean leapt off the spasming cock and watched the thick white fountain spurt up before splashing down across his brown tummy.

The dean moaned with satisfaction and pulled Lucy's face down to his belly. Her own mouth joined Lucy's lapping tongue and the two women sucked every trace of semen off their lover's body.

'Penny!' Amanda cried out, her face a mixture of surprise and guilt, ' I wasn't expecting you tonight. You said you were going to lie low for a few days. If I had known, I –'

'Amanda, I need you. I have just seen something so brutal and nasty, but it turned me on. What is happening to us? I want to try –'

It was no use, Amanda was forced to interrupt her. 'Oh, Pen. This is so awkward. You see, I am waiting for someone.'

Penny's heart fell. She had pounded up the stairs, hoping to fall directly into Amanda's long soft arms and between her satin thighs. Amanda was even wearing that beautiful floor-length gown, revealing her black stockings and lacy suspender belt through its transparency.

Penny's stomach turned upside down with jealousy. She wanted Amanda and considered it her right to have first refusal.

'Oh, Amanda,' she moaned angrily, 'you promised to

wear that gown for me and now you have someone else. I thought I was special.'

'You are, darling,' Amanda murmured, walking forward to stroke Penny's hair. 'Don't be a baby. We have plenty of time.'

Penny bit her bottom lip and frowned, almost enjoying her childish petulance and Amanda's discomfort.

A gentle knock on the door broke the two girls apart.

'Who . . .' Penny gasped, her face white with fear.

Amanda rolled her eyes and put her hands on her mouth. Penny could tell that her beautiful raven-haired lover was scratching for a solution.

'You will have to hide, sweetheart.'

'What!' Penny hissed.

'I am so sorry but, believe me, you don't want to get caught in here tonight.'

Penny's stomach curdled and her head went cold. Surely not, she thought, almost guessing the identity of Amanda's guest with a sudden dread.

'Under the bed,' Amanda whispered, dragging Penny by her elbow to the four-poster.

'I can't –' Penny moaned.

'You have to. Please, Penny, for me. Don't spoil this.'

'Bitch!' Penny mumbled, before sliding across the polished floorboards and into the darkness beneath the bed.

From the shadows she watched Amanda's lovely ankles skip to the door to answer the knock. When the door swung open, Penny's narrowed eyes detected a second pair of high heels entering the equation. She had seen those long feet before, encased either in tight knee-length boots or high-heeled sandals.

Kloster's long and rangy legs strode in to Amanda's room.

'I could have sworn that I heard another girl in here,' Kloster said, with an icy undercurrent to her brittle tone. 'Where is she hiding? Under the bed?'

Penny froze.

'What!' Amanda exclaimed, laughing. 'I think my hands are going to be full enough tonight with you and Mr Klima.'

Penny's throat dried and her head spun with disbelief. How could Amanda even conceive of consorting with Kloster and Klima at the same time.

'I have wine, an excellent Austrian red,' Kloster said, as her spike-heeled shoes brushed against Amanda's.

Penny judged from the silence that they must be kissing. The thought rankled and hissed inside her. She could only see two pairs of black shiny heels and shimmering ankles close together.

They only parted when there was a second knock on Amanda's door. Kloster welcomed Klima's handmade Italian shoes into Amanda's room and Penny was paralysed with anxiety beneath the bed.

'It has been some time, doctor, since we socialised together,' Klima joked.

'Yes, comrade,' Kloster teased, 'I seem to remember us both trying to dominate proceedings. Too many officers and not enough soldiers.'

'Quite right,' Klima answered, and Penny could almost imagine the sly smile on his lips as he stared into the beautiful doctor's arctic-blue eyes.

'Perhaps we will find a balance tonight with Amanda,' Kloster quipped in a low, hushed and sultry voice.

'I think we may,' Klima answered. 'She is an exceptional student and looks so enchanting tonight.'

'Thank you,' Amanda giggled, and Penny nearly screamed 'Bitch' out from under the bed.

Now, with the twins busy on Amber, the dean in her room with two students, and the Klima-Kloster double act with Amanda, Penny knew that the situation would have been ideal for a little exploration of the staff quarters. And yet, here she was, stuck beneath Amanda's bed as the opportunity passed.

How long will I be here? she questioned herself, unable to bear the thought of an entire night on a hard floor beneath the music of busy lovers. To further compound her strife, Penny could not rid her mind of the letter that warned against prying any further into the Academy.

As the lecturers poured wine and drank, Penny's attention was snatched back to the room above her: she noticed Amanda's feet surreptitiously shuffling towards the full-length dress mirror. Discreetly and without a sound, the mirror turned and tilted to offer her a complete panoramic view of the bed.

Despite her annoyance at Amanda, Penny had to stifle a giggle; her friend was going to let her watch the lovemaking. The voyeuristic potential thrilled Penny, making her feel slightly sordid, but her story could only benefit from this twist of fate. She was trapped like a rat and the least she could do was make the most of this most unusual situation.

She heard Amanda flirting shamelessly. 'Oh, Mr Klima, I cannot believe you came, but who could turn two girls down? I think most men would be willing to pay for the privilege.'

'I am sure they would,' Klima said, laughing, 'to drink wine and bask in the elegant company of two such beautiful – but, dare I say, deadly – creatures of the night.'

'And don't you forget it, you slick tongued Cossack,' Kloster added. 'I seem to remember that the marks I left upon your back the last time had you sleeping on your front for many days.'

Penny shuffled closer to the rear wall and pulled her knees up to her chin. What was Amanda thinking of? Kloster was positively dangerous, and she suspected the Russian of unpredictable depths.

With one bottle of wine nearly finished, the doctor made the first move. Her short leather skirt fell to the floor and Penny heard Amanda coo with pleasure. A black see-through blouse followed the skirt and Kloster strutted over to the bed. She came within Penny's line of vision in the mirror, causing Penny's eyes to strain from the shadows to devour the sight: the doctor had stripped down to a pair of seamed stockings and a shiny PVC suspender belt, her ghostly pallor clashing beautifully with Amanda's black silk sheets and the inky shades of her own hair and hosiery.

Amanda followed Kloster on to the bed and began an immediate kissing of the doctor's thin black tattoos, which climbed like spiked ivy around curved marble urns.

Klima took a seat, close to the bed. Penny saw his legs cross and his gentle hands settle within his lap.

The bed springs cracked and wheezed above Penny's motionless body as the two women began to writhe on the bed. She looked back at the mirror and saw two pairs of long black stocking-smoothed legs tangling about each other, swishing and gliding eagerly.

Through the mattress Penny could hear the sounds of their red lips smacking and sucking on tongues and chins. The first few moans started to become audible and Penny shivered in response.

'Slut!' she heard the doctor hiss, and watched her mount Amanda on the bed and tear the gown open with her crimson nails. By the motion of Kloster's shoulders, and the squeals of pain from Amanda, Penny knew that the doctor was kneading her friend's small tight breasts with her evil claws.

Klima rearranged himself in the chair and carefully removed his silver watch. From a side pocket in his jacket, she watched his steady fingers remove a pair of glinting handcuffs.

Penny froze, finding the sights and sounds almost unbearable. Should she cover her eyes? Should she help Amanda if things went too far? How could the girl willingly place herself at the mercy of two such ruthless individuals?

Amanda had introduced Penny to a wonderful dimension of female pleasure, but Penny now knew that she had been wrong to assume she had a complete understanding of Amanda's sexuality. She thought back to how Amanda had taunted Kloster in her study and willed the use of that nasty strap-on device.

Kloster was slapping Amanda's gartered backside now with a brutal power. Amanda sobbed and groaned but the doctor refused to relent; her cold white hands slapped and clawed at Amanda's tight buttocks as if she intended to destroy them.

'Service her, Mr Klima,' the doctor spat, her breath coming in gasps. 'I want to watch her taken assertively.'

Klima undressed without haste, before his naked legs moved slowly towards the bed. Kloster twisted Amanda over and on to her back in readiness. Penny watched Klima's naked and sinewy body, rippling with a dancer's knotted muscle structure, slide between Amanda's legs.

'That's it. Open wide, my pretty slut,' Kloster whispered, and Amanda raised her long legs, flashing her straight seams at the mirror.

Klima's head descended between Amanda's smooth thighs and his hands stretched along Amanda's belly to engulf her red and pinched nipples. Penny noticed that Kloster and Klima had not touched. They seemed to have focused their attentions purely upon Amanda's long and submissive body.

Amanda sighed, delirious with arousal, when Klima rose from between her thighs to attach the handcuffs with the doctor's assistance. With the restraints in place, he moved back to the fleshy feast between Amanda's legs and Kloster concentrated her sharp teeth on the girl's nipples. Amanda's body heaved above Penny, deafening her with a cacophony of jarring wood and stretched spring. 'Bite me! Bite me, doctor! Be hard with my breasts,' she cried.

The request was followed by a shriek as the doctor must have complied. The sound and sight of Amanda's depraved passion spurned Klima on to penetrating her. Penny watched his naked buttocks press forward as he sunk a long and brown penis into the writhing Amanda.

Amanda kicked out and struggled but Kloster held her shoulders firmly down. Klima shuffled across Amanda's chest and smothered her face with his own lips, sealing entreaties for more diabolic treatment inside his own mouth.

Penny found herself stunned with disbelief and immobile with fright. She just stared out from her little floor-level prison, gaping at the strength and fury of the lust above her. Lucy's bondage appeared in her memory as little more than child's play when compared to this spectacle. There were far greater extremes and explorations occurring at the Academy, far beyond her own fledgling trials of self-discovery. Something inside Penny demanded, through the haze of shock and fear, that she too should experience the fullest spectrum of Whitehead's forbidden colours.

In the mirror, she could see that Klima had turned Amanda on to her side, flicking her legs high in the air whilst swivelling his own body behind her. He began to pump her sex vigorously from behind, while clutching her bruised breasts with hands that reached between her arms. Amanda's tear-stained face was visible to Penny for only a few seconds before Kloster changed her position and slipped across the girl's front to stroke her tanned and well-defined torso. From a mere glimpse, Penny knew that Amanda had passed beyond anything that she recognised in the girl. Her thick eyebrows had knitted above screwed-up eyes, as if she was in either great pain or a pinnacle of pleasure. Only the open and gasping mouth suggested the heights of deviant arousal that must have gushed through the girl's soul.

Klima rolled forward and pushed Amanda on to her tummy, face down on the slippery black sheets. He pulled his glistening cock from Amanda's well-pummelled sex and slipped it slowly into her tight anus. Kloster scurried to the side and blocked Penny's vision of the sodomy that thrilled her gasping friend. She could only see Klima's face buried in Amanda's shock of raven hair to one side of Kloster's pale back, and his slowly moving legs entwined around Amanda's sprawling calf muscles on the other. He seemed to be taking her rear slowly and carefully, slipping inside a little deeper each time, forcing louder and louder grunts from Amanda's muffled mouth.

The doctor seemed content to sit back and purr, occasionally stroking Amanda's splayed legs, tracing the creases in her stockings with long crimson nails. When Klima's rhythm developed to a harder and more forceful lunge between Amanda's soft buttocks, the doctor's excitement increased. She clapped her hands and urged him on: 'Harder, *Herr* Klima, take her deeper still, spear her to the bed.'

When Klima's body rose and thrust down in to Amanda's backside with a heavy and fast momentum, the doctor clambered upon his back to force his cock deeper into Amanda with her own body weight. Kloster clawed the Russian's shoulders and shrieked a smattering of broken English obscenities down at the pumping lovers beneath her.

The pile of thrusting hips and kicking legs seemed to collapse and writhe on to its side, with Amanda emerging, drenched in sweat in the middle, still impaled on Klima's spearing penis, which was sunk to the hilt.

Penny knew that he came when Amanda released a final scream of passion. He croaked and sunk his teeth into Amanda's shoulder.

Kloster purred with approval and slithered across both lovers to suffocate Amanda's ecstatic cry with her alabaster sex. To Penny, it seemed to be a final operatic conclusion to a desperately passionate threesome. She had little idea that it was more of a beginning, an entrée before a banquet that she would watch, spellbound, until dawn.

When Miss Barbusse returned to her bedchamber after bidding a dishevelled, drained, but eternally grateful Paris good night, Lucy had become engrossed in her books.

The dean smiled, folding her arms with contentment across her kimono-garbed breasts. 'I can count the people on one hand who have actually been permitted to read my journals.'

Lucy looked up and widened her beautiful tear-stained eyes at her mistress. 'I feel honoured to have been given access to your life, your wisdom, your passions. I have learnt so much in such a short time. No one has ever taken so much of an interest in me.'

Lucy's words were pure Vivaldi to the dean, resonating like beautiful strings inside her cold heart, weaving melodies of love.

'But who is this, mistress?' Lucy cried out, holding the leather-bound volume aloft to point at a faded photograph.

'Do you think him handsome?' the dean asked, her eyes alight from a pyre of memory.

'Oh, yes,' Lucy emphatically replied, 'and so distinguished.'

'He was. Cultured, educated, generous and tender.'

'The master?' Lucy asked in a hushed tone.

'Yes, the master. My master,' Miss Barbusse answered, already feeling the first pang of regret swell inside her throat.

'But was he not cruel? You were his slave?'

Miss Barbusse laughed and walked forward to cup Lucy's beaming face within her cool hands. 'Yes, my sweet, he was cruel and demanding and very strict. But in the most beautiful way, with methods that cast away my inhibitions and taught me about real freedom.'

'But where is he now?'

Miss Barbusse struggled to remain composed. 'He lives on, Lucy. He lives on in my memory, in my books and in my work. From there, I will share him with you.'

The dean was pleased that Lucy refrained from asking any further questions about her master. It had been over twenty years since she saw him last and the pangs of grief would always be fresh.

Miss Barbusse poured herself a glass of scotch and sat down on the bed, close to Lucy. She was content to watch the girl's face as she read several passages from the journal to herself. She was pleased to see her protégée's face pass from horror to astonishment and finally to wonder.

Six

'Not this time,' Penny hissed at the smiling Lucy Harrington.

'Oh, really? Well I don't know about that,' Lucy whispered back with her pretty turned-up nose and shadowy blue eyes pressed close to Penny's grimace.

The door to the gymnasium was closed and the heat from so many heaving, gasping and darting female bodies had perfumed the thickening air. Kloster walked around the two girls, who quivered and tottered in their heels on the soft gym mat.

'Remember, there is a time for gentle caresses and a time for force,' Kloster instructed. 'You will delight your enemies by taking their sexuality between your bright-red fingernails and squeezing it until it screams. You can seduce an opponent with a spiked heel and lacquered nail. It can be just as devastating as a deep kiss or scented massage.'

'Perfect lesson for kicking your slutty arse,' Lucy rasped, with her back to the doctor, as the two girls circled each other.

'Sure you wouldn't prefer to kiss it?' Penny countered. 'I'm sure your anger is just latent bisexual frustration.'

The comment seemed to be Lucy's cue for a lunge. The attack came quick and low, lifting Penny over Lucy's shoulder and depositing her on the mat, red face upward with one stocking laddered.

'Excellent move, Harrington!' Kloster yelled, which infuriated Penny even further. She had slipped out from under Amanda's bed at four in the morning, her body aching from the hard wooden floor, after listening to Mr Klima and Kloster make love to Amanda for hours. Under the bed, Penny had heard enough moans, lascivious demands and obscene suggestions to arouse her own body and mind in ways that now made her cringe.

To compound Penny's discomfort, there had been no one available to assuage her fiery hunger for satisfaction after the lecturers had left Amanda's room. Amanda had been rendered inactive by the furious and thorough onslaught of hands, restraints and a long and seemingly inexhaustible penis. Penny had been left to walk back to her room alone, tingling and wide awake with desire.

The frustration and anger had sent her into Kloster's Friday-morning lesson with war on her mind. Initially, she had been delighted when her sparring partner in 'the aggressive-take-overs lesson' had been Lucy Harrington. In the protection of a formal Academy lesson, Penny had glimpsed an opportunity to even the score with her tormentor without creating waves. The girls had even been allowed to unbutton the rear of their hobble skirts to permit greater mobility when fighting each other.

Now, however, flat on her back and staring at the ceiling with her legs splayed at unnatural angles, Penny began to wonder if her Whitehead slump could actually get any worse.

'You must fight with your mind, Penny Chambers,' the doctor advised from the sidelines. 'You are too fond of allowing your emotions to blur your vision.'

'Got that right,' Penny mumbled as she scrabbled back to her feet and retrieved a high heel.

Lucy stood back, smug and self-satisfied, with her hands on her slender hips. She still looked immaculate, uniformed meticulously with not a blonde hair out of place, even after throwing Penny over her shoulder in the deft wrestling manoeuvre that Kloster had shown them.

In the distance on another mat, Penny watched the radically transformed Amber effortlessly toss the weighty Bessy to the ground before smothering the hapless girl's face with her opened legs.

'Straighten yourself, Miss Chambers, and begin again from the top,' Kloster ordered before strutting off to view another tussling duo.

'Want some more, slut?' Lucy taunted, out of Kloster's earshot. 'Come and get it. If you even get near me, I might tie you up in knots again. I know how much you enjoyed it last time.'

Penny's eyes narrowed and she began to recite the script again: 'You have stalled on the signing of this contract for months. You have wasted hundreds of man hours, you know nothing about etiquette and you have absolutely no knowledge of customer service. We offer you a good deal and you choose a competitor. Well, allow me to change your mind back again. I'll show you what we do to little teases in our company.'

The dialogue felt good, tumbling out of her mouth, the words galloping on hot, lipstick-tinged breath. Penny imagined pretty executives actually performing this ritual on powerful, suited male directors in professional office surroundings. She could imagine their visceral thrill, when boxed, tossed and tied down by a glamorous well-heeled and tight-skirted woman. How many commercial deals, she asked herself, had been saved with this approach by Whitehead graduates over the years?

Penny finished her trial spiel and made a feint towards Lucy's left. The young heir skipped to one side, expecting a move from that direction. This time, however, Penny used her speed and guile: she countered

141

to the right, then back to the left again, right once more, and left for the last time, forcing Lucy to lose her balance in the dancing confusion. Penny completed the tactic by aiming her two-handed lunge straight down the middle, and in for the kill.

Penny's hands grasped the collars of Lucy's silken blouse and she yanked the out-smarted girl forward. She enjoyed the look of surprise and fear in Lucy's eyes for a split second, before initiating her judo throw. When Lucy hit the mat to the tune of a ripping blouse, Penny relished the idea of having Lucy in her power: taking her time with bonds and verbal torments.

She pushed her weight on to Lucy's stomach and pinned her wrists to the ground. Lucy's blouse had been torn free from her right shoulder, revealing a creamy shoulder and smooth breast, cupped in black silk.

'I bet if I pull your knickers down,' Penny teased, 'I will find a big red hand-print on your little white cheeks. I might show the class what a good spanking our heir received last night.'

'Try it!' Lucy stammered.

Penny loosened her grip on Lucy's wrists in order to stroke the exposed breast and really taste revenge. Her hand had not even closed on the soft mound when a hail of saliva, spat from Lucy's beautiful crimson mouth, blinded Penny.

'You dirty –' Penny never had time to finish. Her hands instinctively released Lucy's wrists to wipe her eyes and she felt Lucy's body slither further down between her legs. She was unable to see Lucy's next move but felt the heir's legs rise over her shoulders and slide beneath her chin.

With a pair of high-heeled feet lodged beneath her jaw from behind, Penny's body was pulled backwards and down to the floor. In a flash, the positions were instantly reversed: Penny lay on her back with Lucy's feet now pinning her shoulders to the mat. The young heir sat up between Penny's parted thighs and smiled.

'Got something in your eyes, Chambers?' Lucy taunted.

'You dirty bitch!' Penny shrieked.

A volcano seemed to have exploded somewhere deep inside of her. She struck out and clawed at Lucy's long stocking-sheathed legs, but the Cuban heels had hooked beneath her collar bone and reduced Penny's blows to little more than an ineffectual flailing.

Lucy removed the spearing heels quickly, spinning her legs backward and propelling her body forward to crush Penny. Her nimble hands closed like steel traps around Penny's wrists and banged them down to the mat with a slap. Once again, Penny found herself immobile and useless, her skirt hiked up to her waist, her eyes staring into a haughty and triumphant face.

Penny's eyes were still sticky with spit and her anger threatened to explode from between her firm breasts. The chance had been there to get some revenge on her enemy and she had blown it by reaching for a pretty breast.

'Get off me –' Penny started to yelp, but Lucy's soft lips stole the demand from her mouth with a deep and slippery kiss.

Lucy proceeded to seize an immediate advantage over Penny's shock – she grasped both of Penny's hands with one of her own and used the free hand to reach behind her and finger Penny's knickered sex. The hand slipped between her girdle and tickled her outer lips with a painted fingernail.

The hand only stayed there for a moment; Kloster had reappeared to view the interesting contest and the other girls had all stopped and turned their perspiring faces to watch. Lucy's fingers, however, had lingered long enough to arouse Penny, reanimating the intense arousal she had experienced when bound by the ruthless heir over a footstool in her own room. The hot bolts of desire clashed with Penny's anger and made her desperate for something quite perverse. From out of the most uncharted depth in her soul, something emerged, making Penny shiver and writhe beneath Lucy. She wanted to be punished for her weakness and failure. She wanted to be humiliated and controlled as a way of paying penance for spending a night beneath a bed. She wanted to be lashed for being warned off her investigation and she needed to be spanked for inciting suspicion amongst the staff.

Penny felt like a fool and a failure and she demanded a harsh sentence.

Lucy was the perfect individual to meet that desire.

With her free hand, Lucy unclasped and tore a nylon down and off Penny's left leg. She pulled the smoky wisp of warm fabric across Penny's straining face before looping it around her wrists. Lucy pinched the toe and end of the stocking between her red nails and wrapped the hosiery around Penny's wrists, over and over again, until Penny was unable to move her hands apart.

The other girls crowded around the mat and Penny watched an evil smile broaden across Kloster's face.

'Finish her!' Kloster demanded, and a ripple of shock passed among Penny's gaping and horrified classmates.

Penny, never having experienced anything so demoralising and humiliating, just lay still, allowing the forbidden appetite to rise and burn.

Lucy busied herself before every pair of staring hypnotised eyes: she ripped Penny's laddered right stocking off and bound her naked ankles tightly together. She stood up, with her feet planted on either side of Penny's face, and let her captive stare up a pair of long legs to a shadowy and satin-gripped sex.

'You have a captive, Lucy!' Kloster prompted. 'An important deal is at stake. How will you add humiliation to a victory that the prisoner will dream of for the rest of their lives?'

Kloster's outburst had given the beautiful heir an

idea; Penny could tell by the malicious smile on Lucy's face and the little tremors of excitement that twitched at the side of her smeared mouth. She began to look evil and greedy, almost slovenly with her ripped blouse and smudged make-up. But it was a haughty and devious air the girl had assumed, and one not without a dramatic sexual appeal to Penny.

Lucy yanked Penny's long skirt off and threw it to one side. Amanda stepped forward, white with rage, from the crowd of staring pupils, but Kloster stopped her with one long arm.

Lucy proceeded to slide Penny's knickers down from beneath her silky girdle, over her pale thighs and knees, before ripping the gusset asunder to retrieve them from around her little bound ankles. She then stretched the black satin gauze between her fingers, wrapping it over her thumbs. Another quick wave of mute horror flexed along the column of staring girls and Kloster licked her bright-red lips with pride.

'You thought you were strong but you are weak,' Lucy said quietly, fulfilling the role of a sexual terrorist in Kloster's game. But every girl present knew of the ulterior motives and meaning in Lucy's speech: these two girls had been at war since day one.

'You have decided to take your business elsewhere,' Lucy continued, 'like a slut who cannot choose between lovers and leads both on instead. For this misbehaviour I will punish you and rectify the error you have made. But first, I will gag that devious and tarty mouth. You see, I do not wish to hear any more lies.'

Penny watched her own fragrant panties being lowered on to her face. They were pushed between her teeth and her jaws closed upon them in defeat. She bit down hard and let Lucy turn her tightly bound body over on to its front.

Penny quickly realised that her body was no longer her own: it had been taken by a stronger will. The very

145

thought of such submission thrilled her deeply. Her reason screamed 'No!' and her natural self-respect struggled to take effect. But something inside Penny relished this release from control. Like a gimp in Madam Skinner's cottage, Penny wanted to end the struggle and relax into another's sordid will.

Penny closed her eyes when Lucy began the severe slapping of her naked rear. She kept her thighs tightly clasped together and sensed the little secret pool of moisture that had gathered on her sex and now rubbed between her legs. Every girl in that room was watching her being stripped bare, tied down and spanked ruthlessly as she bit into her own damp panties. It was humiliating, perverse, and it would have been unthink-able in her past life. On this day, however, Penny wanted it more than anything else in the world. She bit down on her satin gag to stifle her cries of pleasure, and pretended that her rotating buttocks were a symbol of struggle and not a sign of heavenly discomfort.

Kloster stopped Lucy after the twentieth lash; Penny had counted each slap from the hard palm in her prostrate world of private bliss.

'I think that is enough,' Kloster said, catching Lucy's arm before another spank could blast off Penny's ruddy buttocks. 'It was, however,' the doctor added, 'perfectly executed and enormously effective. I think you are all ready to embrace invincibility. Your enemies will never fully understand what hit them.'

Without speaking, Amanda and Bessy dropped to the mat and removed the nylon restraints from Penny's wrists. No one else spoke in the room; a total silence had fallen over the stunned pupils.

Close your eyes.

The words had been drawn on the mirror in her room. The author had used a dark-red lipstick to carefully inscribe the second warning in two days.

146

Penny stared at the script for some time, unmoving and inconsolable. It was she who wriggled on a pin before a hidden scrutiny; it was her, the fledgling investigator, who had been exposed. It was only her fifth day at Whitehead and she sensed the chilly twilight of fear casting her dwindling hope further into shadow.

Penny eventually broke from her trance and made her way to the hidden cache of notes and dictaphone tapes between her mattress and bed frame. They were still secure, undisturbed and pressed flat inside a make-up bag.

Her secret visitor, for some reason, had not effected a thorough search of the room. They were content, it seemed, to steal into her unoccupied bedroom and leave messages. If she pressed on with the investigation, Penny reasoned, a warning could quickly transform into a threat.

Something hot began to smoulder inside Penny. The smoke from this inner fire brought the humiliations foisted upon her by Lucy to the front of her mind. The second episode, seen by all, had thrilled her close to a faint, but Penny refused to accept total defeat. Penny had never failed at anything in her life and she would not be beaten. Nothing had gone to plan, but she still demanded the final truth.

The time called for extreme actions. In a crisis Penny had always been able to harness her concealed resources, and it was this reserve of energy and ingenuity that she called upon now. The days of circling reconnaissance were over: the time for daring had arrived.

When the manor clock announced eight o'clock and the dusk powdered her room, Penny departed for the dean's quarters on the ground floor. This time she intended to do much more than listen outside the door.

The sound of high heels, striking out a confident stiletto parade, stopped Penny at the foot of the stairs.

'Be brave, Lucy,' Miss Barbusse's voice said. 'Although I doubt that you will see anything beyond the scope of your intuition.'

'Yes, mistress,' the girl replied in a hushed and respectful tone that Penny had never heard before.

The voices and clacking heels moved away from Penny and out through the echoing Academy reception. She breathed a sigh of relief and propelled herself into the dean's marbled corridor.

At the oak door, she paused and glanced left and right, her nose sensing the discreet wafts of perfume left by the two women. Penny shivered with excitement and turned the brass door handle slowly. The handle cooled her palm. After a click, she pushed the handle away from her tense body and the dean's unlocked door opened.

Penny scurried through the portal and shut it behind her. Not even daring to breathe, she turned round and glanced at the study. Penny instantly remembered her first encounter with the dean.

Penny stared at the chaise longue on which she had sat in shock when viewing the uniform, and acknowledged how much had changed inside her since that moment five days ago. The study was still as she remembered it: polished wood, teak shelving, the vast desk, and Persian rugs ruffled by the dean's exclusive heels.

The curtains were still open, and Penny used the remaining haze of dying midsummer light to guide her search. She made straight for the desk and tried each drawer. They were locked, so she sped to a black filing cabinet. She swore beneath her breath on discovering the cabinet's stubborn refusal to reveal its treasures. Everything in the study was securely locked and Penny guessed that the dean held the keys.

She had to think fast and be quick: in and out without delay. If she was caught then it was the end. Penny shuddered and cast the thoughts of possible discovery and punishment from her mind.

To the far side of the study, half-concealed by a book case, Penny caught sight of another door. The exit was only visible from behind the desk and that accounted for her missing it on the morning of her matriculation at Whitehead.

The door had been crafted from a dark and reinforced wood, as if to soundproof the chamber beyond, but the handle turned smoothly and soundlessly. Penny tiptoed through the doorway and closed it behind her, sealing herself off in complete blackness. The drapes in this room were drawn and must have been thick enough to stop any vestige of outside light from struggling through.

Penny clawed the walls on either side of the door, her fingers scrabbling for a light switch. One hand scurried over a circular dial and twisted it round. A light clicked on in the centre of the room and the switch seemed to function as a dimmer mechanism. Penny turned the dial round one complete circle to fully illuminate the queen's lair.

She was unable to move for several seconds, her eyes struggling to cope with the images bombarding her from the shadowy walls. The heavily gilded portrait frames, their lustre dulled with antiquity, surrounded fine oils depicting bacchanalian lust of such extremity that Penny's first reaction was terror.

Beside the massive canopied bed, an artist had depicted a young dark-haired woman's plight on both a rack and some manner of cast-iron gibbet. The creations were ghoulish and satanic, but also beautiful in the manner in which they captured the mixture of anguish and orgiastic pleasure on a young woman's face. It was the same willowy model, with the creamy complexion, who graced the walls of Penny's own boudoir – the beautiful maiden who grasped a riding crop amidst the folds of thick fur. Penny shuddered when imagining the time the model had spent on the medieval devices until the portraits were complete.

She reached out and stroked the dark silk wallpaper. It felt slick beneath her damp palms and seemed to tickle her nerves with tiny pulses of electricity. She approached the bed and noticed the tiny brass loops and fixtures on the upright posts, designed, she guessed with an exhilarating dread, for supporting thin chains and the weight that struggled within them.

So this was Miss Barbusse's inner sanctum, where the young sacrifices delivered themselves for private tuition. Penny admired the daring of Lucy and Paris, who had been here and called the dean 'mistress'. She half envied them also, for what they had seen and experienced inside these dark walls at the mercy of their icy mentor. They had played a game so seductive in its danger and chance.

Penny shook off the need to just stand, stare and soak up the room's atmosphere. She skipped across to the large dresser, nearest the door, and slid the top drawer out.

She stared down at a sea of wispy under-things, their expensive and exotic perfume drifting up to her nose from the packed compartment. It held all manner of corsetry, brassieres, black lingerie and sheer hosiery. Penny sifted through the orderly drawer with her fingers, careful not to disturb the surface calm. When her fingers brushed across something hard she was unable to prevent her hands from pulling it out and into the light.

The large onyx shaft, crafted expertly, stretched Penny's fingers wide open to cradle its diameter. She turned the object in her hands, estimating its length to be at least ten inches, and wondered how often it explored the dean's intimacy.

She replaced the object in its soft bed, her hands almost reluctant to relinquish the enticing shape, before photographing it and the drawer with her slim-line camera. Penny turned and shot off half a film on the portraits and bed before returning once more to the dresser. The tension of the venture thrilled Penny and stopped her from feeling guilty as she plundered a woman's privacy.

Penny withdrew a black leather attaché case from the second drawer and placed it on the top of the dresser. She flicked the little silver catches upward and opened the lid.

Penny gasped and placed a finger on her slippery red lips, her eyes widening with astonishment. The tools and implements were beautiful and infinitely perverse. Laid carefully in crushed red velvet and mounted within bands of sterling silver, the dean's accessories revealed another of the woman's interests to Penny. There was nothing of Soho or Amsterdam tack in the manufacture of the cuffs and ankle bracelets. They had been created by a master craftsman, made to order, as had the canes, hide whips, polished plugs and shining clamps that glinted back at Penny like evil jewels. She photographed the case from three angles before replacing it in its tomb.

The final drawer was deeper than its counterparts and Penny struggled to slide it out of the dresser frame. As soon as her eyes delved inside the drawer, Penny gave thanks to whichever god provided guidance for junior reporters.

On the left side, stacked neatly, were several photograph albums; on the right lay Miss Barbusse's leather-bound journals.

Penny's entire body scrambled with excitement: the holy grail of Whitehead had been discovered. Her trembling hands hoisted the first album out of the drawer. Penny sat on the nearest rug and opened the volume.

The photographs had browned with age, the colours faded slightly, but the clothes, the cars and period details suggested the mid-sixties to Penny. In each photograph a group of young teens and twenty-somethings frolicked and laughed in Parisian cafés and jazz clubs. They were captured dancing in coffee lounges, leaping into fountains and posing around a yellow Alfa Romeo car.

As Penny's fingers skipped through the pages, the crowds thinned and two characters became central figures: the first was an elegant girl, her head always scarfed and her eyes shaded by sunglasses with pointed black frames. It was a younger Miss Barbusse, tight skirted and narrow waisted and invariably huddled around an older man. His gaunt and angular features – both noble and menacing – seemed vaguely familiar to Penny.

By the end of the first volume, each photograph had become consumed by Miss Barbusse, the man, and the passion that obviously raged between them. Her eyes were always adoring; his seemed to be calculating. Her smile revealed an eager and innocent acceptance of all he had to offer; his stiff face betrayed nothing openly but suggested a hidden spring of carefully guarded knowledge.

In the second volume, Miss Barbusse's face had frozen into a haughty foundation of its present chill, but a new flame danced within her beautifully shaded eyes. Her lover had disappeared from the pictures and Penny presumed that he held the camera, capturing his flourishing protégée now enriched by his experience and tutoring.

He liked her scantily clad with her breasts naked save for the trickle of pearls flowing between her breasts; he adored her on furs in her garters and black nylons; he was partial to her wet from showers and waterfalls, her dark lingerie clinging to her firm contours; and he seemed particularly fond of Miss Barbusse in tightly fastened bonds.

If the camera never lies then Penny assumed that Miss Barbusse held the poses with the gusto of an addict. When she had been bent over a leather couch and her buttocks had been striped by a cane, her face would turn towards the camera and offer an evil but hypnotic smile. When her arms had been stretched wide between cuffs fastened to an iron bedframe, her nylon-slippery legs opened provocatively to entice the camera on to her shaven and profoundly pink sex. The narrow dark eyes and slightly parted red lips always seemed to entice and summon her older lover to explore new limits.

When glancing through the third volume, Penny's back turned to a sheet of ice, and her legs clenched themselves around a sex that seemed to demand a thorough and fastidious attention from something long and hard.

It was the photograph of the dean in the tight and shiny, black, rubber mac that haunted Penny. In the photo, Miss Barbusse stood in an early-morning Venetian square, surrounded by scurrying pigeons, and still offered an air of defiance and an appetite for fresh extremes, despite the intense activities she had obviously experienced the night before. The lapels of the shiny coat had fallen open to reveal soft white breasts peppered with pink love bites. Her slender waist had been braceleted with pure silver chains, with matching suspender straps that hauled her nylons to the very peak of her thighs. Between her legs, something long and two pronged had been sunk into both her anus and vagina. Only the tight and welcome embrace of her illicit openings defied gravity and prevented the cobblestones from claiming the steely plug.

It was the image of her face that stunned Penny more than the props and delicate marks on her flesh; Miss Barbusse's eyeliner had run and her lipstick had smudged across both cheeks. The eyes were insane with ecstasy and the tiny pink tongue pushed at the camera as if to lap and suckle the glass lens; it was the incongruity of that wanton leer, on a face as noble and reposed as any queen, that clawed inside Penny.

When the manor clock struck and chimed across the Cornish estate, Penny realised that she had been busy with the albums for an hour. She knew a retreat now, with the secrets she had glimpsed, would have been advisable, but the dozen or more untouched journal volumes begged her to stay and read on.

Penny began with the third journal, skim-reading and hoping to chance upon the heart of the dean's story. Her eyes flashed across the meticulous French script and struggled to translate the information with only her rusty A-level-French skills to work with. Her reading was patchy and only effective in random bursts of clarity. The volume seemed to express Miss Barbusse's quest for all that sixties Paris had to offer a teenager. There were endless lists of lovers she had discarded, her amorous exploits described with a playful sadism. Towards the end of the volume there was mention of her curiosity about the seedy underbelly of town and several notorious individuals she had only glimpsed from afar in hotel restaurants. In the fourth volume, Penny discovered an involvement with someone the diarist only ever referred to as the 'master':

I never could have known that such a range of sensation was available to a woman. The strength of his bare hands, that have killed men, has reshaped my body. His teeth and leather belt have awoken a giant beast inside me. It can only be placated by his attentions.

Penny's fingers skipped through the fragile pages and her nails trailed down tiny scribbled paragraphs until a detail emerged to slap her face with shock:

He has used the yoke and single glove for three months to aid my posture . . . My corsetry training has created an impossible nineteen-inch waist and my knees and ankles are now hobbled daily by a skirt made in 1932. It prevents me from straying far from his apartment. I watch the Seine each day, while preparing my ultra-long nails and learning to walk for him on heels that push me on to my strangled toes. My stays and fastenings are a delight, and whisper of the impending pleasure that he will bring home to me this evening. We are to receive guests from the valley and I have been promised the jewelled handcuffs. My allure must be impeccable: my seams straight, my boots knee length, and my nails are to be long, curved and lacquered in red at the baron's request.

Penny's blood froze when her eyes licked across a newspaper clipping, pasted on to a page towards the rear of the volume. It featured Jean Enfer, the notorious French mercenary, gun runner and adventurer, photographed in his bush fatigues in the Congo. Penny matched the noble face in the newspaper picture with the man in the dean's photograph album. He was the 'master': the terror of Algeria, the African soldier of fortune, the Cape Horn yachtsman and the most infamous womaniser in Paris. Penny remembered his story and filled in the blanks by reading the early-seventies newspaper article: Jean Enfer had been implicated in a spy circle, associated with the extreme right-wing political rebels who fought for France's colonial interests. Many believed that the charges were trumped up to save the reputation of a diplomat's wife, who had become involved with the gallant in a manner too shocking to ever recount. He had been exiled to the Pacific, where he disappeared, perhaps assassinated by the French secret service.

Beside the newspaper cutting Miss Barbusse had repeated one word: 'Lies, lies, lies!'

On the journal's last page, Penny read a solitary line: 'And now I too must flee.'

Had she been devastated by his exile or his alleged involvement with another woman? Had she been forced to vacate France because of her association with Enfer? Penny's French was too poor to glean further detail, but she suddenly felt an enormous weight of sympathy for the dean.

She could never have hoped for such a sensational story, but now she had more than an article: it was an illicit and perverse love story that smacked of film rights following a best-selling book. It was a goldmine of information that plucked at every mercenary nerve in her body. She would never have to work again; she would be a celebrity; she would destroy Miss Barbusse.

After Penny replaced the fourth volume and before she could reach for the fifth, she heard the study door open and close. Beyond the bedroom, the vibrations of a sudden occupancy froze the blood in Penny's veins.

She closed the drawer and sealed the dean's secrets away before her eyes frantically searched for a hiding place. She raced across to a large wardrobe and opened the mirrored doors. The racks and shelves were thick with all manner of chic dress and ultra-high-heeled shoe – there was no room for Penny's terror-stricken body.

She backed away and fell on to the bed, turned and scrabbled across the mattress, finding her feet beside the heavily draped bay window at the side of the bed.

When the handle turned on the door connecting the bedroom and study, Penny's mouth dried and her heart seemed to stop. She pressed her back against the wall and awaited her end – she could only hope that it would be swift.

The door began to creak open and Penny stifled a scream. She would have to rush the dean, leave through the reception and sprint for the main gate where her car awaited outside. There was no other option than a desperate and hasty flight.

The long fingers that wrapped around Penny's mouth

muffled her cry. The long arm that encircled her trim waist from behind pulled her backward and out of the dean's room.

Penny seemed to fall through a thick black curtain and into complete darkness beyond. Back in the boudoir from which she had been seized, Penny heard the dean's voice: 'The lights are still on. I could have sworn that I had turned them out.'

'Your handmaiden?' Lucy queried.

'Yes, perhaps,' Miss Barbusse replied, before gathering herself. 'Lucy, will you collect the wine and bring glasses. My feet are tired too and I would like a massage.'

'Yes, mistress,' the girl replied.

In the dark a voice whispered into Penny's ear, 'Is this what you seek?'

The voice was deep but purred with a husky feminine tone. Penny felt the slippery lips on her ear and the woman's long soft hair brushing against her cheek.

Penny was unable to reply with the long fingers clamped across her mouth. Her body had frozen within the tight embrace and her back rested upon a large and pointed pair of trussed breasts. Penny was lifted from her feet and carried sideways in the dark. She was placed gently upon her feet and pushed against the wall in front. In the dark she heard a rustle as the long arms passed over her shoulders and fumbled with something in front of her face. Without a sound, a panel slid across the wall and two spots of light met Penny's blinking eyes.

'Go on, Penny, look. See it all,' the voice whispered.

Penny pushed her face forward towards the two beams of light, which were no wider than her eyes, and looked through the tiny apertures.

She was immediately granted a view across the dean's double bed and into the room beyond. Miss Barbusse had reclined along the mattress, propped up on one elbow, and sipped a crystal glass filled with blood-red wine.

She had stretched one of her slender, black-nylon-coated legs forward to where Lucy knelt in supplication. Lucy cupped the dean's ankle and removed the tightly fitting stiletto from her damp foot. She began to rub the reinforced sole of the dean's slippery foot with her fingertips.

The dean purred with approval and lay back on the bed with her eyes closed. 'Umm, that is good, Lucy.'

Lucy beamed with satisfaction before sucking the dean's toes through her black seamed stockings. Her little red lips closed around Miss Barbusse's big toe and her cheeks hollowed as she sucked. Miss Barbusse clawed the duvet with her crimson talons and moved her head from side to side with pleasure. Lucy began to lick across the top of her mistress's foot, sliding her wet tongue over the shimmering stockings and sighing through her nose with pleasure.

'Is this what you want to tell the world about? I think it is best left between two people,' the voice rasped into Penny's ear, and the fragrant breath washed hot against her face.

Penny could not reply; she had no answer and her eyes had become transfixed by the passage of Lucy's hands up the dean's legs, swishing over her shiny knees and disappearing inside the tight folds of her skirt.

Miss Barbusse reached beneath her backside and unzipped her skirt. Lucy eagerly pulled it down the dean's legs and her eyes flashed with excitement at the sight of her lover's stocking-tops and creamy thighs, which were beautifully framed beneath a tight black corset and transparent panties.

'Have you enjoyed my novel, Lucy?' the dean moaned, opening her legs and writhing on the vast bed.

'Yes, mistress,' Lucy replied softly. 'I have learnt so much. It amazes me what the master put you through.

You are so clever, mistress. And it thrills me too, as you said it would. I cannot put it down – it makes me so restless. I think I too am a deviant.'

Penny realised in a flash that the lovers were discussing the notorious book, *The Deviants*, still banned in the British Isles. It had been written anonymously by a French girl, and a source at the *Inquisitor* magazine was certain that royalty payments were wired to the Whitehead Academy in Cornwall.

'You have a long journey ahead of you, Lucy, if you are to become a true deviant,' the dean whispered as she raised her legs and placed them on Lucy's shoulders.

'I have time, mistress,' Lucy replied seductively, before lowering her glistening mouth on to the dean's flimsily knickered sex.

Penny was amazed by Lucy Harrington's behaviour and manner. Where had the foul-mouthed bully gone? Where had this polite and attentive angel risen from? Penny struggled to reconcile the two faces of the heir. With Miss Barbusse she was a paragon of breeding and culture; with Penny she had been a fist-fighting brat with a scrubber's mouth.

'Come, we have a journey ahead of us,' the voice whispered behind Penny, and a hand slipped inside her own, entwining its long fingers through hers and squeezing them tightly.

Penny stole one final glance through the peephole and watched the dean squash Lucy's pretty blonde head between her thighs, trapping it against her sex.

The powerful stranger, who had hauled Penny from the brink of discovery, pulled her through a dark passage and away from Miss Barbusse's chamber. She was unable to see where her feet fell and began to panic. The woman seemed to sense her fear. 'Careful, there are stairs here. We must go up.'

Penny took one step at a time and mounted a narrow and twisting staircase, seeing nothing but grasping the long-fingered hand – her only buoyancy in an ocean of darkness.

The stairs wound upward, twisting round and round. Penny could feel the narrow stone walls pressing on her shoulders and hear nothing save the sound of two pairs of stiletto heels clipping off the thin stone stairs. She realised that the stairwell must have been installed inside the wall space and be accessible only from a hidden portal in the dean's room. When the stairs finished, Penny followed the hand and the clouds of musk that enshrouded its owner into a long and labyrinthine corridor.

'We are above the second floor now, in the attic space,' the voice whispered.

'Why did you save me?' Penny asked.

'Because you are the last one that will ever infiltrate the Academy.'

'The last what?'

'Don't play dumb, girl. You are the last reporter that will ever explore Whitehead. There has only ever been one other and he will never be seen again.'

Penny froze with fear and only managed to speak between an involuntary gulping. 'Sebastian? What did they do to him?'

'We took care of him.'

Penny spoke after a long pause. 'And me, can I expect a similar fate? You know others will come for me, you –'

'No,' the woman interrupted in a curt tone. 'You will leave here and dispel the myths.'

Penny was staggered by the information. 'So the dean knows. She has known about me all along?'

'No. Only I know and I will set you free to save the Academy.'

'What makes you think that I have any intention of saving this place?' Penny queried, becoming exasperated, annoyed at the loss of control.

'Because I have watched you. At Whitehead, nothing

160

goes unnoticed for too long and you have embraced the culture here with a healthy appetite.'

Penny felt her cheeks cloud hotly with shame in the dark.

'Look here,' the voice commanded and the hand tugged Penny down and into a crouch. 'But be quiet, or I will wring your neck.'

Two holes of yellow light appeared on the floor and Penny leant forward to peer through.

The discreet observation holes must have been bored into the ceiling beside the light fittings, to provide a bird's-eye view of the room below. Penny stared down at a rug before her eyes flitted across the antique furniture arranged beneath her. It had similar dimensions to her own chamber, but the walls had been covered in different, though equally provocative, oil paintings.

Through the tiny vantage point, several sounds wafted up towards Penny. She recognised the voice instantly: it was Bessy's deep northern brogue that cried from the bed and pierced the noise of vibrating bed springs: 'Want some more, you dirty little lad? I'll teach you a lesson, my boy, for trying it on with me!'

Penny changed the angle of her head and stared down at a slant to catch a glimpse of the heaving bed, which seemed almost to rise off the floor and crash down again. Her nose picked up the familiar scent of sex, thick and cloying in the hot air below.

On the bed, half-concealed by the canopy, Penny was able to see Bessy pumping her body up and down with some considerable vigour. Beneath her tightly corseted back, crisscrossed with leather laces, a solitary pair of male legs kicked out and became tangled in the black sheets. The legs were long, hairless and tanned. She had seen them once before, when hiding beneath Amanda's bed: Bessy was riding Klima! The notion spun through Penny's excited mind, almost failing to settle into comprehension.

161

It was the manner in which Bessy was talking to the lecturer that particularly shocked Penny. 'I'll give that cock something it'll never forget. You won't be sniffing around the girls when I've finished with you, my lad.'

Klima croaked with ecstasy and Bessy increased the speed of her pumping buttocks across his lap.

'That's it!' Bessy squealed. 'Fuck me! Fuck it into me. Give it to me, you dirty little bastard!'

The peepholes suddenly disappeared. Penny's guide and saviour must have slid something across from the side and once more she had been plunged into total darkness.

'Mr Klima,' the woman purred, 'in a new role. The great seducer has become a pawn beneath Bessy. Isn't it just wonderful?'

'Why me?' Penny hissed, annoyed that the captivating spectacle had been snatched away from her eyes. 'I must be the last person on earth that you should be showing this to.'

'I want you to see it all. Otherwise, you will only try and find out for yourself with disastrous consequences. Look at tonight, Penny Chambers: you were trapped like a rat in the dean's bedroom. Let that serve as a warning to the curious. I am tired of being your guardian angel.'

'You left the messages, the note and the lipstick on my mirror. Who are you?'

'Later,' the voice replied: 'Let me just say that I have a vested interest in both of our futures.'

Penny shook her head in confusion. What did this woman mean? Before she could stutter out another question, she found herself hoisted to her feet and dragged through the attic space.

They walked across a reinforced area in the attic, for a distance that Penny estimated to have been at least twenty feet, before she was forced to squat down and peer through another pair of peepholes.

On this occasion Penny stared into her own bedroom.

She saw her things from above and the painting of the young girl in furs.

'You watch me! You –'

'Yes, Penny. I pay special attention to you, and what an active little madam you have proved yourself to be. Your night with Amanda is one of my firm favourites. I have watched it several times.' Penny detected a hint of playful cynicism in the voice as it descended in to a husky laugh.

'A film!' she blurted out.

'An insurance policy,' the woman replied.

Penny felt the blood drain from her face. The Academy had become a rollercoaster of fantasy quickly followed by nightmare.

'Come on, let us go underground,' the woman invited, seeming to relish Penny's shock.

She allowed herself to be led, dour-faced and puppy-like, back towards the staircase. At the bottom, the woman paused and reopened the peepholes overlooking the dean's chambers.

'How are things progressing?' the husky voice asked Penny.

Penny peered through the wall and saw Lucy, naked, glowing, and busily skim-reading one of the dean's journals. Penny could not see Miss Barbusse and became astonished at the trust that existed between the two women after only five days. The dean was actually allowing Lucy access to her secret history.

When the dean's heels resounded from the study and warned of her readmittance to the bed chamber, Lucy dropped the journal into the dresser and scurried back towards the bed. Lucy's reaction surprised Penny, but her guide closed the peephole and pulled Penny away.

'How can she be so familiar with Lucy? They hardly know each other.' Penny said.

'My mistress is capable of becoming intimate with anyone in a very short time. She can look at you and read your dreams.'

'You seem pretty fond of her. What kind of hold does she have over you –'

In the dark, the woman stopped abruptly and turned towards Penny. She could feel the woman's face pressed against her own. 'I owe her my life!' the voice hissed. 'She has done more for me than any other human being. She has helped me in ways that you are unable to comprehend! And I will let no harm come to her. She is a goddess!'

Penny stumbled backward, suddenly afraid of her guide and this display of fanatical loyalty.

The woman turned again and tugged Penny down a set of wet stairs. They led to what could only be a subterranean passageway, the temperature immediately dropping as they became surrounded by cold earth.

'Quickly,' the guide ordered. 'There is more for you to see. The picture is not yet complete.'

Penny had allowed herself to be blindfolded – she had no other choice and was forced to trust her guardian.

They had walked away from the manor at a quick step, in an underground tunnel with dripping walls. This too was completely dark and seemed to have stretched for over half a mile. Penny, however, had not been completely bereft of her sense of direction. From the angle at which they had left Miss Barbusse's chamber she realised that the mysterious woman was leading her beneath the playing fields and tennis courts, and towards the gamekeeper's cottage.

The very thought of re-entering Madam Skinner's perverse domain after dark filled Penny with an acute sense of unease.

When the underground journey stopped, Penny had heard the unbolting of a door. Her guide had then insisted on the blindfold. She had been led through what must have been a cellar and up into the house.

Penny had seen nothing and perhaps that had been a

blessing. There were sounds assaulting her ears from every direction – booming through the walls and creaking like demonic whispers from the ceiling above. Penny had been able to determine the falling of a lash from somewhere: a hard wet slapping sound and the human cries that followed. Another voice had begged for forgiveness and been silenced by the cut of a cane. From behind her, at one point, she had heard chains slipping eerily through steel pulleys, as if to raise a weight from the floor.

She had finally been led into a warm room and the closing of a door had sealed her mercifully away from the cottage's night-time symphony.

With Penny seated, the woman had continued with more of her cryptic and mystifying dialogue: 'When you remove that blindfold, you will see a shadow from the past. One that becomes more indistinct each day. I can only hope that you have the courage to understand why some of us can never go back.'

Penny sat in silence and took shallow breaths. Her pale skin shivered with expectation but the evening's continual cycle of shock had virtually exhausted her. From her heart she found strength. 'I have broken into the principal's office and read her diary. Earlier in the day I allowed a girl I hate to humiliate me and I still don't think I have fully come to terms with what I felt. You kidnapped me and dragged me through a maze of secret tunnels. You have filmed me sucking another girl's fanny and yet you ask me for courage? I have gone beyond a set of normal human reactions and emotions. The human mind can only take so much in one day, so just try and surprise me.'

The blindfold was whipped off Penny's face and her eyes blinked from the sudden charge of electric light on to her optic nerves. She shook her head and rubbed her eyes. Gradually, the tall and elegant shape of an astonishingly statuesque and beautiful redheaded woman materialised before her blinking gaze. Against dark and leather-studded walls, beside an acre of closet space, beneath a mirrored ceiling and before a large double bed, a female vision stood tall and winked at Penny.

The long and slender legs rose like graceful marble sculptures from out of black, patent, stack-heeled shoes. Across the sole of each shoe a long and feminine foot snaked beneath the tight arches of crisscrossing leather straps. Beneath the sheer toe of the black seamed stockings the toenails were painted a vivid shade of bright pink. Around the top of the woman's thick and softly moulded thighs a tight leather skirt glistened like a second skin, gripping her slender hips with the effect of spray-on paint.

The flat and pale stomach shimmered beneath a transparent black blouse which stretched to tearing point over her large and pointed breasts, which were thrust arrogantly forward in a leather peephole brassiere.

She had hitched her hands and glinting red talons inside the thin belt loops attached to the waistline of her skirt, while her head was cocked in the manner of a challenging streetwalker. The long tendrils of thick red hair flopped down in a silky torrent to the Amazon's pierced belly button.

When Penny's wide eyes found the woman's face, they remained there for some time. The eyebrows were pencil thin and arched around two heavily painted blue eyes, which were perched attractively close together above a long and thin, feminine nose. The lips were glistening wetly with thick red paint, offset beautifully against a pale complexion. A solitary beauty spot rested above a sensual top lip.

Penny saw the barstool tart of every man's wildest fantasy. It was hard to equate the husky and knowledgeable voice with this street-smart dress code. It was even more difficult for Penny to parallel this raunchy creature with the formally attired Whitehead Academy staff.

'Who the . . .' Penny tried to ask, still struggling to cope with the pronounced sexuality before her.

'Who am I? Is that what you wish to know? I suppose it is time that we were properly introduced. It has been some time, after all, since I put that flower on your desk at work. It was your first day at the *Inquisitor* and you were terrified. My, oh my, how you blushed when the office hunk gave you that flower.'

'You, you –' Penny's words tripped, fell and scuffed their knees on the uneven path of disbelief.

'I, I –' the woman teased. 'Yes, I was once a rather popular chap in a silk suit who the girls used to drool over. But Sebastian is no more. His secret twin, Sabrina, who had hidden in the dark for twenty-six years, kind of took over at Whitehead. It was the perfect opportunity to disappear and start all over again, to be reborn.'

Penny could only vaguely connect the tall and handsome Sebastian, the *Inquisitor*'s ace reporter, with the perfumed creation before her. The eyes were the same colour, but more alive now. The quiet and almost sullen temperament had vanished, giving way to the husky cigarette-smoking vamp in five-inch heels.

'It cannot be,' Penny stammered. 'How – how did it happen?'

'The dean saw through me straight away. That woman is a genius. I never took my eyes off her legs for a moment, or her shoes, or skirt. I was not leering; I was envious. She had style and she saw my hunger; she sensed my deepest curiosity. Do you know what she asked me after only one hour in her study?'

'No,' Penny replied, unable to stop shaking her head.

'She said, "Sebastian, I think you deserve the best of both worlds. I will issue you with two uniforms, one for a boy and one for a girl." And that was that, she did not pry or mock. She understood. She kissed my cheek and the doctor took care of the rest.'

Penny's mind swivelled and swooped. She wanted to cry with relief and laugh with elation. 'I thought you were dead. The boss knew you were stressed out: he thought you had cracked after one too many undercover cases. We . . . I thought they caught you and, well . . .'

'Murder? Never. Whitehead is concerned with the living and the pursuit of our most private selves. The enemy is on the outside, Penny, and not in here. I used to be the enemy, but how could I bite the hand that feeds, after so many years in the closet? I decided to stay here. I never even told Miss Barbusse that I was from the *Inquisitor*. I just pretended that I was a regular student who discovered a bizarre vocation here. No one here knows beside you, and no one will ever find out.'

Sabrina paused to watch Penny's shaking disbelief, before adding in a playful tone, 'Know why I didn't date the girls at work?'

'Why?' Penny stammered and gulped.

'Because under my trousers my legs were silky smooth, completely waxed, and my toenails were painted. Imagine that?'

'I can't. I never would have guessed.'

'No one could. Living as a man was my biggest role, the greatest lie of all. In all that inner confusion I just threw my life into my work until they sent me to Whitehead, and that was definitely the last case.'

Penny stared at Sabrina's tight leather skirt. Her eyes hovered of their own accord over the beautiful creature's crotch.

Sabrina threw her head back and laughed. 'Did I go the whole way and lose my little chap too? Is that what you are thinking?'

'Well . . . I mean . . . If you are a girl now, it only stands to reason –'

'It can be argued, Penny, that gender is a state of mind and soul. I live and love as a woman, but at least one part of Sebastian remains.'

Sabrina pulled the hem of her leather skirt up to her neatly trimmed pubic hair. Beneath a tiny pair of black see-through panties and between an arch of leather suspender straps, Penny saw the penis cradled in its dark and silky hammock.

Someone knocked on the door and Sabrina smiled. 'Before you go home, Penny, and try to sleep, I would like to show you one last little scenario. After all, it's only fair: I have spent many a night watching you have fun.'

Sabrina laughed naughtily and skipped towards the door, her behind wiggling as temptingly as any nightclub good-time girl Penny had ever seen in London.

Sabrina opened the door and pushed her head through the gap. Penny heard her whispering and the smacking of eager kissing lips. She reached through the partially open door and clutched a hand.

Penny passed fleetingly close to a swoon when Sabrina tugged Rupert into the room.

'Hello, Pen,' the blushing and clearly uncomfortable figure stammered.

'Hello, darling.' Penny grinned, with mirth quickly replacing her horror.

'Our paths keep leading back to this place, don't they?' Rupert said, and wiped his handsome face with a handkerchief.

'They seem to,' Penny answered.

'And we know a good thing at the cottage when we see it,' Sabrina added, licking her sultry red lips. 'After Madam Skinner's rave reviews of Rupert, the frisky tom, I just had to meet him.'

Rupert looked at his feet and Sabrina pinched his cheek with affection.

'I am wearing your favourites, sweetheart,' Sabrina whispered to Rupert. 'I have dressed to order. A girl likes to please her man.'

Rupert's face blushed a deep crimson. His lips moved as he tried to say something to Penny, but no sound was forthcoming.

'Don't worry about Penny,' Sabrina advised. 'She has a very open mind, haven't you, girl?'

'Oh yes, absolutely,' Penny replied, shifting uncomfortably on her chair as Sabrina stroked Rupert's erection through his trousers.

'She won't be staying all night though, you greedy boy,' Sabrina hissed at Rupert, through a smile, and fell to her knees.

Rupert's penis was freed from his slacks before Penny had time to prepare herself.

A wide and slippery mouth, thickly coated with red lipstick, hungrily devoured the young man's erect penis. Rupert closed his eyes and began to sigh, running his fingers through Sabrina's glossy red hair. It was almost too much for Penny to comprehend: that long cock that had filled her own sex and anus now slipped quickly in and out of her ex-colleague's radically transformed mouth.

Rupert began to moan and gyrate his hips, pumping his groin on and off Sabrina's lapping mouth. He clutched the back of her head and stabbed his cock forcefully into her welcoming mouth. The conclusion to such a startlingly mutual desire was not long in its powerful and spurting arrival.

Penny could tell by the ecstatic expression on Rupert's face that he had emptied his desire deep inside Sabrina's mouth. She purred like a cat and Penny heard her gulping throat, sucking every last drop down.

Rupert fell back on the bed and Sabrina rose to her feet, pulling her hemline down to conceal her stocking-tops.

'Time you went home, Penny,' Sabrina said with a smile. 'I think you have seen enough for one night.'

Sabrina collected Penny, who was now astonished and flushed, and led her to the door, before adding in a serious tone, 'And you have a great deal to consider, my girl, about your future options.'

Penny nodded and followed Sabrina out and into a warm cottage corridor.

Sabrina looked back at Penny and raised an eyebrow. 'You're not jealous about Rupert, are you?'

'No! Not at all,' Penny blurted out. 'He's lovely and it was just a one-off between us, but I am curious as to . . . well . . .'

'How far he goes?' Sabrina laughed and winked.

'Yes,' Penny answered breathlessly.

'He goes as deeply into my tight little pussy as he sank into yours,' she replied, and squeezed Penny's hand with anticipatory excitement.

Seven

Gulls cried and swooped over the distant Cornish cliffs: black silhouettes before a gold and purple sunset. The green Academy lawns were licked with playful breezes, teasing an unquiet ocean inside Penny; on this night she had a decision to make.

She watched the object of her fascination strike the stem of her empty glass with a desert fork and call for attention.

'Congratulations on the successful completion of your first week at Whitehead,' Miss Barbusse began, in the centre of her elegant audience. 'The staff and I have decided to award tomorrow as a day of rest. We are all very pleased with last week's progress and have agreed to further reward your efforts with this lawn soirée, on this most glorious of Saturday evenings. In four days you should all be looking forward to a well-deserved graduation, preceded by the highlight of your stay, the masquerade ball. Now, please eat, drink and enjoy yourselves.'

Miss Barbusse melted from the centre of the gathering, after her welcoming speech, and floated in her ankle-length dress to the refreshment table. She appeared even more graceful and beautiful to Penny than ever before.

Penny followed the dean with her eyes, watching her serene posture and elegant profile as a champagne glass was lifted to those impeccable red lips. Penny walked across the shorn and pale-green grass towards the table, a hundred secrets bristling beneath her skin. She moved between the other students: the men clean-shaven and stiff collared, the women perfumed and sultry – every waist had been pinched, every nail painted, every hair groomed into place.

It struck Penny that, to an observer, the genteel gathering would have appeared as a glimpse into the past, where well-heeled and groomed guests mingled and laughed before a sprawl of ancient stone and fragrant rose bushes. It was, however, like everything else at Whitehead: one woman's memory, repainted in immaculate detail within the boundaries of her tiny retreat, protected from the bustle and madness of modern living by high walls and forbidden rituals. Penny desired to know more about this woman; she wanted to breathe her air and hear the cultured words that swept through that noble mouth. Penny wanted to be sure.

She had taken a hasty glimpse into the Academy's heart the night before. It had stung her appetite and created longings, some new, some reinvigorated. But, above her own growing inner awareness, and the confusion of newspaper ethics speeding through her mind, Penny needed to get to know this woman.

The *Inquisitor* fact-finding mission had little to do with this new quest; she desired instead to fill her soul with deviance, to gain a conclusive insight into an institution that, if she chose, could be destroyed with a few thousand words.

Amanda slipped into place beside Penny, her raven hair swept up and tied in a luscious arrangement upon her head.

'What's on your mind?' she asked.

'She is just so beautiful,' Penny replied, unable to remove her eyes from the dean.

'My, you have changed your tune. I thought you hated her.'

'I was mistaken, that's all. Mistaken about a lot of things.'

'Well, this place guarantees a new angle on most things. I told you it was best to just go with the flow and not fight it. You know, don't knock it until you've tried it.'

Penny smiled and gave Amanda's hand a little squeeze.

'But what about Amber?' Amanda prompted. 'She has just blossomed into this high-heeled hussy. She's delightful. She has promised to rub my back later and you should join us. After walking up and down those stairs today and swinging my hips with that bloody encyclopaedia on my head, I need a bit of TLC. And wasn't that lesson on disembarking from a car in a short skirt agony on your hips. "Too much clit and not enough tact!",' she mimicked Kloster, making Penny laugh. 'How about you, sweetheart. Are you going to join us?' she restated her invitation.

'Maybe, but for now I just want to watch Miss Barbusse.'

'OK, but don't go too far, we hope to sneak away. You don't want to miss out on Amber,' Amanda whispered, and pinched Penny's bottom before moving off towards the flirtatious American.

Penny stood a few feet away from the dean and watched a cloud of young men materialise around their principal.

'You boys are all looking very smart this evening,' Miss Barbusse purred, smiling softly to each in turn.

'Thank you, dean,' they all muttered, edging forward to inhale her narcotic pollen and to gaze at the banquet of silky contour before them. Penny thought of them as gazelles, rushing to a cold and satisfying drink, aware of and yet exhilarated by the presence of a dangerous feline.

She watched Miss Barbusse occasionally stroke an

arm to electrify a spine beneath its blazer, or tilt her haunting beauty to bestow a flattering glance at a stammering young man. They wanted her, desiring that mouth that had consumed their peer in a lecture; they needed her touch to slake a thirst for extraordinary experience.

Miss Barbusse watched them drink heady champagne for confidence and she baited her quarry like a conjurer. Her moves were subtle, but not lost on Penny. Something was happening; the dean was weaving her illusions. The growing atmosphere of desire sparked against Penny's skin, which was pale and expectant beneath shiny nylons, a sheer blouse and tight skirt.

The neckline of the dean's long gown plunged in an elegant V, revealing her snow-white cleavage, and she made certain that all four of her young admirers were offered the occasional glimpse inside that musky parting of soft breast. When she moved forward to take a green olive from the buffet, her hemline would be raised to offer a whispering spectre of sheer-hosed calf to their eyes. The olive would then be sucked slowly by thick crimson lips and chewed casually, her intentions always shaded by dipped eye lashes. Every man had imagined a part of his anxious body into that olive and dreamed about the motions of that soft pink mouth.

Miss Barbusse strolled away from the table and across the shadowy lawn, eagerly followed by her train of suitors. Penny glanced behind her and watched the other pupils, who were flushed with drink and mingling freely amongst each other for the first time in a week. Kloster and the Celeste twins, the latter uncharacteristically chic in matching electric-blue gowns, policed the activity carefully, watching for stray hands or quickly passed notes.

Lucy Harrington was nowhere to be seen, and Penny counted that as a blessing. Beyond the main throng, Klima and Bessy walked alone. Ahead of them, Rupert drifted warily towards the gamekeeper's cottage and Amanda ducked out of view with Amber, carrying a bottle of champagne and two glasses. The magic was penetrating all of them: one week of complete celibacy or unashamed hedonism now spun and danced its lures amongst the revellers – the dynamite only needed one spark.

Unobserved, Penny slipped away from the main throng and followed the grass trail that had been gently crushed by the shoes of the dean and her admirers. When she turned the corner, the party she pursued had drifted towards a small ornamental privet maze behind the manor. Miss Barbusse's melodic laughter drifted high and above the deeper male tones, as they followed her perfumed goad into the secret den. Penny waited until they had disappeared inside the hedgerow before scurrying in after them.

The walls of the hedge threw a cool evening shadow over the tiny paths, but her eyes were still able to determine the direction of their footsteps. Penny wound around the maze and crossed inwards to find new paths that spiralled towards the centre. As she approached the maze's heart a complete silence descended. She began to fear that she had lost sight of the group and that they had left the maze by a discreet exit. The quiet voice of the dean, seeming to float from behind her, stopped Penny in her tracks.

'And the rest, all of you. I wish to see every stitch removed.'

Miss Barbusse must have been on the other side of the hedge, no more than a few feet away, but concealed from Penny's eyes. Penny crouched down, so that the top of her head would not be visible over the flat hedgerow. She pressed her ear into the cold leaves and spiky foliage and listened without taking a breath.

'That is good, very good. You are all so well-developed and perpetually eager. I like appetite in a young man, but so much the better if it is channelled by a woman of some experience. Don't you think?'

'Yes,' the boys mumbled in agreement.

Penny imagined their quickly disappearing discomfort at having been made to strip before each other and this powerful woman.

'There are four of you, and yet there is only one woman. Perhaps, you feel that these odds are unfavourable,' the voice continued, assertive and in control.

'But let me tell you,' Miss Barbusse continued, 'there is a time in a woman's life when her own hunger would startle any man. If he was able to see into her heart, he would be amazed by what she craved. There is a dark place in each of us. Would you like to fall into my shadow?'

The voices of the boys came in hushed whispers, almost pleading entreaties: 'Oh, yes, dean . . . take us there . . . we are yours.'

'Good,' she replied, her voice no more than a husky draft.

There were two sharp cries of alarm, and another that drifted into bliss.

The dean's voice began to pant, as if rising from underwater for air: 'Gather around me quickly and stand with your shoulders together.'

There was the sound of hidden activity and an emphatic suckling danced into Penny's ears. She crept forward on her hands and knees, desperate to glimpse the spectacle.

The cries of passion were louder now, resonating like drum beats. Penny crept before a small entrance that provided an access to the maze's centre. Nervously, she nudged her face round the corner and stole a glance.

She saw the white backs of two naked men and the faces of those two who faced her; all four huddled together, quivering in rapture.

Between their shaking legs, like a wild animal behind the bars of a cage, Miss Barbusse had knelt down and turned her face upwards. Between the hips of the two men closest to Penny, she could see her beautiful face moving quickly from one groin to the other as if feeding from two separate dishes. In her hands, raised beside either of her ears, the other two glistening penises slipped and glistened though her long pale fingers. The pink heads of two engorged organs stabbed through the palms of the dean's hands in their haste to spit on her sleek hair.

Miss Barbusse swivelled round and began to suck the two penises in her hands, simultaneously reaching behind herself to grasp those slippery members that had previously resided in her mouth.

The boys gasped and moaned, their tight backsides rotating and pressing forward towards the centre of pleasure. Penny could see the back of the dean's head moving quickly, several inches forward and several back again, as she devoured and swallowed the firm flesh.

One of the boys with his back to Penny ejaculated and launched a white spiral of cream on to the dean's shoulders and hair. He fell back from the group and collapsed on the grass, panting and covering his red face with his hands.

Another shrieked out loud and filled the dean's mouth with his fragrant seed, before he too fell away to crumble on a small stone bench.

When the third man came in the dean's soft hand, she pulled her mouth off the other penis and turned her head to catch his semen on her face. She made no attempt to swallow the offering, allowing it to splash on her mouth. When she turned round to suck the last remaining cock, Penny saw a long tendril of cream slip off her chin and drop in her lap.

The last man standing, his back arching and every muscle tensing across his shoulders, lowered his head and gripped the dean's smooth face with his hands. She clawed his pale buttocks with blood-red nails and began thrusting her mouth on and off his solid manhood. He ground his hips on to her face and she lapped furiously at the organ filling her mouth.

'I – I – am coming!' he roared, and Miss Barbusse pulled her face from his groin, milking his quivering balls empty on to her cleavage. The semen fell, splashing like hot wax between her breasts and staining her beautiful silk dress with pearly smudges. She rocked back on her heels and cast her wet face towards the sky, breathing deeply and savouring the reservoir of young seed on her tongue.

She had been anointed with the passions of her young pupils, offered wet gifts in praise of her beauty, and she had excepted these donations with enthusiasm.

Penny struggled to take a breath: the scent of sex poured from every leaf and hung heavily in the darkening evening air. She wanted to throw herself into the circle and take immediate part in this ritual. She suddenly desired the weight of four strange male bodies pressed on her own, biting her nipples, licking and spearing her sex. She could feel the dean's satisfaction at being desired so ardently and worshipped with fresh young vitality.

How could any human, presented with so many temptations and lures, ever escape from the Academy? On every night and in each turn along a polished corridor, you could fall across the sensual delights when men and women fulfil their darkest fantasies. You could fall beneath a spiked heel or loving whip, disappear between the legs of a maiden or ride across the flanks of a young buck. There were no limits, no loves that dared not speak their names – only deep and strange oceans to drown in, for ever.

Penny rose to her feet, unsteady and dizzy. Her heartbeat blasted through her chest and echoed its frantic rhythms inside her ears. Her dancing vision watched Miss Barbusse undress to a leather corset and sheer black stockings. She saw the woman assume a doglike position on the grass and invite the young men to ravage her.

It was a feast of muscular arms and stamping feet that engulfed the dean. The men jostled and pushed each other, desperate to unleash their frustration and passion. They fell around the dean and pulled her this way and that as she screamed and laughed in utter and total abandon.

'Take me!' she cried. 'Have me! Use me! I can take you all! I demand that you –'

A thick penis stopped her words and filled her mouth from the side. Her slippery ankles were raised in the air and her shoes were pulled off. One man lapped at the soles of her feet and stroked the dean's stockings roughly. Another crept through her legs and sank his penis into her freshly shaven sex. The fourth emerged over her head and pushed his cock between her trussed breasts to pump at her warm cleavage.

Penny fled from the maze, tripping and falling several times before she found the quiet lawn outside. She had no particular destination on her mind. Other lures in the Academy twilight awaited, and Penny was only aware of her desire to hurl her spirit into the Academy's melting pot.

She fled past the main manor and looked at the lawn furniture that had formed the centre of the soiree. Only four figures remained at the party, the rest having fled to pursue hidden liaisons now that the staff had been distracted. Penny did not stop running but could see that it was a powerful diversion that kept Kloster and the twins busy.

'She gave you to us, my boy!' Kloster screamed with excitement. 'She said you were fond of manipulation. Taste the depths of submission!'

Paris had been tied down: his head, hands and feet

forming the peaks of a five-pointed star upon a table stripped of cloth and utensils. His limbs had been fastened to the table legs with knotted stockings. His face appeared as no more than a red smudge.

His torso was bared between the lapels of a torn shirt and the two naked twins bit his nipples. Kloster, stripped to her transparent black undergarments and black stockings, yanked at his stiff penis with a leather-gloved hand. When the young man's organ had achieved a solidity of which she was fond, she clambered on to the table and impaled herself on the shaft.

Paris cried out and a twin scurried around the table to pull at his hair and lick his face. Her gigantic partner scratched his stomach with her nails, shouting abuse at him before clutching a thick candle. She greased the hard tallow with her lipstick and spit and held it in front of the man's eyes. His lips released a groan of pleasure and the twin moved behind the pumping doctor to search between his buttocks.

Penny did not stop to watch and carried on racing across the manor lawn, her head turning left and right, her ears straining for the sounds of opportunist love. In the distance, she heard the high-pitched echo of Paris's delight. To her right, she heard the half-muffled cooing of two distinct female voices.

She staggered towards the soft voices, which came from a tiny grotto of shrubbery beside the tennis courts – the place where she had thrown away her inhibitions beneath the heat of a young man.

An empty bottle of wine lay amongst the discarded clothes and high-heeled shoes. On a patch of flattened grass, the two women had abandoned themselves in a frenzy of intense lust. Amanda and Amber tongued each other's painted lips. Their shaded eyes were closed in rapture and their long fingers slipped over scantily clad curves and erect brown nipples. Their giggles and sighs came between hastily taken breaths.

The urgency of their passion startled Penny. They feared, perhaps, that intruders would interrupt their action, or the bells would sound to summon the students home. Or maybe, Penny decided, these two beautiful, perfumed lovers were just completely lost to an illicit passion beneath a sanctioning moon.

Amber climbed up and down Amanda's body, forcing the raven-haired beauty to her knees. Amber's stocky legs, coated in sheer black hose, rubbed themselves over Amanda's back, shoulders and arms. Amanda had slipped three of her fingers inside the young American's dewy slit, and rotated her wrist to keep the girl boiling and ravenous.

They smeared each other's face with wine-tinged saliva and bit at petite noses and tiny chins with snapping teeth. Amber pulled Amanda's head back by her dishevelled hair and forced her own moist sex on to her mouth; she clambered upward and stood on her little tiptoes, forcing Amanda to rape her sex with that luscious mouth.

They were beautiful: tussling, clawing, wanton girls clutching at an intense abandonment and all it had to offer. It would have been wrong to have stopped them, or to have added more petrol to this fire. Penny gave the slippery and half-clothed mass one final longing stare before passing on and towards the stern silhouette of the gamekeeper's cottage.

The very sight of that distant and gaunt edifice propelled one enduring image across Penny's brain: in her mind's eye she saw the statuesque Sabrina standing tall at the end of so many men's secret night-time journeys. She thought of those long feminine limbs and that fountain of auburn hair, of that insanely beautiful face and hungry mouth. Finally, Penny's mind recalled an image of that delicate white penis, cradled by sheer black panties. She was a creation that had to exist even though she was offered no light in the outside world.

Sabrina, above all of the others, deserved her freedom inside this dark kingdom.

Penny wanted to see her beautiful and magically transformed guardian angel. She needed to tell Sabrina that she had made a decision: the love and fury of the Academy must never be destroyed.

Penny grasped the iron handle on the front door and tugged at it.

The door was firmly shut and locked tight.

She groaned and fled to the rear of the cottage. She caught sight of the stable, attached at a right angle to the cottage proper, and heard the caged human animal inside skipping with delight beneath a crop.

'Stand still while I attach the bridle!' Madam Skinner's muffled voice demanded over the squeaks of a spinning wheelchair.

The human pony must have cantered to a halt, because Penny heard Madam Skinner soon whispering to it with affection, stroking its mane, perhaps, or brushing its soft flanks with her smooth white hands.

The wooden rear door to the cottage was unlocked and Penny let herself into a whitewashed reception. She stood still and gathered herself; this place had previously terrified Penny, shocked her senses and forced her mind to expand its borders. Fear could not cloud her mind now. Penny needed her ex-colleague's crazy humour and wisdom. She followed her inner compass, remembering that Sabrina's room was situated on the ground floor. She had left that room the night before, exiting through the front door, and she now used her senses to uncover the redhead's chamber.

Penny knocked on Sabrina's door quietly, glancing left and right in the unusually silent cottage, desperate not to be disturbed. There was no immediate answer and she pressed her ear to the door, able to discern a distant groaning. Penny knocked again, this time a little louder.

'Come in,' a husky voice groaned, as if distracted by something more important than a visitor.

Penny pushed the door open and tiptoed gingerly into the leather-studded room. Sabrina had a guest: the same naked male lover, Penny presumed, who visited here on a regular basis.

Rupert, the quiet and unassuming young pupil, continued to sample the diverse range of delicacies on offer at the Academy. Sabrina had bent her long body over a chair. She had stripped off every vestige of clothing save for a pair of sheer tights and her high-heeled slip-on mules. The shimmering nylon haze on her legs, tantalisingly revealed the smooth shape of her tear-drop calves and strong thighs to Rupert's mesmerised face. The legs seemed to descend for a league from her shapely backside, which had been pushed upward to tempt her panting lover.

'Come and join us. Things are getting really interesting,' Sabrina gasped, turning her face to look over her shoulder at Penny.

Rupert merely smiled and rubbed his hands over Sabrina's tight buttocks.

'I'll . . . I'll just take a seat,' Penny stammered.

'OK.' Sabrina winked and blew a kiss from her thickly coated lips to Rupert.

Penny sat down on the bed and watched the spectacle from the side.

Rupert fell to his knees and stroked Sabrina's long legs through her tights, groaning, seemingly amazed at the acres of leg on offer. Penny's eyes were propelled towards Sabrina's chest, which was partially obscured by the one arm that supported her body. The gorgeous creature's breasts were large and soft, the skin smooth, the nipples hard and brown.

How? How did she get such beautiful breasts? Penny queried, unable to tear her eyes off the alarming sight until Rupert tore through the rear of her tights.

184

He had gripped the thin nylon between his hands and ripped apart the thin black seam over Sabrina's buttocks. He dipped his tongue through the shredded fabric and nuzzled between the little portion of exposed white buttock.

'Mmm,' Sabrina murmured through her nose. 'Does my little pussy taste good?'

'Yes,' Rupert gasped, flicking his tongue around her clean pink anus.

Sabrina dipped the painted fingernails on one hand to the front of her tights, to stroke her little frontal gift. She closed her heavily made-up eyes and parted her lips to moan with pleasure.

Rupert rose to his feet, his slim musculature gleaming under the subdued lights. He pressed his long cock forward, between the temporary slit in her sheer black tights, and nuzzled it against Sabrina's furrowed anal whorl.

Rupert turned his flushed face towards Penny and made an astonishing request: 'Pen, will you pass the tube of lubrication to me.'

'Oh, yes, do me, Rupert!' Sabrina squealed.

Penny seemed to float towards the bedside cabinet, her eyes locking on to the tube of cherry-flavoured jelly that lay between two vials of nail polish. She picked the tube up and handed it to Rupert.

'Thanks,' Rupert replied, wasting no time in unscrewing the cap and squeezing a pale-pink gel along the length of his quivering shaft.

'Will you do me the honour, Penny?' he asked, grinning mischievously at Penny.

She was unable to find her voice but walked across to Rupert and let her soft hands encircle the cock that had felt so good embedded deeply within her own rectal passage. Penny rubbed the cream over his penis, smoothing it over the gleaming end and down to the hairy base.

Rupert gasped, becoming breathless with anticipation, 'That's it, rub it all the way down. Sabrina likes deep penetration.'

Penny complied, feeling stronger, slipping into an aroused haze and kneading the cream all over the cock.

'Good, now I am ready,' Rupert said, and pushed his long penis back between Sabrina's splayed buttocks.

'Do it, Rupert. Don't tease me, please slip it in. Oh, yes, all the way down. That's so bloody good!'

Penny stepped back and watched Rupert's deep and agonising strokes sinking into Sabrina's stretched pink rim. He would push his shaft right into Sabrina's tight cavity and then withdraw the slippery pole back to the tip, repeating the motion in a steady rhythm, gradually developing his speed.

Sabrina sobbed, shaking her red mane about, her legs starting to buckle.

Penny acted on impulse, falling to her knees and sliding between Sabrina's legs and the back of the wooden chair. Sabrina moved her ankles back to allow Penny more room on the carpet beneath her. Penny looked at the erect white penis, hanging between two smooth balls, and licked her lips. The cock was stiletto long and Sabrina's groin had been completely shaved. Penny stretched out her little tongue and traced it along the fine nylon that hugged Sabrina's shaft.

'Oh yes, Penny!' Sabrina cried. 'Suck my tail!'

Penny pushed her face into the fragrant tights and lapped at the penis, rubbing the trapped balls with her hands at the same time.

Rupert must have adored the spectacle of Penny on her knees, sucking his transvestite lover through her tights: he began to pound his well-oiled penis in and out of Sabrina's anus with a fresh vigour.

Sabrina screamed with pleasure and gripped Penny's hair with her free hand, pulling her face up and down along the silky shaft. Penny smeared it with lipstick and spit and slipped her hands over Sabrina's long, firm legs, clawing her nylon tights and laddering the fine fabric.

'That's good. That's great,' Rupert panted, slapping Sabrina's buttocks as he thrust and ground himself inside her stretched pink tunnel.

'Fuck me. Fuck me like a tart!' Sabrina rasped, her whole body shivering from the onslaught of delirious sensation which iced her pale skin from toe to wanton mouth.

Rupert collapsed along Sabrina's back, his buttocks clenching as his sex pumped its seed inside the tight glove that gripped his softening erection.

'Oh, that feels good. I can feel it splashing up inside me!' Sabrina shrieked, and ripped Penny's blouse off her shoulder with one taloned hand.

Penny slipped out from beneath Sabrina, shuffling across the thickly carpeted floor, and watched the couple collapse across the chair, both panting and gasping for air. 'That was so bloody horny,' Penny squealed with satisfaction, surprised and yet delighted by her participation.

'Oh, he has such a lovely cock,' Sabrina gasped. 'As well you know, my dear. I just love to be screwed like a hussy, in my high heels. You have no idea how much I used to dream of this.'

'And your pleasures will always remain a secret,' Penny whispered, smiling at Sabrina.

'Good. I am so pleased, Penny. There is no other way,' Sabrina replied, as Rupert moved off her buttocks and regained his unsteady feet.

'What do you mean?' Rupert asked blinking the sweat from his eyes.

'Nothing you need worry about, stud,' Sabrina answered, laughing. 'And it is high time that you had a treat, Penny. You must be desperate for something hard between your lovely legs.'

'You better believe it,' Penny gushed, elated by her new resolve, and clambered on top of the soft bed.

Sabrina followed in hot pursuit, still in her heels and black tights. She slipped on to the bed and began freeing Penny from her outer garments.

Penny writhed and giggled under Sabrina's long fingers, whispering to her bizarre lover, 'I wanted to fuck you every day at work until you disappeared. I used to imagine you taking me into the toilets and giving me what for.'

Sabrina laughed and kissed Penny's face, her long penis pressing up to the waistband of her tights. Penny slipped her hands down and rolled the sheer tights to the top of Sabrina's thighs, freeing the eager cock. Penny opened her legs, wrapping them around Sabrina's waist and trapping her between her thighs.

'If only the editor could see us now,' Sabrina giggled, and pushed her shaft between the lips of Penny's moist sex.

Penny adored the forceful passage of the cock inside her: parting her dewy walls and sinking to the heart of her craving. She stared at the beautiful feminine face looking down at her: the feline eyes, rouged cheeks and slippery red lips reminding her of some glossy magazine starlet.

'Fuck me,' she whispered to Sabrina, who instantly complied with a quick thrusting.

Sabrina held Penny's shoulders down and banged her shaven sex in and out of Penny, fulfilling that tingling quest for utter depravity that had driven her around the grounds of the Academy.

Penny thought of the dean, consumed by male lust in the maze, and of poor Paris, electrified beneath the beautiful dominatrix trio; she dreamed of Amanda, pounced upon and taken by Amber, and rejoiced that she too had managed to find her own special brand of Whitehead deviance on Saturday night. The secrets of self-discovery were beyond the understanding of the uninitiated and Penny knew that it must remain that way.

Sabrina rifled through Penny's welcoming vagina and pumped her towards orgasm. The decision had been made, the guilt assuaged; it was time to soak in hedonism.

'Harder, Sabrina, just take me! Go on, do me,' Penny squealed.

'Oh, you little tart!' Sabrina gasped, banging in and out of Penny's sex with all the force her thighs could muster. The bed rattled and thumped against the wall; sweat ran into Penny's eyes and she clawed Sabrina's soft back.

Above Penny, on the mirrored ceiling, the sight of her own screwed-up face and this exotic creature's long white back, moving upon her, plunged Penny into a choking and clenching orgasm.

Penny's mind and body joined, and a warmth of satisfaction spread through her, dissolving tension. There would be no more sneaking or worrying or taking chances, only deviance under the tutelage of Miss Barbusse.

Eight

'I don't believe it. This cannot be happening to me,' Penny shouted.

She shook her head and looked under the bed a second time.

They were still there, stacked neatly, having no rightful place beneath her bed in her room.

Miss Barbusse's leather-bound journals and photograph albums had been slipped under the bed frame. When Penny pulled the duvet back to retrieve her research notes, intending to alter her story and present Whitehead as nothing more than a glorified health farm, she had seen them: dark volumes, trapping sinister ghosts between their pages.

Penny put her hands on her head and walked around the room, half-dressed, trying to fathom out this strange offering.

Who could have put them there, sneaking into her room the night before and placing the sensational epic beneath her bed? Sabrina had been busy with Rupert and would never, Penny was sure, have removed the diaries from the dean's study. It did not make sense.

That left only Miss Barbusse and Lucy.

'Oh, my God! That scheming bitch!' Penny cried out.

She ran immediately to her wardrobe and ripped her suitcase out. She flung drawers open and began a hasty and disorderly packing of her personal effects. She tripped over the rug and fell forward, banging her shin on the footstool and landing on the bed.

'My notes. Oh, no. Burn the bloody things.'

When Penny stumbled and scratched for a box of matches she heard a sound that froze her soul.

The long and eerie wail of an ancient air-raid siren clawed its way around the manor house and the echoing grounds. The sound seemed to reverberate with doom, heightening Penny's panic until nausea gripped her stomach.

In the distance, dogs began to bark. Below her room and outside in the corridor, she heard the other girls' bedroom doors opening. There was shouting and cries of surprise as the female dormitory was rudely disturbed on a bright Sunday morning.

Penny looked at her suitcase and imagined the considerable distance between her room and the main gate. She had not even dressed and there was just too much evidence to destroy. It was no use; escape was out of the question and a hasty flight would only make things worse.

She flopped back down on her bed and her jaw began to quiver. It was over.

'Stand outside your rooms immediately! This is an emergency! I repeat, this is an emergency!'

The crackling voice, filtered mechanically through a megaphone, belonged to Doctor Kloster. It rose at a terrifying pitch from the ground floor and began to work its way up the stairs.

Penny stood up and looked through her window. She saw the Celeste twins jog past in black jumpsuits, a Doberman dog straining on a leash from either hand. Penny's throat tightened with fear. She scraped her kimono gown from the floor, kicked her suitcase to one side and made her way to the bedroom door on unsteady feet.

Stay calm. You can explain this. It will be all right.

Just stay calm, she whispered to herself, trying to control her breathing and stamp on her fear.

Penny walked into the corridor and saw the other bleary-eyed girls, wrenched from sleep, clutching gowns around themselves and babbling incoherently with alarm.

'What is this, a fire alarm? I don't smell smoke,' Amanda shouted down the corridor to Penny.

'You will do,' Penny whimpered, her face ashen, her voice choking out with a hiss.

Kloster bounded up the stairs, dressed in a long leather trench coat, swinging her baton. Her face had stiffened with rage and one eyelid twitched as she barked at the top of her voice, 'Your rooms are to be searched! Stand with your backs to the wall beside the door!'

Jade had appeared in the corridor in just a pair of panties and a bra, her face stricken with panic. She turned to re-enter her room, but Kloster caught her by the arm and screamed, 'Did you hear what I said, girl?'

'Yes. But, my clothes –' Jade stammered.

'Damn your clothes, girl. You will stay in your panties all day, if necessary. There is an investigation in progress. You –' Doctor Kloster paused and glanced into Jade's room. 'I see that you have something to hide.' Kloster pointed into the room and shouted, 'Come here!'

A red-faced and bowed Roberto shuffled into the corridor in just a pair of hastily gathered trousers.

'On your knees!' the doctor barked.

Roberto dropped to the floor, shaking his head, and Jade began to wave her hands in the air and pace back and forth.

Every girl jumped and winced when the thin wooden baton made contact with Roberto's rump. It descended twice more at full force and Roberto's eyes began to water.

The flogging only ceased when Miss Barbusse, elegantly clothed and fully made up, rose from the stairwell and looked across her girls. Behind her, Lucy Harrington, her face a portrait of spite, followed like an obedient pet.

Penny felt her spleen rise to her mouth. She opened her lips but nothing besides an angry gasp escaped. She raised her hand, attracted the dean's attention, and stammered, 'I know what you are looking for. It has turned up in my room.'

Every pair of eyes turned towards Penny.

Kloster bounded forward, shooting passed Penny and into her room. Miss Barbusse walked forward slowly, never removing her entrancing eyes from Penny's pallid face.

'In your room, Penny, of all places,' she said quietly. 'You cannot imagine my disappointment, but I will not flatter you with my surprise.'

The dean walked into Penny's room, but Lucy stood back, keeping out of Penny's reach. She winked at Penny and whispered, 'You're fucked.'

Penny clenched her teeth and raised her hands, determined to wrap her fingers around the girl's throat. Only the voice of the dean stopped her: 'Penny, in here, if you please.'

Penny turned and walked back into her room.

Miss Barbusse stood by the bed with one arm held across Kloster's chest, as if to restrain a wild animal. On the ruffled bed clothes, her journals had been spread out.

'All here, nearly thirty years of my life. All hidden beneath the bed of a traitor. And these –' Miss Barbusse held up Penny's dictaphone and notepads. 'I bet you have quite a story. I have already been forced to flee from my native country once. Did you think that a slut could make me desert my second home.'

'I can explain it all –' Penny stuttered.

193

'Sure you can!' the doctor hissed. 'The evidence is here, written in your own hand. A suitcase about to be packed on the floor. I will look forward to hearing this.'

Miss Barbusse, cool and seemingly unruffled by the whole occasion, just smiled at Penny, lowering her voice. 'There will be a time and a place for you explanation. But not here and not now. Your room is no place for a trial.'

Penny's skin tingled from an icy dread.

Miss Barbusse teetered on her heels towards the vast oil painting of the girl in furs. She smiled at the portrait before turning to face Penny. 'And I thought that you had embraced her. You were such a promising student, Penny, but I suppose that you have taught us one of our own lessons: that you can never trust anyone in the bedroom. There is always the risk of ulterior motives.' The dean turned towards the enraged Kloster and quietly added, 'Take her away, to the cottage.'

Kloster's face lit up with something approaching orgasmic excitement as she approached Penny, her patent stiletto heels seeming to click like the hand of a clock in a condemned man's cell.

Penny stood, having dressed in her uniform, before the three seated figures in the main room of the cottage. Behind her, trembling with anticipation, were her jailers: the Celeste twins, resplendent in tight knee-length boots, black nylons and matching leather reefer jackets. For the formal occasion of Penny's trial, they wore their leather police caps, adding a sinister aspect to their severe beauty.

Penny had to admit, it was the most bizarre judicial situation she could ever have imagined: Madam Skinner sat proudly in her black wheelchair between the doctor and dean, whose tiny behinds had found a home upon the backs of the two rubber-suited cottage gimps. The three severe-faced women were content to stare at Penny for some time, as if struggling to comprehend that the Academy had actually been infiltrated.

After several moments of complete silence the dean spoke. 'We have no way of establishing exactly who you are, where you are from, and just exactly what you have uncovered here. But, I warn you, if you answer our questions candidly, then much unpleasantness can be avoided.'

Penny took a deep breath and began, 'I will tell you that I came here as a journalist to assess the rumours about this place. I came here for a story, but I found something else. I ... I saw certain things inside myself that I had always denied. I suppose my shock gave way to relief, and, well, I changed my mind about exposing the Academy.'

Each face before her refused to betray any emotion; the cold eyes just continued to study her face.

'You do not work for Polycorp,' Miss Barbusse said her eyes narrowing. 'But I wish to know who your employers really are.'

'I am not prepared to reveal that,' Penny replied, the heat rising from her collar – the *Inquisitor* being the most ruthless and well-circulated magazine on the tabloid scene.

'Can I remind you,' Kloster snapped, 'that you are in no position to begin refusing to answer any of our questions. You have no place to run or hide and you will never be allowed to leave the Academy. Your fake employers signed the declaration of secrecy and you are aware of the repercussions. Why make this more difficult?'

Penny, becoming indignant, replied, 'I did not steal the journals. I will admit to reading them, after breaking into the dean's room. And that was wrong, I know, but I did not steal them. They were planted in my room last night.'

'So you read my private diaries and then decided not

to expose us?' Miss Barbusse countered, her face awash with disbelief. 'And you say that someone planted them in your room. Who? And why?' she added.

'You would not believe me and I will not be a part of this sham that you call a trial.'

Kloster laughed; Madam Skinner shook her head and Miss Barbusse covered her eyes with her hand.

'I knew,' the dean said, 'that this day would come. That the world would intrude upon my work, but I never could have imagined that the spy would concoct such an appalling defence.'

'The truth is not something that you wish to hear, dean,' Penny blurted out, becoming enraged at the impossibility of her situation.

'The truth, what do you know about truth?' she replied in astonishment.

'I know that Lucy Harrington planted those books in my room, but I do not know why. Unless, of course, it was just petty malice.'

The doctor gasped; Madam Skinner's knuckles whitened around the armrests on her chair and Miss Barbusse raised a face shimmering with white rage.

'Even in defeat you have no honour!' she cried. 'I have never heard such a preposterous lie! You will face the inquisition, my girl, and learn something of truth!'

'The inquisition!' Doctor Kloster echoed joyously.

The Celeste twins sighed in rapture behind Penny, and Madam Skinner licked her glossy red lips.

Penny exploded: 'Give it to me! Give me everything and you will learn that I am telling the truth!'

'You shall have it, my girl!' Miss Barbusse roared, abandoning her composure. 'You will descend into hell and feel a caress so wondrous that you will betray even your most hideous secrets!'

The twins grasped Penny's arms and pulled her towards the door.

'Do what you like!' she spat at the dean. 'But soon

enough, Miss Barbusse, your pride will take a tumble when you find out who your enemies really are!'

'Silence!' she countered. 'Get that slut out of my sight. Now!'

'I knew there was something wrong with her, right from the start,' Lucy whispered breathlessly, close to Miss Barbusse's ear, in her study.

'Lucy, you must be certain. There is nothing that you are not telling me? This is no childish prank to humiliate an enemy?'

'No, mistress, I swear. I have seen her at home with another reporter and that aroused my suspicions. I did not say anything because I had to be sure. And now this just confirms her guilt.'

'Yes,' Miss Barbusse replied, her eyes glazed. 'I still do not want to believe it. That one of my students would betray me – the thought is so ugly. She is in very serious trouble. Everything is at stake. You understand that I have to be certain.'

Miss Barbusse paused to stare into Lucy's eyes. She stroked the girl's shiny blonde hair and shook her one frail doubt away. 'But I do believe you, my pet. I only wish that you had brought your suspicions to me earlier, and I am sorry for having to question you in this matter.'

Lucy's bright face filled the dean's heart with something warm. Beneath every stone, she decided, there was clay and something more precious. And this girl – this compliant, loving and insatiable angel – was the diamond.

Lucy slipped her arms around Miss Barbusse and tickled her neck with her little tongue.

'Oh no, my sweet. They need me over at the cottage. I cannot possibly become distracted . . .'

It was too late; Lucy's gentle fingers were caressing her breasts through her flimsy blouse and the dean's nipples had tightened beneath the sheer black bra. There had not been time that morning to prepare a corset, so Miss Barbusse had chosen black French silk to slip beneath her dress. Lucy's hands created a spark of electricity beneath her gauzy under-things. The girl rubbed and caressed her hips, breasts and buttocks with waltzing hands, relaxing her, untying her inner knots, making her languish in the bright morning light.

She let Lucy guide her over to the desk and stretch her body across the flat top, upsetting paper and pens. Miss Barbusse reclined along the expansive surface and watched the girl remove her high heels, licking her feet, knowing that her mistress adored such ministrations. She basked beneath the sudden blanket of cool air that prickled along her legs as Lucy raised her skirt and began kissing her stockings and the naked peaks of her thighs.

There was love in those kisses, admiration and respect. Miss Barbusse was certain of this, and drew her breath sharply when Lucy's shiny red lips found her sex.

If this was punishment, then Penny wanted a life sentence.

But it was not designed to make her pay a penance; it had been crafted by her captors to open her soul.

The shiny black crop in Kloster's hand contrasted dramatically with the pale skin of her thighs and the mist of sheer black nylon on her legs. Her body had been harnessed into a shiny leather basque and her knickers were both brief and transparent. On her feet she wore patent sling-back stilettos and her black bobbed hair had been tucked beneath a leather cap. The tall and indifferent creature strode around Penny in the containment cell, disappearing from sight and making Penny's back stiffen when she moved behind her.

The doctor surrounded her with slowly narrowing circles, drawing closer and closer to Penny's bound shape, which had been strung inside a large, rectangular, iron stock. Her legs were pulled apart and cuffed at the base, while thin steel chains pulled her wrists above her head. A wooden brace, padded with soft leather and attached to the sides of the frame, restrained her neck, enabling her to only look forward. She had been stripped of her uniform and dressed in black see-through French knickers, which were slit at the front and back. Her suspenders passed beneath the flimsy shorts and clutched her seamed stockings; her upper body had been left naked and Madam Skinner had painted her face and teased her hair in the manner of a harlot.

About her in the dark room, lit by dim red lights, the captors had gathered their props: Madam Skinner had restocked the rack with canes and flails from elsewhere in the cottage; a black silk mattress had been laid on the floor before Penny's stretched body and something representing a sinister black dentist's chair, with a reclinable back, had been wheeled in. The jailers had made certain that her eyes were able to see every device.

They had left Penny with her thoughts and expectations for an hour, before the doctor had re-entered the room alone to begin her pacing. Penny maintained a haughty and indignant face but, despite her aloof facade, she trembled. In the previous silent hour, her mind had filled itself with random images of the Academy staff and what she had witnessed of their capabilities and tastes. She had stretched to view the collected implements and wondered about their various purposes. Now her secured limbs and every nerve ending thirsted for a peculiar range of sensation.

She had been caught; there was no way out and yet some distant part of her seemed to rejoice with guilt and hiss with excitement at the prospect of punishment.

A cool draft tickled her thighs and the doctor's hot breath licked across her shoulders from behind.

'Pretty slut, you smell good. You appear ready for anything. Deeply penetrating, rabid sex. Mad sex: the love of the sinner and the insane. Is this what you crave?' the doctor whispered.

Penny remained silent.

Kloster's stern face appeared before Penny's. She stared into Penny's eyes, so that Penny was unable to look away. The doctor licked her own glossy red lips and rubbed the hard crop against Penny's naked ribs. She flicked the leather loop across Penny's navel, tickling her sensitive skin, while still letting her flesh know that the hard tool could unleash a terrifying pain.

Kloster lit a cigarette and raised it to her thick lips with dungeon-white hands and blood-red nails. She narrowed her eyes and drew the smoke into her lungs.

'Umm . . .' she purred. 'To think of what we can do, for hours, for days, for weeks, for ever, if we choose.'

The leather-tipped crop slipped between Penny's legs, parting the silky slit in her knickers, and furrowed through her delicate lips.

Penny inhaled sharply and could not prevent her eager sex from chasing this vague flicker of pleasure. Kloster removed it quickly and washed Penny's face with a richly scented plume of cigarette smoke.

The crop dropped again to begin a more insistent probing through Penny's pubic curls and the curtained folds of her moistening sex. Kloster slipped her other hand round Penny's shiny backside and began to rotate Penny's hips gently, in little circles, so that her clit danced over the firm crop.

'Oh, Penny, would it not be good to just abandon yourself to all of this, to feel the caress of a whip and then the softness of a mouth on your pretty breasts. Would you not enjoy the sharp sting of a cane on your buttocks and then the passage of something smooth and long inside your little pussy. Something big, of course, that would stretch you, and push right up into you?

There would be no recriminations or shame – just us girls in private, enjoying each other. All I need is the name of your employer and those pleasures are yours, delivered by the hands of experts.'

'No names,' Penny replied.

'Why such loyalty? You are expendable to them, and yet we have shown you our secrets, our will to power.'

'I told you: no names. And I decided to end my investigation –'

'Sure, sure,' the doctor cooed softly, her lips sliding against Penny's ear. 'And Lucy is to blame. We hear you, Penny, we hear you. But now we want to hear you softly sighing with pleasure, and between each gasp we want to hear the truth.'

The doctor moved away from Penny, and with her went the crop, leaving Penny to ache for its tender stimulation.

Penny heard the door open and two new pairs of feet enter the gloomy chamber. The footsteps approached her rack, padding softly, and emerged within Penny's line of vision.

A naked Paris walked beside the lovely auburn-haired and scantily clad Felicity. They gripped each others hands and smiled, unperturbed by the presence of others.

Kloster appeared beside Penny, oiling one naked hand.

'My pets would like to show you something,' the doctor whispered.

Penny watched Felicity, the beauty upon whom the twins feasted in the gibbet, the girl who was always at their mercy. What could she show Penny? The mysterious girl, her identity hidden even from Madam Skinner, the gourmet cook, the night-time slave. She was beautiful: pale and supple, her veil of innocence haunting and shimmering with desire. Penny did not want to look; she did not want to ache for whatever Felicity was about to receive.

Felicity slithered across the black sheets, unabashed and giggly, writhing her nylon-slippery legs across the smooth sheets, her face smiling and flushed with anticipation. Penny knew that feeling, that delightful expectation of sex, the tingling moments before the first touch.

Paris offered the first touch: the slender young man fell into Felicity's arms, their lips meeting immediately, their tongues slapping excitedly. The two young shapes wriggled and moulded around each other, Felicity reaching for his stiff cock and sliding her legs around his waist, Paris squeezing her breasts and biting her neck.

A slick finger found Penny's sex. It tickled her lips and disappeared inside her damp entrance. It began to tickle her inside and a thumb flicked across her tingling clit. The doctor's pale digits worked on Penny; without invitation or prompt, they rubbed and circled, getting faster, their momentum matching the writhing lovers before Penny's eyes.

Penny eyed the long cock on the mattress as Paris twisted within Felicity's embrace. Penny was unable to stall her desire or fight the arousal: the doctor seduced her honey out and made her clinging vaginal walls beg for a thickly girthed companion.

Paris raised Felicity's legs and rested her pretty feet upon his shoulders. He eased her body round so that the captive could watch the slick passage of his trembling and dewy shaft inside the expectant sex.

Penny cried out with pleasure when Felicity moaned in rapture.

The doctor's fingers operated in quicker flurries, producing a hot friction against Penny's clit. Penny shoved her waist forward and her legs rattled within the tight chains. Her arms pulled uselessly against the upright supports. She had never felt so naked and exposed and vulnerable; she had never desired satisfaction with such an intensity.

Paris pounded in and out of Felicity on the mattress, making the girl's breasts shudder and quiver. She grunted and croaked with her eyes clamped shut. Penny squinted through her own heavily painted eyelids, her throat straining with an animal whimper. She could almost feel the dimensions of the man's cock inside her, almost sense Felicity's ecstatic approach to orgasm as Paris thrust and banged against her cushioning pelvis.

'Is it good?' the doctor shouted down to the lovers.

'Oh, yes,' Paris grunted.

'Yes, yes, yes! Fuck me, fuck me harder, Paris. Do it hard –' Felicity was unable to finish; the force behind her lover's deep and rapid thrusts had stolen her breath.

Penny's mouth panted in empathy; the doctor's fingers pushed her to the very edge of orgasm, and then stopped.

'No!' Penny cried. 'Don't stop, finish me!'

'A name,' the doctor whispered through gritted teeth. 'A name and you will have the cock.'

Penny's head clouded with confusion and anger, her body screamed in desperation for succour.

'Which newspaper, and I will deliver you,' Kloster prompted.

Down below, Paris grunted and began to weep from the power of his climax. Felicity's slender legs swished over his buttocks, her little painted toes arching within their nylon folds, her muscles holding him fast, claiming his seed, planting him deeply.

'Not a newspaper ... a magazine,' Penny gasped, willing to sell her soul for Felicity's passion.

The doctor's hand refused to return and the sound of her heels signalled her exit from the steaming room.

'You bitch,' Penny mumbled, and felt a tear roll down her flushed cheek. 'You teasing bitch.'

The scent of the lovers still hung in the air, embracing and taunting Penny's own keen fragrance of arousal.

Her body seemed to vibrate in the darkness and her glossy lips panted with frustration, her clit still echoing from the imprint of Kloster's hand.

The door opened but the visitor did not reveal their identity to Penny's forward stare. Her eyes whipped about but she could not see the new phantom that had come to be part of the inquisition.

Within seconds, aftershave drifted beneath her nose and a naked male chest glanced across her own; she could feel the taut chest and tiny nipples denting her shivering skin.

'I was so disappointed when I heard that the spy was you, Penny,' Klima whispered over her shoulder. 'I too was a shadow skulker and bedroom creeper, so I understand your plight, the contradictions and frustrations. But there is a release, an escape from hiding and acting. There is a path to relief.'

Two fingers circled Penny's nipples. They had appeared from behind her and were content to brush and tickle her little pink gems, nothing more. But more was what Penny demanded. Her breasts betrayed her and revealed their instant susceptibility to assertive pressure; her nipples hardened and pointed forward.

'I really want to help you, Penny,' the smooth Russian voice offered. 'I want to release you from a burden. I would like to caress these naked white breasts. Would you like that?'

'No!' Penny hissed.

'I would like to squeeze these soft jewels. Would that not be good?'

'Yes! Damn you,' Penny shouted.

'Perhaps they would prefer a painful grasp and hard teeth to bite them?'

Penny panted through her reply: 'Grope me! See if I care. Be hard with my tits, or just tease me like that German . . .'

The hands closed around her breasts. The fingers were long and hard, the palms rough and demanding.

Penny whimpered and thrashed within her chains: her weakness was exposed and revealed to the dark.

Klima squeezed and mauled her soft breasts. She could imagine his tanned fingers clashing with her pink nipples and white curves, raising red bruises. The pain was exquisite and her sex wept in response.

'That is good. Is it not?'

'Yes, you bastard, that is good,' Penny gasped.

'But I feel you would welcome a little more. It would be a shame to neglect another of your treasures,' Klima whispered, his words hot on Penny's ears.

The hand crept between her thighs from behind. It entered the flimsy black knickers and found her moisture. The other hand continued, unabashed, on her breasts, pinching her with cruel fingertips.

Penny shut her eyes and listened to the blossoming symphony inside her sex: how it rose and gained amplification in the chambers of her quickly beating heart. She lost her mind for a few seconds; she misplaced her resolve and ignored her moral restraints. 'Fuck me! Fuck my cunt! Do it to me. Come on, be a man and take me, have my arse too –'

Three fingers pushed inside her sopping vagina, no more than an inch. The hard thumb flicked across her clitoral bud and Penny fell towards the fire of orgasm.

'Please let me release you, Penny. Let me bite your breasts with white teeth and slip my cock inside you. Give me permission to end the craving – with one word.'

'The *Inquisitor*! The fucking *Inquisitor*!' Penny shouted. 'Is that enough?'

'It is enough for now, my pretty spy,' he whispered, and removed his hands from her body.

'No! Don't you dare leave me like . . .'

Klima appeared before her, his eyes hungrier than a wolf. His mouth fell upon hers and bit her slippery lips; she pushed her tongue forward and slid it around his cavernous mouth.

'Want my cock?'

'Fuck me.'

'How hard?'

'Really hard. Hold me and fuck me really hard.'

'Right in and up?'

'Yes, you bastard, screw me until I scream.'

The long and thick appendage shot through the slit in Penny's gauzy knickers and parted her tender lips. It hurt; it stretched; it reached further than any other cock she had taken before; it made her scream.

Klima bent his knees and lifted Penny as high as her chains would allow. His steely fingers sank into her soft buttocks and clawed for a purchase. She felt her little stocking-clad feet rise from the cold iron frame as her sex swallowed the whole of the solid pillar.

Penny was unable to speak; her vocal chords could produce little besides a series of random chokes and grunts.

'Right up, Penny, really hard now, making your teeth rattle and your tears flow. Faster, fucking you faster, as if you were against a wall with a stranger.'

'Yes,' she managed.

'You know he will be savage and yet you want him.'

'Yes!'

'You want that stranger's cock inside you. You want no mercy!'

'Yes!' she squealed and shuddered with an orgasm that quickly flowed into another.

But the pounding did not stop; it plundered her on and over into a special pleasure. Penny was lost in space and time; her mouth would offer anything for one more second in this glorious place.

Klima's voice drifted through her daze: 'The stranger wants you, needs to leave his seed wet between your lovely thighs. But who else, he wonders, have you told of your discoveries.'

'No one . . . I have had no contact . . . everything is in my room.'

'Can the stranger trust you?'

'Yes! I swear! Just keep fucking me!'

'He believes you! He must reward you! Can he leave his cream inside you?'

'Yes!' Penny screamed, and nearly passed out from another searing climax.

The delightful thing that filled her pulsed and quaked, over and over again, releasing a hot stream to mingle with her own wine.

Something eased Penny out of sleep; something moved around her in the darkness; something rustled across the black silk sheets that Klima had left her exhausted body upon.

Penny could see little: the sole window in the containment cell had been barred and locked. It could still have been day, or was it Sunday evening? There was no way of knowing and little point in caring.

Strong arms made her sit up in bed before a long hand raised a cup of cold juice to her lips. She tasted passion fruit, orange and mango: chilled and revitalising, quenching her thirst and replacing the fluid that had wept from her every pore during the inquisition.

Soft strawberries were placed upon her hot and expectant tongue, followed by warm buttered rolls that she devoured, her hunger climaxing when a delicious banana ice cream dissolved in her mouth.

She finished her meal and the long arms, now doubling to four soft stroking limbs, eased her back down to her thick and soft bed. A cool hand stroked her forehead and hair, while skilful fingers tidied her knickers and smoothed out her stockings.

Two long bodies eased against her from either side of the mattress, pressing intently and cradling her soft contours with assertive hands. Penny could feel naked flesh against her flimsily clothed body; breasts nuzzled against her shoulders and cold thighs touched her legs before their stockings rasped with static across her own.

In the dark, whispers passed through her head and across her tingling skin:

'She has such soft hair.'

'Umm, it smells so good.'

'Have you touched her breasts?'

'Yes, I have them now. So big and soft.'

'She is pretty, but I can smell her lover.'

'Umm, she has had a cock. Do you think he was thorough? Has he worn her out?'

'No, she is insatiable. She has been with Amanda and Lucy.'

'Yes, she enjoys pretty girls. She is like us.'

Penny relaxed; she let the tension flow from her limbs and licked the sugar from her lips. What more did they want? What more could they learn? A stronger force of will surrounded her; her limbs were now free, but she could not even think of escape. The warmth seduced her; the sensual textures against her hot skin lulled her; the hand between her legs thrilled her.

'She has read the diaries,' one voice began again.

'There are so many, though. I wonder how much she was able to take in and understand,' her partner added.

'How much?' The first voice purred, its lips sucking on her cheeks like an insistent anemone.

'A few pages,' Penny murmured.

'Ooh, so elusive, but which pages?'

'I know of the master and what he put her through —' Penny gasped, unable to finish when a pair of hands squeezed her breasts to rival the fire in her sex.

'What was he like?' the first of her captors asked, her voice quivering with excitement.

'Cruel,' Penny panted. 'And hard.'

'How did you feel?' the other countered, as the fingers on her clit whipped around in tiny frenzied circles.

'Good,' Penny spluttered.

The first voice slipped a question into her ear; the tone was sharp, the breathing strained: 'But did the dean enjoy it?'

'Yes!' Penny moaned.

'Was she a deviant like you?' it asked, now losing its own control.

'Yes!'

Penny writhed beneath the interrogating hands; they dipped into her damp sex and tickled the tight rim of her anus. A long tongue tasted her face; teeth nibbled her ears; fingers pinched her hard nipples and nails clawed her raised buttocks.

'Why was she a deviant?' the insistent succubus demanded.

'Because she displayed herself to men, and took the lash and thrived on their animal passion. But she was free to walk away at any time, but craved it more and more,' Penny cried and raked the black swishing silk beneath her.

The voices swirled in unison, taking a line each and crafting their verdict:

'Just like you, Penny. When Lucy tied you up and Amanda thrust her toy inside you.'

'You loved it, worshipped it, the sinfulness, the hedonism, the love of being fucked and licked and stroked.'

'The power and freedom was yours too.'

'Yes,' Penny shrieked, challenging her lovers, feeding off their mounting excitement.

'Want to feel the way she did?' the first voice both asked and informed Penny at the same time.

'Oh yes, yes,' Penny whimpered, falling back into those luxurious swoons of desperate need that she had felt beneath Lucy. Her memory filled her mind with images she desired to replicate: she saw Miss Barbusse on all fours in the maze; the twins banging between Amber's thighs; she saw breasts and long legs, soft skin and pretty faces flushed with desire. Penny saw the very centre of her soul and wanted it enriched with every dark shape and fancy that had ever intrigued her.

She was lifted from the mattress and her stomach was placed over a soft leather cushion. It must be the chair, Penny's mind screamed: that sinister throne that had tickled her curiosity while she hung in the stocks.

A pair of hands massaged her soft buttocks through the silky panties and a voice moaned with appreciation behind her. Further away, in the dark, she heard something unclipped from a mounting before it was tested in the warm air with a swish and smack. It sounded like leather – soft leather, shiny hide.

A bright white spotlight clicked on and illuminated the shiny black chair. Penny blinked and stared around the room. Only the chair had been lit up; the remainder of the room was lost in impenetrable shadow.

Penny glanced over her shoulder and saw an eager-faced Celeste twin kneading her shiny buttocks, her nose wrinkling and her lips pursed with anticipation. From out of the swirling blackness, her partner emerged dressed in tiny leather shorts, which were laced at the side and fitted with thin black suspenders that fell across white thighs to clasp glossy stocking-tops. Both girls had dressed identically. Their little leather waistcoats only enhanced the pale colour and the shape of their small hard breasts.

Their blonde hair flowed freely around square jaws and heavily lidded eyes, adding a softness to the angular cheekbones. They were beautiful but mad; each pair of sparkling blue eyes had become insane with passion.

Penny wanted their teeth and power; she wanted her smaller and softer body to be crushed against their muscle tone and straddled by their long stocking-clad legs. They made her feel petite and dainty, a flushed and womanly morsel for aggressive lesbian appetites.

Penny lifted one of her legs between her captor's

knees and tickled the twin's sex and inner thigh. She looked back over her shoulder and pouted at the Celeste twin, who immediately turned to her compatriot and smiled with amazement.

The leather strap smacked against Penny's silken behind, the noise startling her ears and the tiny specks of pain exhilarating her body. She wriggled her hips and let a long sigh drift from her tiny nose.

The strap lashed down again, followed by the other twin's hand. They were soon belabouring her cheeks with hand and strap, delivering a blow each in turn. Penny dug her face deep into the soft leather padding and hooked her shiny calves around the twin's legs, pulling them in closer, trapping them against her ruddy cheeks.

A twin gasped, almost breathless with excitement, 'Is this what you want?'

'Yes, mistress,' Penny sighed, delighted at her use of the word.

'You like a tough girl to slap your pretty arse?'

'Yes! I want it every day. From now on, I want some tough bitch to slap my naughty tail.'

The twins moaned in delirium before falling about Penny's prostrate shape and devouring her.

They twisted her on to her back and sucked her breasts forcefully; one hand cupped her bush and rubbed it firmly through the frontal slit in her panties. Penny slipped a foot between either girl's legs and slid her shiny nylon-wrapped toes against their damp lips.

The twins began to gasp and moan, squeezing her hips and thighs, laddering her nylons with their black claws.

'Did you steal the journals?'

'No,' Penny stammered.

'Don't lie, Penny.'

'No, it's the truth.'

'Stop it, girl, tell us!'

'They were there when I woke up. It's true and please use that thing on me. The thick black cock.'

The twins stared at each other in mute shock, before one peeled off to collect a fresh device: Penny's implement of choice.

The twin gripped the astonishing length and swollen diameter with both hands. She greased the long rubber pole with her lipstick and spit, staggering forward on her tiptoes to elevate the shocking dildo to the correct height.

She paused as it nudged against Penny's sex, and looked down, grinning broadly at Penny's trembling face. Penny slipped her legs up and across the tall girl's shoulders, sliding one foot under her nose and across her wet lips.

When the hard cock entered her stretched realm, Penny's toes bent back and a deep groan throbbed from out of her throat. The device seemed to burrow through her, ever widening, ever searching for every spare fraction of space inside her sex.

The other twin raced round the chair to kiss Penny and hold her shoulders down. Penny imagined herself back at university, taken by force in the showers by these two beautiful athletic women after netball. If only it had happened. If only, she thought, they could have released her then, or carried her off from a party when she was giggly and flirtatious and deflowered her amongst the cold blades of grass. But at last it had happened, and at last it had opened a chasm begging to be filled in every new tomorrow.

Penny climaxed within minutes, hoisting her entire body off the leather bench and kicking her legs towards the ceiling. If her vocal chords had been capable of anything other than groans, then Penny was certain that her language would have shocked even these two aggressive lovers.

* * *

212

The twins left Penny in the same position that greeted Miss Barbusse's eyes.

Her ankles had been secured, a foot apart, to the soft leather straps at the base of the curious chair; her wrists were trapped at her sides, cuffed into the seat. The headrest and back of the seat had been raised slightly, to offer Penny a view of her entire body. The spotlight still remained on, illuminating her like a sacrifice to some alien ritual.

The dean moved into the circle of bright light, her head cowled by white wool, her cream silk dress cut to her knees.

'I am amazed at your endurance,' the dean said, looking intently at Penny's flushed face. 'Not even the twins were able to extract the final detail of your confession, and this has never happened before.'

Penny tried to reply: 'I have told you every –'

Miss Barbusse raised one hand to silence her. 'Even after all of this, you still hang on to your story. I admire your tenacity, Penny, and your stealth in unveiling so much of Whitehead. I cannot, however, show any leniency.'

'What is to become of me?' Penny asked, her face deadpan, her voice strong.

'The jury has made a decision. Madam Skinner, Doctor Kloster and I have agreed that you will never leave Whitehead. You are to become a slave.'

A silence reigned between Penny and her judge.

'You will throw off worldly ambitions and serve our purpose here. In time, if you prove efficient, a greater responsibility may be granted. We can always use a pretty and intelligent girl at the Academy, even if she is a rogue.'

Penny gasped. 'But what of my employers, my friends –'

'The letters you will write will convince them of a change in direction. It has happened before. These will be composed after the ball and graduation, both of which, I am sorry to say, you will miss.'

'You cannot just imprison me, chain me up in this bloody cottage –'

'Why not? You threatened to take my livelihood and freedom away, so I will remove yours. The decision is made and, you never know, if your performance under the inquisitors is anything to go by, you will soon feel right at home.'

Penny was unable to speak. She watched the dean light two black cigarettes; one was for herself and one she slipped between Penny's dry lips.

'Relax, it is not so bad. Where else in the world would a spy be spared with such generosity. There are even people who would pay to become one of us. I consider you lucky.'

Miss Barbusse smoothed her hand over Penny's legs. 'Look at your nylons. Ruined. I will send someone tomorrow with fresh underwear and hot water. You smell a little . . . how can I say . . . fertile.'

Penny allowed Miss Barbusse to remove the cigarette from her lips and tap the dead ash on to the floor. The dean produced a shiny red lipstick and re-applied the colour to Penny's mouth.

'Umm, much better. We have yet to find make-up that can reach the finish line.' The dean laughed to herself and brushed Penny's damp fringe from her forehead.

Miss Barbusse leant across Penny, making her skin bristle from the intimacy.

'There is something you will have to do though, Penny, to cool my temper. You see, it has taken me all day to unwind even a little. I am still very angry with you.'

Miss Barbusse slithered off the leather chair and unzipped her skirt.

Penny's eyes widened at the greatest shock of all.

'Your spirit appeals to me, girl, and your green eyes have a certain passion that I am not entirely insensitive to. But you must be humbled, you must learn to taste the clean and pure discipline of Whitehead.'

Miss Barbusse's slender legs had been meticulously covered in shiny white stockings; her little shaven sex appeared pink and moist beneath her delectable sheer briefs.

The dean sauntered around behind her head and lowered the chair enough to present Penny's body in the horizontal position.

'I am so sorry that an enmity exists between you and Lucy. It is tragic, and I hope that one day you can become friends. But, for now, I want you to taste the wine that has slipped across her tongue on this very day.'

It was the final humiliation to be forced to take a sex that Lucy had enjoyed in freedom, but Penny's eyes refused to turn away from that shiny triangle of invisible gossamer covering those pink lips.

The dean kicked off her heels and climbed gracefully upon the chair, straddling Penny's breasts. She smiled at Penny and tickled her little chin with one long painted fingernail.

'You have been mastered, bound and unravelled,' Miss Barbusse whispered. 'You are an exemplary slut and I will enjoy your mouth.'

The tiny silken triangle of fragrant sex wafted above Penny's moistening mouth, before lowering itself upon her lips and teeth.

Penny closed her eyes and tasted obedience.

Nine

Penny opened the black drapes in her new room, housed within the gamekeeper's cottage. She had slept late, the inquisition having delivered her into the deepest slumber she had enjoyed in years. Across the sun-warmed lawns and in the distance, she could already see some of the cottage staff preparing the masquerade ball for Tuesday – the final celebration, which she was destined to miss. Outside the old ballroom they had strung the chestnut trees with Chinese lanterns; a candy-striped marquee tent was forming around thin metal poles and the speaker system was undergoing a test.

Her female classmates walked out of the main manor building in a long and orderly column behind Miss Barbusse, teetering across the lawns and disappearing through the ballroom French windows. On the corner of the playing field, Penny watched the men jogging by with a Celeste twin positioned at either end of the running pack, their long legs setting the pace and their stern eyes herding the breathless stragglers.

Lessons as usual, Penny mused, but their numbers had been depleted by one, their former peer now on a sabbatical at the cottage.

Her door had been securely latched from the outside and someone had delivered breakfast and hot water through a small iron grille at the foot of the door. This was to be her new home: a Spartan, though comfortable, room at the cottage. Goodbye to London, her career, her friends: this had been Miss Barbusse's decree.

Penny, however, did not climb the walls in anger, or spit, or rage and tear her bed to pieces. The thought of remaining safe from the stream of human affairs and rush-hour anxiety, of residing instead in a hidden world of continual arousal, appealed to a part of her. The Academy had unlocked her, brought fire and inspiration where doubt and anxiety had been before. She could stay at Whitehead for years and experience any avenue of pleasure; she would be a slave and earn extra responsibility with her beauty and imagination. It could be an ideal existence, safe within high walls, satisfying any number of exotic fantasies.

It could not happen, though; not for her. Despite the Whitehead Academy's many lures, Penny knew that she would not let herself stay.

Her business was unfinished: Penny had been beaten by Lucy Harrington and those heated clamourings for revenge would not dim. Penny demanded justice, to unearth the truth. Above all else, though, Penny wanted to see the outside world through her new eyes – the eyes that Whitehead had opened.

The heavy iron bar slid through the latch on the other side of her door.

Penny flitted back to her crumpled bed, her hair tangled, stockings laddered, and French knickers still clinging to her softest parts. After Miss Barbusse had finished with her, Penny had been too drained physically and emotionally to strip off.

The door creaked open and Serbio, the laundry gimp – whom she had seen sleeping peacefully amongst the girls' dirty under-things – shuffled through the door with his head bowed. In his hands he held a neat stack of new lingerie and a clean uniform.

He tried to avert his eyes from Penny and walked almost sideways to place the fresh laundry on the foot of her bed. His little mouth parted and released a nervous whisper: 'I have a fresh outfit for you and I am to take your dirty clothes away.'

Penny narrowed her eyes, a large grin creeping across her lips. 'About time too. I am just desperate to get out of this underwear. I've been in it for ages. I even fell asleep in my lingerie. And look at the state of my stockings. You cannot imagine what they went through yesterday.'

Serbio stopped moving; his small plump frame shivered beneath its leather suit, and he closed his soft brown eyes.

'That's why I need . . . I need to take them away. If you will give them to me now –'

'Sure, right away,' Penny replied, smiling and raising one leg, pointing her toes towards the ceiling.

Serbio's eyes darted left and right, seeking sanctuary.

Penny unclipped her left nylon and rolled it down her leg, slowly. She rotated her toes close to Serbio's chest and yawned as if from relief. 'Oh, they are so clingy and damp. They have almost become a part of my skin.'

Serbio began to fret: his face clouded red, perspiration droplets formed on his bushy eyebrows, and Penny detected a thickening within his leather-hugged groin.

'Do you have a laundry sack to put them in? I certainly would not want you to touch my soiled lingerie. I think it smells.'

Serbio's throat tightened; his mouth trembled; he struggled to gulp; he had become incapable of speech.

Penny removed the ruffled stocking from her little white foot and held the fragrant nylon up to the light.

'I am afraid there is no saving these: they're all laddered. It's a shame though, they must be very expensive – so shiny and silky. They're lovely to wear, to feel close to your skin under a skirt. And they make that little whispering noise when you walk or cross your legs, a little siren song.'

Serbio snatched out a hand towards the stocking, but

Penny anticipated the act of desperation and gently moved it out of his reach.

'It's so good of you to wait on me like this but I wonder if I could ask for a little favour.'

'No favours,' Serbio panted. 'I am not permitted to even communicate with you. Fraternisation with a new prisoner is forbidden for months.'

'Now that is a pity, but rules are rules and don't I know it. I was just hoping that you could carry a little message for me, but don't worry about it. It's nothing really and I can't possibly let you have my soiled underwear. A girl has her pride, and handwashing them will keep me occupied.'

'No,' Serbio whimpered. 'I wash them.'

Penny hung the stocking over the bowl of warm soapy water on her dresser and nonchalantly said, 'But they smell: all that perspiration, and hot leather, perfume, and lord knows what else has been spilled down these –'

'No!' Serbio shouted. 'I will take care of them.'

'What! That's too much work for one man. There are my panties too, still damp and ... Well, it's too embarrassing to talk about with a total stranger.

Serbio's body had crumpled in on itself; his large eyes stared hungrily at the black see-through knickers covering Penny's white buttocks and musky sex.

'OK,' he muttered. 'Just one message I will deliver, but the underwear – I must have the underwear.'

'You will: two long stockings that have been on my hot legs for twenty-four hours and my damp panties – the marks on them alone tell an epic story.'

Serbio stretched his shaking hands out towards Penny. She laughed coquettishly and removed her right stocking in an agonising and exaggerated motion.

Penny draped the two stockings over Serbio's trembling hands. He stared down at the nylons as if they were sacks of gold. His nose quivered and he seemed ready to plunge his eager face right into the gauzy fabric lying across his rough palms.

'The knickers you can come back for, when I know the message has been delivered,' Penny added and licked her lips.

Serbio's face blanched, becoming annoyed.

'You will go and tell Sabrina that she must visit me, nothing more,' Penny instructed. 'Just slip a note under her door. No one will know it even came from you. When I am satisfied that the errand has been run, these silky briefs will be ready to drop into your little hands. And then you can smooth them through hot water, and rub them over hot frothy soap, scrub the tiny little slits and –'

'OK, OK. I will deliver the message,' Serbio panted, and fled from the room with Penny's stockings clutched to his heart.

Penny lay back on her bed and giggled for a very long time.

'The men have showered after their run. They are drying off now,' Miss Barbusse told her class.

Every girl sat elegantly and cross-legged in the ballroom, their pretty faces raised to receive the next instruction.

'You have learnt a great deal here in a very short time,' Miss Barbusse continued. 'You have become warriors; you have learnt the foundation skills that will stay with you for the rest of your lives. The men you will work with, in the course of your careers, are all potential targets. You will develop my lessons in your own unique ways in any given situation, and you will acquire power. So much power it will make you dizzy. You will watch the tides turn. You will create slaves and pathetic begging serfs that plead for a favour, promising anything for one moment more spent in your precious fragrant company.'

The girls all seemed to glow back at Miss Barbusse. She knew they were imagining the possibilities, the rivals and clients – all targets for Whitehead's craft. The shooting season was ready to begin.

'The male students do not know it yet, but this afternoon they will all receive a very special visitor. They think the massage they have been promised and are expecting is to be delivered by the twins. It is not. The massage techniques, that you were shown this morning, will be executed by you.'

The girls all appeared shocked; their glossy lips parted and painted eyelids fluttered wide open.

'Each of them will receive one of you, unsupervised and on your own, in their room. You will be a true Whitehead madam. You will be seductive, feminine, graceful, elegant, insistent, clever, devious, and above all you will be demanding!'

The girls began to smile with excitement and lick their lips with expectation.

'But you have a mission, a final test before graduation. You will each seduce their most private, questionable and sincere sexual experience from them. You will use your hands and your mouths and whatever additional means you feel are appropriate. Each of you, however, must deliver a report to me by the end of the day and I will know if it is genuine. I will determine the authenticity of the confession by its very depravity and its passion. These are secrets that no one has ever heard, perhaps not even their best friends. But you, my elite, will deliver that guarded information to me.'

Sabrina's husky voice wafted through the grate and tore Penny from her nap: 'Penny, Penny, wake up, it's me.'

Penny sat up in bed. 'Come in, Sabrina, I was just dosing.'

'No. No one is to speak with you. I have only managed to slip up the stairs because Madam Skinner is busy in the nursery.'

Penny crept over to the grate. 'It will be OK, Sabrina, no one will know.'

'Penny!' Sabrina hissed. 'For crying out loud. You're in it up to your neck and I will not be dragged down with you. I bloody warned you, girl. What were you even thinking of?'

'I did not steal those journals. What I told you was true. I decided to close the investigation. Those diaries were planted in my room!'

'Shh, Penny, keep your voice down. What do you mean by "planted"? Are you out of your –'

'Lucy planted them in my room.'

'Are you crazy? She's in love with the dean. They are inseparable.'

'It's an act. It has to be. I don't know why, but I know she stuck them under my bed. She hates me.'

'Penny, this is just ludicrous. I am so disappointed in you,' Sabrina whispered, her words heavy with remorse.

'Listen, Sabrina, I will prove it, to you all. I just need to get out of here –'

'No way. I am not releasing you. I like it here. I will not risk the dean's wrath.'

'You don't have to: just deliver a message to Amanda – she will help me. No one will know that you had any part in it.'

'Penny, I am so sorry, but I can't. I have too much to lose. You dug this hole, sister, you will have to lie in it. You will be caught again and the inquisition will not be so friendly. You will expose me and then –'

'Sabrina, I could have done that already. I never even mentioned your name yesterday and, believe me, I said a lot of things that shocked me. I could have blabbed about your warnings and the tour you gave me, not to mention that you were originally from the same magazine, but I kept my mouth shut. I know who my friends are.'

Sabrina fell silent beyond the door. Penny could hear her breathing and smell the redhead's delicious scent.

'OK, Penny. One message for Amanda and then you are on your own.'

'Thanks, honey,' Penny whispered, sighing with relief. 'And please don't worry, things are going to be all right for both of us. I only want you to pass a note on. Just ask Amanda to bring a gown over tomorrow night and a mask for the ball. That's all.'

'They have begun,' Miss Barbusse whispered to herself, smiling with pride in the dark attic space above the male bedrooms.

She lit her path across the reinforced ceilings with a little pen-sized torch. It was all she needed: she had walked along this discreet path so many times before and yet, each term, the revelations from her male pupils never failed to surprise her.

Miss Barbusse knelt down on her tiny velvet cushion and opened the first pair of peepholes.

'You like that there, right between your shoulders?' Amber asked her tall blonde partner, who lay face down on a couch in nothing besides a white towel wrapped around his waist.

'Yes,' he murmured, his voice just audible to Miss Barbusse. 'Yes, that is so good. I feel dizzy. Where did you learn how to do this?'

'Right here, silly!' Amber replied, giggling. 'We have all been instructed to practise on you hard-working boys after that long run. You must be so tired.'

'Knackered,' he replied.

'Poor darling. But Amber is here to melt all of that away. Just drift off and dream; relax and let my fingers do the work.'

'You treasure,' he moaned.

Miss Barbusse smiled, sighing through her nose and biting the end of her finger when Amber's face slipped between his shoulder blades.

'Oh boy. Amber, don't ... your tongue ... it turns me on,' the man panted.

'Ssh, it's all part of the technique. I can't help it if

you're so horny, and who cares: no one is watching. We can do anything we like. Have you had an Academy girl yet?'

'I'm not telling you,' the man chuckled.

'Go on, don't be coy,' Amber probed, slipping the towel off his waist and rubbing her hands over his tanned buttocks.

She tickled the parting in his tensing buttocks and licked the base of his spine.

The man's head moved from side to side and he raised his buttocks to give his erection room to swell against the couch.

'You really want to know?' the man moaned.

'You bet,' Amber whispered. 'Tell me and I'll tell you a little secret.'

'Well, it's kind of unusual.'

'Nonsense, don't be ashamed. You would not believe what I did the other night.'

'Ooh, Amber, can I roll over on to my front?'

'It's about time that you did.'

Miss Barbusse wet her lips at the sight of the fresh erection, rising no more than a few inches from Amber's mouth.

'Well, Kloster sent me over to that freaky cottage one night to deliver a package through the back door. I was intrigued by the place: I had run past it in the morning and saw this lovely older woman coming out of the front door in a wheelchair.'

'Go on,' Amber prompted, gently stroking the man's penis at the base and tickling his golden balls with her other hand.

'She was lovely and I wanted to speak to her, but I lost my confidence and was on a run anyway. But she smiled at me and winked. She is really handsome – you know that type, like Anne Bancroft or Diana Rigg – really handsome and sultry.'

'Yeah, I know the type.'

'Well, I just had to go back and look her up. When the doctor sent me over in the evening I thought it was fate, a lucky break.'

Amber's head began moving in the man's groin and he clutched the back of her blonde head. His story became hushed and broken, but Miss Barbusse relished the detail.

'Man, I have always had a thing for older women. She invited me in and made me a cup of tea.'

'Go on,' Amber pressed, temporarily removing her slippery lips off the head of his phallus.

'And she sucked my cock. It was beautiful. And then she put it between her breasts, and they are so big. I just slid my cock through her big warm cleavage while she said the most sexy things. She said she liked young guys and liked to fuck at least six every term. I . . . I just blew up and came all over her breasts.'

Amber's head sprang up and down his thick shaft and her hands pumped the base. The man began to writhe and thrust upward with his buttocks. She removed her mouth to coax a greater confession. 'That sounds so sexy. Oh, it has turned me on. Did you fuck her?'

'You bet, three times in her room. It was the greatest.'

'Is she the first older girl you have had?'

'No, there was one other, but that is a secret. Amber, I could have gotten into a real fix the first time.'

'Tell me.'

'No way.'

'Please, please. Tell me and I will do something to this cock that will make you faint.'

The man gripped the couch and moaned, becoming lost to his arousal, willing to reveal anything.

'When I was seventeen and the head boy in the sixth form, at this all-boys school in Sussex, I did something so perverse with the headmistress. She was married and at least fifty, but boy was she sexy.'

'Go on, honey,' Amber cooed. 'Tell me, I want to know.'

225

'OK, but promise me. Promise you'll keep it secret.'

'Of course,' Amber whispered and licked the shiny head of his cock.

'I used to go and see her every Friday after school, in her study. She used to dress up like a prostitute for me and we used to play this game. She would wear a peephole bra, and no knickers under this leather miniskirt. Just stockings and high heels and . . . she . . . she . . .'

'What did she do?' Amber insisted, pumping his penis through her hand.

'She liked me to take her forcefully. To shove her over the desk and slap her backside.'

'Wow, that is so sexy.'

'Oh it was. And then I would fuck her against the bookshelves and she would bite on this leather strap. And on the floor, on all fours. And I had to call her a slut and really slap her backside. It was so sexy. She was married and so respectable, so clever, but we had this game.'

'Did you fuck her hard. Harder than her husband with your young cock, loaded with all that cream.'

The man began to approach orgasm, nearly choking with excitement. 'Yes, really hard. And we used to leave the phone off the hook, so he could hear at home!'

Amber covered the end of the spasming penis with her wide mouth and noisily swallowed his offering.

Miss Barbusse closed the peepholes, dabbing her forehead with a tissue and loosening her blouse.

Serbio was back for something he held in the highest regard.

'Did she come?' he asked through the slot in the base of Penny's door.

'Yes, and thank you for being so good,'

'The panties – push the panties through the slot.'

'Why don't you come in and get them,' Penny teased,

sensing the desperate need on the other side of her prison door.

'No, through the slot.'

Penny giggled; he was afraid of her power: what she might attempt or coax him to do. She relished the situation, never having realised that a man could become so compliant over a pair of soiled panties.

'OK, I am just slipping them off now. Hang on, they are just a little stuck, I have to peel them down.' Penny heard the sharp intake of breath beyond her door and smiled. 'They will probably fall apart in a machine. You had better do them in your hands. You know, wrap them around something hard and soak them.'

'Please,' he gasped. 'The panties.'

'Sure, the black see-through knickers. I'll be sorry to see them go. They were so comfortable and sexy. Made me feel so naughty, not to mention what they did to the others.'

'The panties!' he demanded, his voice nothing more than a shriek.

Penny dangled the knickers before the hatch, out of his reach but well within his view. She heard a whimper creep through the hatch and shook the flimsy briefs about.

'Here they are. Take good care of them,' Penny said, and tossed them through the slot.

There was a scrabbling sound, a quick panting, and then he was gone.

Miss Barbusse watched Lucy smearing oil over one of the young men that she herself had taken in the maze. He had always been the last to come on that night following the soiree, the most thorough and insistent in his brutal loving, even continuing after the others had lain around exhausted and thanking the stars. He had thick dark hair and an olive skin: he was of French descent, a fellow countryman.

227

Lucy rubbed the glistening oil between his toes, up the rear of his calf muscles and into his strong thighs. He moaned and clawed at the armrest on his couch.

Miss Barbusse shuddered and her teeth ground together. She bit down upon the demon that whispered inside her chest.

'More oil for your shoulders. Lots of it. Your shoulders are so broad and you have the skin of a woman – it is beautiful,' Lucy whispered.

'Thank you, Lucy, and your hands have a magic all of their own. You have lifted the world off my shoulders with your fingertips,' he replied dreamily.

Lucy giggled and kneaded his shoulder and neck muscles with her long white fingers. 'It is so good of the dean to allow us to practise on you guys. It makes things more intimate, more vivid, don't you think?'

'Oh yes, Lucy, and I will be the envy of every man, for having you as my partner.'

Miss Barbusse closed her eyes and loosened her blouse. She stood up for a few seconds and wriggled from her skirt. She had selected this man especially for Lucy; no other pupil could have tortured her as much when given access to her young lover.

'I bet you have many girlfriends at home,' Lucy said, slipping her fingers over the side of his ribs, tickling his waist with her long red nails, forcing his buttocks to clench.

'Not so many,' he replied, his voice shaking.

'Why? I imagine you to have had more lovers than you can remember.'

'That is nice of you to say, but I dedicate my time to my work.'

'How admirable, throwing all of that energy into your career.'

'Yes, but sometimes it can be lonely.'

'Sure, and you become desperate at rare moments, in flash floods of emotion, and do unexpected things. I have been in similar situations.'

'You are very intuitive, and beautiful.'

Lucy smiled and turned him over to lie on his back. His face reddened as the thick erection beneath his loin towel became evident.

'Don't be shy. I have seen those before,' Lucy giggled, and traced her hands along his inner thighs beneath the towel.

'But we hardly know each other. I do not usually display myself to girls for a very long time.'

'Not usually, but sometimes I bet you have slipped up.'

The man grinned, and then closed his eyes when Lucy unwrapped his thick brown penis. She oiled the shaft and stroked it slowly, moving her face nearer to admire the length and breadth of it.

'My, this is beautiful. Sorry to be so forward, but you have a lovely cock.'

The man tensed when Lucy said 'cock'. She had said it beautifully: hushed and open-mouthed, as if ready to slip something between her crimson lips.

'Thank you,' he gasped, staring at the long white fingers with blood-red tips caressing his length. Beyond the hand, a mouth lay in wait: the lips moist, the little pink tongue flicking impatiently.

Miss Barbusse slipped her hand inside her black panties and lay down against the hard attic wood. She pressed her face to the ceiling holes and began to tease her clit.

'What is the sexiest, dirtiest thing you have ever done? Tell me. You are so handsome and tall, I bet you have had some wonderful propositions,' Lucy said, stroking the shaft a little quicker, her mouth approaching slowly, her eyelids lowering.

'I cannot say.'

'Oh, you can. I can keep a secret. I have many. It just turns me on when I know what a lover has done.'

'But we are not lovers, Lucy.'

'No, not yet, but I think I would like to lie with you after the ball. You remind me of a Greek god: so handsome, so strong and yet so gentle. Will you hold me in your arms after the ball and slip my body out of the dress? Maybe drink champagne from my shoe and bite my neck?'

'Oh, yes. I have been watching you since day one.'

Lucy replied through a melodic giggle, appearing embarrassed: 'The admiration has been mutual, but I have been too shy to speak to you.'

'Oh, I could lie next to you for ever, Lucy.'

'Mmm, I would like that, but tell me the story.'

Lucy removed her hands from his trembling penis and unbuttoned her blouse. The man's eyes strained to take in the sight of her beautiful silk-cupped breasts. Her skirt fell to the floor and he reached out a hand to stroke her shimmering thigh, tweaking a suspender clip between his finger and thumb.

Lucy smiled and crouched down beside him, blowing a little kiss up to his eager face. She licked the top of his phallus and clawed his stomach.

'Tell me a story,' she whispered.

Miss Barbusse slipped another two fingers inside her welcoming vagina and panted softly above.

'It was a terrible thing to have done to my best friend, but it was so exciting,' he began, his whole body trembling, his cock seeming to enlarge even further as the memory slid back across his mind.

'Your friend?'

'Yes, my oldest friend. We grew up together, went to school together, loved each other.'

'You slept together.'

'No. I . . . I took his bride.'

Lucy sucked her breath in sharply but focused her attentions on his penis with a greater vigour. 'How?' she asked, making quick little passes over the dewy head of his phallus with the tip of her tongue.

'Before his wedding night, after the ceremony. She was so pretty, so innocent. Such a tiny black-haired beauty. Her hair was cut short, like a man's, and she had a laugh, so rarely heard, but more beautiful than a bird. I always told her jokes, just to hear her laugh.'

'What did you do?'

'We were in a hotel. The reception lunch continued downstairs and I left to smoke and think upstairs in my room. I met her in the corridor; nothing was planned. She had run upstairs to fetch something for my friend – a list, I think, of all the people he wanted to thank in the speech.'

'She seduced you.'

'No, the meeting was accidental and so was the passion. I had been working so hard I had not had a lover in over a year but, when I saw her in that white gown with beautiful pink flowers crowned around her head, I became lost.'

Lucy sucked his penis with relish, coaxing, imploring and seducing his greatest transgression into the light.

'It was her lovely pale skin and those pretty little features, her tiny hips and slender legs. I had been in love with her for the entire year of her courtship. I dreamt of her every night, loved her. I could not help envying my friend. She was a virgin. He was her first lover.'

'But not that night!' Lucy hissed, lapping his shaft greedily, becoming aroused by the very nature of his confession. She stood up and slipped her panties to one side, clambered over the man's crotch and eased the long erection inside her sex.

Miss Barbusse winced and swore, but rubbed her little tingling bud with a fresh passion.

'Tell me,' Lucy moaned. 'Tell me how you took her innocence. Upstairs in the dark, when the others were all below.'

'We had to be quick. She would be missed. I grabbed her shoulders and kissed her with all my might.'

231

'How did she react?' Lucy demanded, riding him slowly and digging the heels of her stilettos into the side of his legs.

'She was stunned at first, shocked. What had I done? I could not think. But then she took my hand and led me down the corridor, to her bridal suite.'

'You fucked her!'

'Yes, quickly and savagely. I took her virginity up against the wall, on the floor and on the bed. I pulled her skirts up and sucked her, in that innocent place where not even the bridegroom had been.'

'She loved it!' Lucy cried out, banging on and off his thick cock, throwing her contorted face up towards the ceiling as if to taunt her mistress.

Miss Barbusse began to feel the first tremors of orgasm.

The man gasped, struggling with the words, 'She did. She wrapped her legs around my waist and told me to "fuck her hard".'

'And you did.'

'Yes, harder than I had taken any woman. So that she shook and nearly broke. She was such a delicate little lover.'

'And now you can see her again – you think I am her. In my bridal underwear, committing adultery only hours after the wedding. Fuck me like her, really hard!'

'Yes!' he shouted and grabbed Lucy by the waist.

They fell to the floor and rolled across a rug. He stabbed his cock between her legs, in short aggressive lunges, making her scream as she came. Lucy wrapped her stocking-clad legs around his oily back, pulling him in further, demanding the deepest penetration.

The man collapsed across her chest as he climaxed, pumping his seed inside of Lucy and sobbing with relief. Lucy regained her own breath and smiled, stroking his ruffled hair and glowing with triumph.

Above the exhausted lovers, Miss Barbusse could watch no more; she closed the peephole, turned off the torch and pleasured herself in the dark. She rolled to one side in the hot attic and thought of what she would do to Lucy that very evening. She would flog Lucy, whip her until she became insane with desire. She would punish the girl and love her until the first glimmer of dawn.

The night brought a chorus from the cottage. It resounded with the unrelenting and savage cries of the gimps. The distant sounds of lash and cane were like native drums on this isle of the banished – the final destination for the eager slaves of extremity.

Penny sat alone with her thoughts and plans, her little room illuminated by a bright moonlight that crept across the bed and washed her nakedness. She had barely touched the meal beneath the silver tureen; her stomach wanted to do nothing but growl with its ominous mutterings. Everything would be decided tomorrow – Tuesday, the eighth day – doomsday for the deceivers.

She sipped her coffee, tossed her book, *Delta of Venus*, down for the third time and sighed. Was it possible to right the wrong? They seemed so strong, so organised and quick to mobilise. She was a mere prisoner, praying that Amanda could slip through the lines and deliver her. The odds seemed too high and the obstacles unscalable but, maybe, Penny hoped, her salvation lay there – in surprise.

The dean would not anticipate her escape; no one would. They had caught her, interrogated her, and locked her away to be dealt with when the others had left for the outside world. No one could predict Penny's second coming.

She would have to be swift and assertive, aggressive if necessary, think on her feet and respond to a night of edge and danger. She would have to be a Whitehead girl. Failure was not an option.

* * *

'You are a masterpiece, Lucy,' Miss Barbusse whispered, pausing with her evening sketch to slip her lips around the black cigarette holder. 'A moment, all by yourself, when life becomes art.'

'I feel like a sculpture, mistress. I can hardly move,' Lucy replied.

Miss Barbusse continued with her Indian ink, re-creating the shiny texture of Lucy's knee-length boots. 'Do you not think it is odd, Lucy, that even our feet are the same size?'

'Maybe it is a sign, mistress.'

'Yes, I would like to think so,' Miss Barbusse replied, and added a detail to the slender waist that her tight rubber corset had created above Lucy's tiny hips. 'You know, Lucy, I wore those boots for my master in Paris, beneath an ankle-length skirt. You see, only he knew that my young skin had become numbed by their strangling caress, only he could imagine the tiny piercings on my labia. We were quite ahead of our time. It was a practice he learnt of in the Orient.'

'Were you uncomfortable?'

'Yes, but the thought of what he would do with me later served as a tonic. He had made me dress in Hansom nylons, the sheerest stockings. They were like spiders', webs, as if woven by a nylon spider. He only had to breathe upon them and they would run.'

'Did you wear this corset?'

'No, Lucy,' the dean replied, laughing. 'That is only a training garment, to induce a straight posture, but you will progress to a more sophisticated model in time.'

'Were you this hot?'

'Hotter. Your kid-skin gloves only reach your elbows. Mine stretched right up my arms and were attached to a shoulder harness.'

'I do not think that I would have liked that.'

'Oh, you would have done. To feel his tongue tasting your salty skin, once the rubber and leather had been peeled off. To have your damp buttocks suddenly released to the air, so sensitive and soft and ideal for the lash.'

Lucy shuddered and the dean laughed to herself, adding a red ink to match the shiny lipstick on Lucy's pursed mouth.

'I would like you to wear those boots tomorrow night, Lucy, beneath your gown.'

'I will, mistress, but my underwear will be a treat – like my dress and mask, a secret. You will not be able to recognise me amongst the other girls.'

'What will you do at the ball?' Miss Barbusse asked, thinking back to the young man who had buried himself deep inside her slave that afternoon.

'Oh, I will avoid you, make you seek me out.'

'Will I find you first?' the dean asked, an edge of anxiety to her words.

'Yes, you will find me, eventually. And nothing will prepare you for what I will demand, mistress. My new limits will astound you.'

Miss Barbusse crossed her slippery thighs and gritted her teeth, imagining the young thing flaunting her beauty in her boudoir after the ball – high on champagne and just a touch slutty. Pouting that pretty mouth, a mouth that will have kissed men all night long, and, perhaps, have taken one in a dark corner to relieve his excitement.

'Can I move a little, mistress?' Lucy asked, without moving her head.

'No. Keep still until the preliminary sketch is complete. The lacing on your corset is very intricate. Are you that uncomfortable?'

'Just a little on my cheeks, mistress. They are still tender – you were very strict tonight.'

'Yes, sometimes you should not tease me so. You incite me with little looks and with your wayward affections. It is a strange relationship between mistress and slave. One can never tell who really holds the strings.'

Miss Barbusse added a few final details to the sketch and slipped off the bed, her naked breasts gleaming in the candlelight, her stockings and heels shining in little starbursts. In her approach to Lucy, who stood tall and erect in her bonds, Miss Barbusse was unable to remove her eyes from the girl's smiling mouth.

Ten

The choice of music surprised Penny; it drifted across the lawns and crept through the trees before it halted and pawed outside her window. The drums were gentle and weaved behind curious guitar and keyboard effects. It was dark music, Gothic music, haunted by an operatic female voice. It was a pure and beautiful vocal: it would rise, trembling with passion, through the hypnotic vampiric rhythms and make the hairs quiver on the back of Penny's cold neck. The voice seemed to call Penny, inviting her to the dance.

From her cell, Penny gazed towards the gathering and the red glow of the ballroom. The Chinese lanterns were purple and threw gigantic shadows of the flitting revellers. It was an inferno and the very thought of entering that realm terrified her. She could imagine the hordes of costumed pupils, and the china-faced staff weaving through the throng to select their prey. The music, champagne and lights would be working their magic, right now, creating a temple of love.

'Come on, Amanda. Don't let me down,' Penny whispered, clawing the window sill, unable to occupy her hands or fill her mind with anything besides the pounding music. She could not be too rational: she would have to feed off her adrenaline like a dark and hunted panther.

The day had clawed by, every minute producing a fresh doubt and imagined catastrophe. She needed to act, to get moving out there in the night before her thoughts drove her crazy.

The latch sprang back on the outside of her door. Penny turned and crouched down, her breathing shallow, her muscles tensing. She could not wait any longer: if this was Serbio again with food, then she would rush him, overpower him and fly to the ball.

It was the head of a fox that slipped through the gap in the door: a magnificent head created from crushed brown fur with a wicked smile and clever blue eyes. Eyes Penny recognised: passionate, fearless eyes.

'Amanda. You beauty,' Penny whispered, and threw herself into the tall girl's arms.

'My, oh my, are you pleased to see me.' Amanda giggled and wrapped her long naked arms around Penny's trembling waist. In one hand she clutched a pillowcase stuffed with something soft.

'You came! I knew I could count on you.'

'It was hard. I had to wait for ages, for the sun to go down and for the cottage to empty. Both outside doors were locked, so I snuck in through the stable. These cottage people are freaky, they are all serving champagne over at the ball. You should see it – what a party! I have never seen anything like it in all my life.'

Penny stood back to survey Amanda's outfit: her long, brown, ankle-length gown was velvet, sleeveless and tightly pinched around her waist. Her pale back was also bare and criss-crossed with tiny laces.

'You look terrific, and what a mask!' Penny gasped.

'Oh, Pen, you should see the costumes. No one knows who anyone is. It's really mysterious and scary.'

'Good,' Penny gasped, becoming more resolute. 'I have my work cut out over there.'

'Is it true though, Penny? That you are a reporter? That you stole something of the dean's? I did not believe it – you would never hurt us.'

Penny sat back on the bed and shook her head before

replying. 'It is true, Amanda. I came here to find a reporter we lost two years ago and to investigate the so-called training Academy, but it changed me. I killed off the investigation. I decided, I swear, that this place should carry on undisturbed. But Lucy planted the dean's journals in my room before I could destroy my notes. It was terrible. I don't know why she wanted me out of the way but I intend to find out, tonight.'

Amanda studied Penny. 'Was it real? You know, our time together.'

Penny sprang across the room and stroked Amanda's hair, reassuring her with words of sincerity: 'Yes, the greatest night of my life. It started everything: the way I now feel and what I want out of life. That first night had nothing to do with the job, and it is something I want to do with you, over and over again, when we leave Whitehead.' Penny kissed the fox's nose and blinked back a tear.

'Good,' Amanda whispered and handed Penny the pillowcase. 'You had better get changed – it is nearly ten o'clock.'

Where was she?

Miss Barbusse, resplendent in white, glided through the coloured smoke and thick drum rhythms, the sound of her six-inch heels lost amongst the anarchy of dancing. Had Lucy dared to occupy a discreet corner in the ball, or to lead a young man out to the damp grass, in order to feed?

A girl in an electric-blue gown teetered past. On her face she wore a colourful plumed mask, the blue-green feathers of exotic birds forming a veil that covered her blonde hair. Miss Barbusse stopped the girl, letting her lacquered nails slip across her pale arm.

'Lucy?' she whispered into the mass of perfumed blonde hair beside the girl's ear.

The girl paused and knocked back a glass of

champagne. 'No, it's Amber,' she replied, giggling. 'Who are you? Have you seen Amanda?'

Miss Barbusse smiled, her sensual mouth just peaking out beneath the owl mask on her face. 'No, I have not seen Amanda. Do you know which outfit Lucy chose?'

'Sorry, no. I don't know anyone from Adam,' the girl replied, shrugging and laughing before she drifted back into the excited mêlée.

Many of the students were dancing, circling around the tall woman in the tigress outfit. She wore a tight gown, tiger striped and crafted from satin. Every time she performed a daring and athletic move, the rear of her gown parted and a long leg slipped through, shimmering in seamed nylon and shoed in a dangerously high, red, strappy sandal.

Miss Barbusse smiled and whispered to herself, 'The same costume every year, my dear doctor. Do you never tire of being the tiger?'

It was the only outfit that never fooled Miss Barbusse at a graduation ball. The doctor would always select it, having first pick from the Academy wardrobe, where the styles flashed back to the twenties. The doctor danced like a fiend, kicking out her long legs at the young men, wiggling her behind and throwing her dagger-like nails up towards the chandeliers. It was her unwinding, her pagan ritual, where her stone façade would melt – but only slightly.

Miss Barbusse watched Kloster select her prey: in the cloying dance-floor smoke she seemed to be focusing her attentions on a tall man, his face covered from the lips upward by a porcelain *Phantom of the Opera* mask. He danced gracefully around the doctor, his unblinking eyes devouring her slender contours beneath the sparkling tigerskin.

The doctor shimmied towards him, on her tiptoes, close enough for her hard nipples to press against his tuxedo, near enough for her tiger whiskers to brush his cheeks. The man slid his hands on to her narrow waist and stroked her hips as he danced. The doctor pirouetted in his arms, her red nails flashing above her head, her tight backside grinding into his tummy and along his cock. She eased her head back on to his shoulder and whispered something in his ear. His hands tightened on her hips and he tried to bite her neck, but she pranced away, beckoning to him with one long finger. The doctor disappeared into the mist and he followed close behind.

Miss Barbusse moved forward, through the dancers, smiling: the great cat had circled her young victim and now she would drink his blood.

The doctor skipped through the red smoke, which became pink over the floor lights, and disappeared through the wide French windows. The youth followed, unthinking, his hands trembling with desire.

The dean threw her head back and laughed. She would wait for a few minutes and then view the carnage; the doctor worked fast at celebrations. Would the young man even be able to stand up at the graduation ceremony?

Miss Barbusse looked around to give the doctor time. There were too many silhouettes, too many masks. Would she ever find Lucy? A cool evening breeze washed across the left side of her face and the night called. Her slave would have to wait. The dean scurried from the hall, determined to see the doctor at play.

The man's cries leapt from around the corner of the ballroom and Miss Barbusse followed the sound. She raised her skirts and ran to a group of dark chestnut trees; she flitted between the shadowy trunks to watch the spectacle from the side.

In a little stone alcove, set within the building's walls, she could see the man's white flesh peeking between an untucked shirt and the trousers ruffled around his ankles. He writhed across the cold grass, moaning and

241

occasionally kicking out a leg. Above him, the proud tigress indulged her appetite. As the music softened to only organ sounds, Miss Barbusse heard the sounds of submission: 'Suck it! Lick it, right inside. That's it. Harder. Harder, I say!'

The tigress moved briefly from the shadows and Miss Barbusse smiled: the doctor's claws had embedded themselves in the hair beside the man's ears, her long legs had straddled his smeared face and his hands had been rendered useless by the cuffs that secured his wrists. The tigress spiked his hard stomach muscles with one of her shiny red heels and thrust her wet sex across his mouth.

'Lash it!' she cried, sliding her leg across his naked chest. 'Suck it hard, you little shit! Thought you would fuck me, eh? Ram your cock inside the tigress?'

The man mumbled and lapped at the sex lovingly, making the tigress shudder. She dropped his body to the floor and wrenched his black briefs down to his ankles. She removed her own see-through panties and stuffed them between his lips to gag his excited yelps. The doctor stood above his dishevelled shape and hissed, her lips snarling beneath the tiger mask's white nose.

'Of all the girls to chase, of all the bottoms to grope, you laid your hands on mine.' Without another word, the doctor fell upon his lap, raising her dress as she squatted across his thick cock. She remained balanced upon her tiptoes, her naked bottom hovering a few inches off his groin.

'Now, thrust!' she ordered, and the man moved his lower back off the grass, digging his elbows and heels into the ground to attain leverage. His penis disappeared inside the doctor and she snarled with pleasure, before encouraging him in a softer voice, 'That's it, right in . . .'

He held the position and kept his cock inside her, before falling back to the earth. 'Good,' the doctor gasped. 'When I say "fuck", you will thrust.' The man nodded and squirmed beneath her. 'Fuck!' the doctor shouted, and he stabbed his cock upward and into her descending sex. She pushed his buttocks down on to the lawn and screamed with delight, before raising her behind and repeating the same command.

The man continued with his upward thrusting and the doctor repeatedly pressed down and met the rifling passage of his shaft.

'Ah, so deep,' she cried. 'But I need it harder. When I remove my cuffs you will fuck me hard. Backwards, do you understand? You will thrust your cock into me as hard as you can from behind. Is that clear?'

The man spat her panties from his mouth and shouted, 'Yes!'

The doctor uncuffed his hands and stood against the wall, half in shadow, her heels spread apart, her dress hiked up around her waist. The lad clambered from the floor and shuffled behind her, grasping her hips.

'Not there, you fool. In my arse!' she screamed, drowning out his whimper of pleasure.

The man pushed her body into the shadow of the alcove and against the wall. The doctor's slender upper body disappeared from view; only her seamed calf muscles and shiny scarlet heels remained in the pale moonlight.

'I knew it was you in the tiger's mask,' the young man cried out. 'I have been waiting to make a pass at you all week.' The doctor moaned from the shadow, pleased with the confession. 'And now,' he continued, drawing his hips backward, 'I am going to screw you against a wall, until your legs give way.'

'Yes! Do it!' the doctor screamed.

Miss Barbusse watched the heavy thrusting for several minutes; it made her claw at her breasts through the white chiffon gown and pant into the cool night breezes.

'I will have this too, good doctor, before Lucy discovers the true meaning of worship,' Miss Barbusse muttered, and fled back to the ball.

Penny entered the reception of the second Whitehead building, which housed the ballroom and male dormitory. The patio, which Amanda had entered by, was too dangerous, lit up by those swirling red lights, so Penny chose the dim indoor corridor leading towards the ballroom. There was a fire exit at the end of the passage providing a more discreet access to the ball.

Amanda had selected a cat outfit for Penny, from the Academy wardrobes, and the black tail now swept across the marble tiles behind her as she scurried towards the fire exit. The velvet mask covered her hair and face, with only the eyes and mouth cut away. She had tied her hair up beneath the pointed cat ears, concealing her identity. She intended to take advantage of the smoke and shadow, as an extra precaution, just in case a staff member became curious about the silent cat in black.

Penny held her breath and approached the door. Through the reinforced glass, set within the top half of the door frame, she could see the red glow dimming and then suddenly flaring up like embers in a fireplace.

She had no clear plan of attack: she would find Lucy first, watch the girl and maybe wait for her to slip up. There seemed to be no other method of approach: the dean and staff were convinced of her guilt. If no option availed itself to her, Penny decided she could always run from the Academy. Her car was still outside. Maybe she should just run now, while everyone was preoccupied. The thought had crossed her mind repeatedly as she had approached the pounding celebrations – but would that not jeopardise Amanda and Sabrina, who had engineered her escape?

No, she had to fight at all costs; she had to make an attempt at rousting Lucy.

244

As Penny hovered by the door, gaining her confidence, a brief silence parted the music before the next song began. In the temporary pause, Penny's ears detected a rhythmic groaning floating from her right.

She spun around in the dark, terrified of being observed, and faced a harmless wooden door. She pressed her ear against the door, but the music had started again, obliterating the soft moans. Penny tried the handle gently. The door was unlocked and clicked open. She peered through. It was only a staircase, leading up to the first floor, but the sounds of passion were louder with the door open.

She had to see. It was just after ten – had the carnal activities already begun?

Penny passed through the doorway, quietly closing the door behind her. She removed her high heels and crept up the staircase, moving closer to the sound.

Before she turned the first corner, Penny heard the dean's voice: 'You are the one who took Lucy yesterday.'

'Yes,' the man panted.

The dean moaned in response.

'How did you know?' he asked.

'I sent her to your room, to practise on you. Was she good?'

'Oh yes, my dean. You taught her well, but it was nothing to how you feel around me.'

The noises of ecstasy followed: the man's tones were gruff and insistent; the dean's high-pitched and strained. Penny slipped her head around the bend and watched the duo making love on the stairs.

The dean had dressed in a long and slinky white gown, sequined around her cleavage. An owl mask covered most of her face, but her mouth was still visible to Penny. Her scarlet lips had parted and she clutched the man's head within her soft cleavage. Her legs, in shiny flesh-coloured stockings, were wrapped around his

245

tanned waist, untucking his shirt and forcing his trousers down. His hands had clasped her buttocks and, with each pump from his hips, the dean slid up and down the staircase wall.

'Oh . . . that is good . . . I want you to come to my room later . . . Lucy will be there too. You are to save yourself after you come inside me. Save yourself for the two of us. You will be brutal with us both! . . . Yes, that's it, harder now, use your thighs. Really fuck it into me!'

The man complied, pounding the dean against the wall. She appeared so petite and malleable in his long arms, squashed against his chest and speared by his shaft. He cradled her in his arms and laid her on the stairs so that he could thrust downward with a greater power and vigour.

'Oh, good! Do it hard!' the dean squeaked.

'This is the second time I have had you, dean. I want you again after this week – how can I survive without this tight love on my cock?'

'If you please me, maybe I will invite you back to service my hunger.'

The thought of returning to the elegant Miss Barbusse spurred the man on to a greater speed. She wrapped her legs and arms around his back, losing a shoe under the force of his thrusting.

Penny swung her body back behind the corner. She wanted to stay and watch the spectacle until it reached a groaning and shuddering climax, but the time was too precious to waste; an ideal opportunity to find Lucy had arrived. Penny scampered back down the stairs and through the stairwell door. She slipped her shoes back on in the corridor and, before her nerves could rise, she plunged through the fire exit and into the ball.

Nothing could have fully prepared Penny for the sight that stretched out before her eyes: the Academy ball had descended into an orgy.

Dark figures stumbled and laughed, skipping through the mist hand in hand to find an unoccupied refuge. They kicked up the smoke and it clawed after them, chasing shiny seamed calf muscles and slick trouser legs. Between the heavy bursts of guitar and drum from the sound system, Penny heard gasps, squeals, cries of passion and panting entreaties. The free-for-all had produced an incredibly loud and salacious soundtrack all on its own.

'Would you like a drink?' a man shouted from her right.

Penny turned and saw an item of cottage furniture holding a tray of champagne glasses. His entire body had been covered in shiny rubber and his face was partially masked. About his throat Penny noticed the dog collar and a long chain that ran from it to a table, cluttered with green bottles.

'Thank you,' she replied, before swiping two crystal champagne flutes off the tray. She knocked the fizzing contents of one glass straight back for courage.

'Perhaps my service is lacking,' the voice piped up from behind its black mask.

'No, it is fine,' Penny replied, raising one eyebrow in puzzlement.

'If it was slow or clumsy, then feel free to correct my failings.'

Penny shook her head, perplexed by the apology. The man lowered himself to his knees and began begging. 'Forgive me, madam, for bothering you.'

Penny smiled and raised her voice so that he could hear her above the noise: 'I should damn well think so too! I shall complain to Madam Skinner about the terrible service! Now get back to your corner!'

The rubber-suited creature fled back to his little table and cowered, exposing his rear.

'What the hell,' Penny muttered, and strolled over to his nook.

247

A cane had been placed behind the table and the man shuddered excitedly when Penny raised it and surveyed its length. 'This is very hard and seasoned,' she said aloud and flexed the springy wood.

The gimp peered back over his shoulder, the little eye-slits in his mask revealing the two gleaming orbs beneath. Penny had never hit anyone with a stick before, but she was curious and unable to ignore the diversion. She let the first blow sound off his tightly clad rear with a quick little flick from her wrist.

The sound of the cane seemed to echo from above her. Penny stared about the ballroom; surely she had not hit him that hard. She glanced down at the servant, who had raised his backside again and shook it excitedly. Penny caned him harder and the sound reverberated through the music and cacophony of human cries. She bent over and stared beneath the table, spotting two little coloured wires and a receiver: the ball had been wired to catch every impassioned sound from the corners of the dance and to relay them through the sound system, creating a symphony of ecstasy. Penny dropped the cane, half in disbelief, and walked off, craning her neck and straining her ears to catch the ghostly words that floated around her.

A voice she half recognised drifted from the vaulted ceiling: 'Oh, Amanda, that's so . . . good . . . yes.'

Penny turned round, amazed, seeking Amanda in the heated confusion. But it was too dark and everyone was masked. She set off again, shaking the tempting diversion from her mind, determined to find the enemy, but other voices whispered within the music:

'Fuck me, fuck me!' a girl cried.

'Is this what you want, you . . .' a young man shouted excitedly.

'Umm . . . harder . . . fuck me like a . . .'

A hand tugged at her skirt and Penny spun round. It was the gimp she had just caned, straining at the end of his leash. The bright white teeth flashed through the opening on his mask as he spoke: 'Madam, I feel as if my crimes outweigh the punishment. Two strokes from a cane is hardly sufficient.'

Penny rolled her eyes before replying, 'My, you are a persistent little creature. I am afraid I do not have the time to spend –' Penny stopped herself as an idea tumbled into her mind. She reached out and fingered the man's collar, unfastening the chain.

'Listen,' she instructed, knowing that two pairs of eyes were better than one. 'If you find Lucy Harrington for me, I may strip your backside bare and give you twenty of the best.'

The man's eyes lit up with triumph. His words came quick and excitedly: 'Twenty, you say. I will find her, madam.'

The rubber shape darted off into the fog and Penny continued to teeter around the hall, pleased with herself, but biting down on her susceptibility to the orgiastic sounds that filled the smoky air.

She nearly ran into Klima on the dance floor, stopping just in time and changing her direction before he saw the solitary figure dressed as a cat. Penny doubted whether his eyes would have been concerned with her; they had become locked on to the two large breasts almost beating in his hands. His dancing partner, Bessy, had unlaced her gown at the front and allowed her handsome chest to fall upon the Russian lecturer's outstretched palms.

Penny moved off the dance floor – it was too open and occasionally the lights would flash brightly and illumine her presence. She moved towards the wall and hugged the shadows. Up ahead, through the now waist-high smoke, she spotted two tall blonde girls, clad identically in snakeskin dresses with cobra masks on their faces, cornering a girl attired like a pretty bird. It was the twins, about to pounce on a female student.

The captive's bright-blue dress had been raised at the front by one of the gigantic predators, so that she could inspect the muscular legs and knickerless sex beneath. Penny recognised those smooth and firm legs; the twins had captured Amber. Her breasts were freed in seconds and a cobra-masked head dropped between her thighs. Amber squealed and raised her legs, draping them over the lapping snake's shoulders. The other twin bit and mauled Amber's naked breasts, pressing her captive against the wall while holding her wrists tightly together.

Penny sped past the trio, forcing arousing thoughts from her clouding mind, glancing left and right for any figure that resembled Lucy Harrington in size and shape. She tripped over a pair of legs and staggered forward. When she turned to apologise, she caught sight of the rear of Amanda's head moving in the smoke beneath her. Penny's eyes traversed the length of the body that Amanda knelt before: the man had dressed in a tuxedo and his eyes were covered by a black pantomime mask. In between the flurries of dry ice, Penny saw the stem of a glistening penis disappearing inside Amanda's mask.

Penny stood back and surveyed the sight, envying Amanda who had become lost to her sucking affections, and curious about the young man who writhed in his seat and clawed the walls.

A flurry of activity and a burst of female screams erupted behind her. Penny turned and watched two men, their faces concealed behind red devil masks, carrying a shrieking blonde girl in a harlequin outfit above their heads. Could it be Lucy? Penny gave chase, following the kicking high-heeled feet and broad male shoulders that hoisted the perfumed trophy aloft.

The men found a table and swept it clear of glasses and plates, before gently lowering the kicking girl upon the shiny wood. She struggled and slapped at the men, her cries swirling down into breathless laughter. Penny approached and crouched down, so that only her cat mask hovered above the still-thickening dry ice.

One of the men held the girl's arms down and stole rough kisses from her scarlet mouth; his companion raised the girl's black and white diamond-patterned dress and shiny ivory slip, exposing her smoothly stocking-clad legs. The girl tried to push the man away with her high-heeled feet, but he clasped her shiny ankles with both hands and cast her shoes away before spreading her knees.

Penny gasped, watching the man unbelt his trousers and massage his stiff cock. The girl pulled her face away from the impassioned kissing and stared down, across her dishevelled body, at the thick organ moving between her thighs. She squealed and slipped her legs around his buttocks, pulling his eager shaft towards her sex. At the moment of penetration, Penny moved forward to take a look at the moaning blonde beauty: was it Lucy?

'Give it to me!' the girl cried out.

'How hard? How hard do you want it, Jade?' the man shouted back.

Penny sighed with exasperation but found it impossible to remove her eyes from the spontaneous and brutal loving before her.

'Fuck me hard, really hard!' Jade screamed.

The man plunged his buttocks forward and Jade fell back into the arms of the man behind her, her moans amplified across the hall. She placed her little feet on the shoulders of the man between her legs, bending her toes right back inside the reinforced soles of her nylons. The man standing behind the table and holding Jade's craning neck, unzipped his own cock and manoeuvred his body across the surface of the oak table to slip his erection between her parted red lips.

The moans ceased but Jade's body continued to writhe and shake between the thorough rifling of two

hard cocks at either end of her body. Penny averted her
eyes, her face now hot and flushed beneath the velvet
mask, her body shivering and pleading with her to stop
and take on an anonymous lover. The dean could
re-enter the equation at any time, though, and she still
had not found Lucy. Penny staggered off, away from
the writhing threesome, and moved towards the other
side of the hall.

On the far side of the celebrations, the crowd seemed
to have thinned, as if afraid of the tall tiger-striped
woman seated upon a cushioned chair.

Penny recognised the laugh and froze: it was the
doctor. Kloster appeared flushed, relaxing, Penny
thought, after some enforced pleasuring on a hapless
victim. The smoke parted briefly and an image of total
subservience flashed back towards Penny. A male
student had fallen to his knees before the doctor; his
naked back had been striped red with claw marks and
his hair had become ruffled. The doctor had attached a
chain to his wrist cuff and the silver leash lay coiled
around her left leg. The other leg had been grasped
firmly between the male slave's caressing hands; the
spaghetti-strapped shoe had been removed and the
doctor's shiny nylon-covered toes had been stuffed
between his wet lips. The doctor sucked on a cigarette
and cooed encouragement down to the lapping pet, her
blue eyes narrowing through plumes of cigarette smoke.

Before Penny could move, a hand fell upon her bare
shoulder.

'Lucy, is that you?' Miss Barbusse asked from behind.

Penny froze.

Her stiffened limbs and locked joints rendered her
immobile. The dean's hand trailed down her back and
stroked her hips questioningly. It must have been too
dark for Miss Barbusse to detect the subtle difference in
their hair colour but, soon, her hand would reveal the
true identity of the girl before her.

Penny fled, the moment of indecision gone, her heels skipping across a surface obscured by cold fog. She turned her head quickly: Miss Barbusse had been taken aback by her flight; she squinted through her mask at Penny, before raising the owl mask to study her more carefully. The look of shock on the dean's face hit Penny like a bullet from a high-powered rifle, but she struggled on, raising the hem of her clingy cat dress to aid her longer strides.

Does she know? Has she recognised me?

Penny did not wait to find out; she threw herself against the fire doors and burst through to the tiled corridor. Before she could catch her breath, a small black shape, shiny and as compacted as a cannonball, skidded to a halt and fell at her feet, its little naked fingers already caressing her high heels.

'I have found her, madam,' the man panted, recovering from his own exertion. 'She is in the main building. The dean's study was open and I heard a noise – she is in there clearing out papers.'

Penny dropped to her knees and cupped the little mummified face in her hands.

'Papers? What kind of papers?' she asked.

'Don't know, just papers and folders and things. Now, about my punishment, madam –'

'Shut up!' Penny shouted. 'When was this? When was she there?'

'Just now, madam. I came straight away. Have I displeased you?' he asked, his eyes widening expectantly.

'I'll say!' Penny replied, smiling. 'How would you like to suck my high heels clean? And massage my feet after I have slapped your insignificant little arse raw.'

The man became speechless; his entire body trembled with excitement.

'Go and wait in the room of Penny Chambers and do not move until I get there!'

'Yes, madam,' the man panted, and fled down the corridor.

'Wait!' she shouted, leaning against the wall and removing her heels.

Speed and mobility would be important: the shoes would have to go and, besides, Penny thought, the rubber-clad gimp deserved a down payment after the information he had supplied.

Penny fled past the cowering man and threw her shoes into his hands, giving orders as she ran: 'I want those clean. You hear? Clean them with your tongue!'

Penny sprinted across the cold grass, made pale and milky beneath a three-quarter moon, and heard the music sinking behind her as she approached the main manor house. She careered to her right and ran across the front of the building, past the unlit study windows. At the end of the building, next to the main reception, she saw a light blink out – in the dean's study.

Penny ducked behind a bush next to the reception door and waited, taking desperate breaths after the sprint and listening to her pounding heart, which was about to explode with an adrenaline overload. She was just in time.

Lucy emerged from the main reception, teetering on high-heeled leather boots and weighed down by a heavy leather case. Lucy flashed her masked face left and right, before speeding down the main gravel drive towards the Academy gates.

'You little bitch,' Penny whispered, her target in her sights.

Penny sauntered out from behind the bush, shaking her hands and limbering up. She walked on to the path and immediately winced, the little hard pellets of granite cutting into her stocking-clad feet. She skipped back to the grass verge bordering the path, and followed Lucy, slowly at first, lettting her anger build up, but gradually increasing her pace as her sense of injustice heightened.

Lucy seemed oblivious to the presence of Penny shadowing her closely from behind. The beautiful heir, tightly wrapped in black satin and displaying a glorious raven-feathered headdress, staggered down the path, one tiny step at a time under the weight of her load, while forced on to her toes by the extreme heels of her boots.

Penny drew, in soft footfalls, within a few feet of Lucy before speaking. 'Those books are on restricted loan, not to be removed from the library. I wonder what –'

The heavy case struck the side of Penny's head and knocked her world upside down. She hit the grass heavily and a thousand tiny spots of bright light danced in front of the red veil that was her vision. She clambered back to her knees, tried to stand up, but fell head first on to the cold lawn. At the back of her startled mind, she heard the sound of feet, passing away, crunching across the gravel.

Penny slipped in and out of consciousness and the dizzy swoops inside her head refused to go. She managed to sit up, sliding her cat mask back into her hair, and put her wet face between her knees. She focused her concentration and took deep lungfuls of clean evening air into her shaking body. When she opened her eyes, the dark landscape settled down to a horizontal plane. She looked up the path, but Lucy had disappeared beneath the shadows of overhanging oak boughs.

'Shit!' Penny swore, and staggered to her feet. She tried to run but overbalanced and started zigzagging on buckling knees.

She is getting away. With the journals. The one's she planted in your room.

This thought lit the fuse inside Penny and through the heat of anger she found the strength to run madly towards the night-curtained main gate. Penny staggered and tripped, but her teeth were set and her fists clenched. She ran and ran, her feet becoming numbed with cold, her nylons rubbing together and producing a friction that only served to aggravate her nerves.

The giant umbrellas of oak branches, rich with wide leaves, killed the moonlight, but Penny stumbled on through impenetrable blackness. Ahead, no more than a hundred feet away, she saw two shining globes – the lights on the main gate – and focused her frantic chase towards them.

As she drew nearer, the eerie silhouette of the stone gates leapt up, stark and rigid against the star-dotted sky. Above her own laboured breathing, Penny heard a noise: it was the sound of a heavy bar being tugged through iron slots.

Penny nearly screamed with relief – she was in time. Lucy was still struggling to open the heavy gate. Penny walked into a circular halo of light created by the buzzing glass globes of the two entrance lights, which were perched upon wrought-iron poles. Against the dark wood of the gate, her keen eyes detected a movement and she heard a soft female voice panting from the exertion of grappling with a heavy burden.

Penny walked into the centre of the circle of electric light and shouted across to Lucy, her voice trembling with emotion, 'I'm down but not out. Get in the ring!'

The movement by the gate stopped and Lucy's voice spat from the shadows, 'You again! I am going to break your bloody neck!'

Lucy walked into the circle of light and peeled her dress up and over her head, the garment taking her raven mask with it. Penny followed suit: unzipping her cat gown and letting it fall around her feet, revealing her soft, white flesh and black underwear.

The girls circled each other, resplendent in suspenders, black seamed stockings, bras and French knickers. Lucy had the height advantage because of her tight leather boots and Penny eyed the severe heels anxiously – they could do a lot of damage.

Lucy's beautiful face froze into a hateful sneer and she plunged across the narrow space separating the combatants, catching Penny's slender waist with her crimson claws. Penny danced back and buried her own strong red nails in Lucy's shiny blonde hair.

The momentum from Lucy's charge spilt them on to the grass, where they broke apart and scrabbled away from each other. Lucy attacked again, kicking out with her dagger-like heel; Penny wheeled to the side, avoiding the silken lance, and clutched out for Lucy's long leg before it could bend. Her hands closed across the slippery stockings and slid down the leg, before her nails found a purchase on the top of Lucy's boot. Penny yanked at the leg with all her might and pulled Lucy on to her backside with a thump.

'Bitch!' Lucy screamed, before sweeping her other leg around and taking Penny's ankles out from under her.

Penny joined Lucy on the grass, releasing the boot to break her fall. The spitting heir was on her in a second, punching her with one hand and tearing at her hair with the other. The pain on her scalp blinded Penny and a brief moment of superhuman strength pulsed through her arms. She punched out in anger and felt her blows land on Lucy's shoulders and forehead, knocking the girl back.

Lucy rolled across the ground before springing to her feet with a surprising alacrity. 'You will pay for that, slut!' Lucy squealed.

She ran towards Penny at full speed, not having time to stop when Penny dived to one side, leaving one of her own legs out to clip Lucy's heel, sending her off balance and on to her face.

Penny scurried across to Lucy and pushed her foot on the back of the girl's head, grinding her face into the luminous grass.

'Enough!' a German voice barked from the dark.

Penny leapt away from Lucy and eyed the main gate.

Miss Barbusse walked unsteadily into the circle of light with Doctor Kloster close behind. Other footsteps crushed the grass behind Penny; she turned and watched the two cobra twins emerge from the shadows. She was surrounded.

Lucy spat the grass from her mouth, sobbing, her voice coming in grief-driven spasms: 'I – I caught her again, mistress, stealing your books – They are by the gate. I caught her just in time –'

Miss Barbusse, her face solemn, raised her hand and silenced Lucy's explanation. Doctor Kloster rattled a pair of silver handcuffs and the twins appeared on either side of Penny, holding brass ankle hobbles.

Penny gulped as the twins shuffled closer. She was worn out, grubby and dizzy from the fight. It was over; she could not go on.

Miss Barbusse, shining in her white dress and elevated to a spectral beauty under the lights, nodded to her staff, her face betraying no emotion.

Penny closed her eyes and felt the wind as the twins rushed past her. She waited, on the verge of tears, for the cold metal to slip around her ankles and wrists. She heard the metal clasps opening and shutting tight, but felt nothing on her own limbs.

She opened her eyes and saw Kloster and the twins busy around the kicking and clawing Lucy Harrington on the grass. Kloster released two powerful slaps across Lucy's pantied buttocks and subdued the spitting vixen.

Miss Barbusse, not even deigning to look at Lucy, walked across to Penny and held out a long white hand. Penny stared down at the pale fingers stretching out to her – in friendship. Something tightened inside Penny's throat. She gulped, but it would not disappear; she was unable to speak. Penny wiped her eyes and began to cry with relief. The dean's soft arms passed around her bare shoulders and pulled Penny's face down to her fragrant breasts.

Eleven

'Graduating with first-class honours: Amanda Jane Bennet.'

The students all applauded and Amanda beamed, striding across the ballroom stage. Her passage was a flash of white blouse, shiny raven hair and strong teeth, which stopped before Miss Barbusse, taking the Whitehead diploma from her hand.

Penny watched her friend with pride: the long legs and straight back, the beauty who had introduced her to a realm of natural pleasure on that first Academy night. Amanda shook every robed staff member's hand before leaving the stage. Even Kloster was smiling, pleased with the young apprentice.

For the graduation ceremony, the staff had all dressed in the black Whitehead gown, red lined with scarlet hoods, and formed an orderly column beside Miss Barbusse at the podium. The students had also attired themselves in Academy graduate gowns, black but with silver hoods. They stood before their chairs, two rows deep, waiting for the dean to summon them. Only one chair was vacant; only one student missing. Lucy Harrington had not graduated. The rumours concerning the events of the previous night had flown about the dining room at breakfast, and nobody required the exact details to guess where the young heir was currently residing.

'Paris Simmons: graduating with first-class honours,'

Miss Barbusse called from the stage, managing an extra-special smile when the young man bowed before her and accepted his scroll.

Penny smiled, a little sad, but elated as well. She watched her new friends and acquaintances, who were smartly attired and rising to the formal occasion, receiving the fruits of hard work, unconventional training and some dramatic self-exploration. She would miss them all. Bessy's humour and hidden depths, Amber's spontaneous nature, and Rupert's deceptively innocent manner would no longer be daily highlights. They had exchanged addresses at breakfast, but it would be so different back on the outside without the quickly taken illicit opportunities of Whitehead. None of them, Penny was sure, would ever see the world in the same way again; they had been unlocked, freed, and equipped with the Barbusse will to power. It was their mission to take these skills out to the unsuspecting world and to open a few more doors.

Behind her, as Rupert rose to approach the stage, Penny heard him mutter, 'My honours degree means nothing compared to this.'

Penny smiled, applauding and listening to the ripple of mirth behind her. It was true; Miss Barbusse had imparted her lifetime's study, the combination of salacious experience and perverse theory, and, somehow, it worked wonders out there on the other side.

'And, finally, graduating as the most exceptional student, and gaining not just the Whitehead Masters but also the keys to the Academy, Penny Chambers!'

The hall erupted with triumphant whistles and deafening applause. Penny rose to her feet, blushing in the excited din, and made her way, on freshly polished five-inch heels, towards the stage. She sensed that every other pupil knew of her original mission, her change of mind, her trials and her victory. They smiled and encouraged her, clapping and rising to their feet in salute.

It was the greatest moment of personal triumph that Penny could remember; she had become the saviour of that which she had intended to destroy. She climbed the polished oak steps beneath the grand chandeliers with every sign of the decadent ball now removed.

Miss Barbusse smiled at Penny, kissing her on both cheeks, before whispering, 'You may return whenever you wish, Penny, and I hope you will never forget us.'

Penny smiled back, squeezing the dean's soft hands before replying, 'Just try and keep me away, and thank you for all that you have shown me. It is worth preserving, for ever.'

Penny pressed a role of film, which she had hidden in the chimney breast, into the dean's hand and whispered, 'I won't be needing this. I'm so sorry for reading your diary, but the secrets are safe with me.'

Miss Barbusse kissed Penny again, this time lingeringly and on the lips. The students below cheered with a fresh vigour and several men wolf-whistled.

'But the inquisition – what we did – how can you forgive us so readily?' Miss Barbusse queried.

'Don't mention it,' Penny whispered through her smiling lips.

She winked at Miss Barbusse and walked on to shake Kloster's hand.

Amanda reclined on the bed watching Penny, who packed her things slowly and reluctantly.

'You know,' Amanda said, unbuttoning her blouse and peering down at her silk bra. 'I am really going to miss this uniform. I mean, it's really weird, but I have grown to love it in – what – only ten days. It makes me feel so haughty and feminine and strong.'

'It makes you look that way too,' Penny replied, after turning towards the languishing Amazon and smiling.

'Thanks,' Amanda whispered, winking at Penny and drawing on her cigarette with shining cherry-red lips.

'They are letting us keep the uniform, you know,' Amanda continued. 'I was thinking of wearing it to work, but I think I may save it instead for special occasions.'

Penny teetered back to the canopied bed, her eyebrow cocked and a naughty smile turning her lips. 'What kind of occasion?' Penny asked, and slipped on to the soft duvet to lie alongside Amanda.

'Well, you know, when someone special comes over for dinner, to talk about old times and Academy nights.'

'You mean like Amber? When she flies in from New York.'

'Yeah, like Amber, or one of the guys,' Amanda teased.

Penny rolled on top of Amanda, who squealed and fought back, but Penny trapped the girl's wrists on the mattress. She lowered her face and licked Amanda's mouth, which opened immediately and sighed.

'You have my number,' Penny whispered, 'and my address. I was hoping that we might see a lot more of each other on the outside.'

'You can put money on that, you little tease,' Amanda whispered, and slipped her long tongue inside Penny's hot mouth.

Penny let her body collapse across her lover and Amanda's arms slithered down to unzip her skirt.

'Do we have time?' Penny muttered, before continuing to bite at Amanda's neck.

'An hour before the farewell dinner,' Amanda panted in reply.

'Good. Do you have that toy with you?' Penny asked, her breath coming fast and her pulse thundering against her panty girdle.

'Would I come in here without it?' Amanda whispered.

Penny groaned and rolled on to her back, raising her buttocks to wriggle out of her skirt. Amanda's hands were sliding over Penny's legs in seconds. Her face had flushed beneath her heavy make-up and her eyes were seeking Penny's knickered sex.

'You said you liked to take a girl in her undies,' Penny teased. 'Well, suck me through these. Miss Barbusse gave them to me. Put your tongue on a thousand pounds' worth of gossamer.'

Amanda moaned, her forehead wrinkling before her face descended between Penny's parted thighs. The thick curly black hair, bustling between her legs, tickled Penny and excited her. When Amanda's tongue reached her gauzy and perfumed sex, Penny clawed the bed and slipped her elegant legs over Amanda's back.

'Ooh, that's it, right there. Do it in tiny little circles with your tongue. Yes, oh, Amanda!'

Penny could feel her panties dampening with her own juices and Amanda's saliva; the fabric clung to her tingling slit and forced her to push her sex into Amanda's face. Amanda moaned with approval and slid her hands around Penny's thighs, reaching for her breasts. Penny unclipped her bra, removed it and let Amanda's fingertips find her hardening nipples.

'Oh, you dirty slut,' Penny joked.

Amanda removed one hand and spanked Penny's girdle-hugged hip in punishment.

'Mmm . . .' Penny moaned. 'Do that again.'

Amanda's grinning face, her lips glistening, rose from between Penny's thighs. 'You want me to give you a spanking, don't you? You randy tart.'

Penny smiled and nodded.

Amanda swivelled Penny on to her tummy and clambered up the bed. Penny giggled and moved her buttocks about, taunting Amanda with the white flesh that shimmered beneath her black see-through girdle.

Penny felt the hand slap across her soft cheeks and she moaned with approval, grinding her face into the soft goosefeather pillows and reaching one arm beneath herself to tickle her clit.

'That's good, but you can hit me a lot harder than that, bitch.'

'Ooh, you have asked for it now, madam!' Amanda squealed and laughed at the same time.

Her hand fell in long and considered arcs, blasting off Penny's smarting buttocks. Penny could even feel her little golden ring, on the underside of one finger, indenting her flesh with a glorious and soothing pain.

'Oh yes, Amanda. Give it to me now!'

Amanda whimpered from an overload of excitement and rummaged around for the long rubber shaft.

Penny felt it move her panties and nudge through her labia before finally sliding through the red dewy entrance to her warm sex. It slipped inside, widening her lips, probing further and further, until it paused and withdrew to begin the motion and delicious sensations again. Penny croaked with pleasure and pushed her body down the bed to swallow the hard tool and Amanda's nails right inside.

'I need this every day, Amanda.'

'We can arrange that – it's only a short taxi ride from Hampstead to your place.'

'Will you come over after work?' Penny panted, relishing the smooth passage of the toy inside her.

'Every single night. But what about men? We are going to need a real cock now and again.'

'Mmm,' Penny sighed. 'We can share boyfriends.'

'Oh, yeah,' Amanda squealed, thrusting the shaft into Penny more rapidly. 'Without them knowing. Seduce them and wear them out.'

'Sounds perfect, I'm not the jealous type.'

'That's good,' Amanda whispered, while gliding across Penny's back, 'because I am going to fuck anyone you bring home.'

Penny clenched her teeth, thighs and eyelids, and whimpered through her climax.

* * *

Miss Barbusse unlocked the door and walked into Lucy's cell. The beautiful prisoner was lying face down on her cottage bed, unmoving, her little hands clenched tightly around fistfuls of white pillow.

It had been a strange journey on that final morning, through the underground tunnel and cottage cellar: a walk through her own dark kingdom, transformed from a crumbling estate to a fortress of heightened sensuality by her own will and discipline. It was the kingdom she had hoped to share with Lucy: its every secret and hidden passage, its routines, long history, and its acres of opportunity. Instead, her disappointment weighed heavily beneath her jet-black corsetry. Her damaged heart felt more than the anguish of mere deception.

'I was a fool,' Miss Barbusse said.

Lucy rolled on to her back and stared blankly back at the dean.

'I thought you were me, so many years ago, a kindred spirit, someone with whom I had a real empathy. I was wrong. I would never have betrayed the master.'

Lucy sat up and stretched out her legs. Her skirt ruffled up around her mid-thigh and Miss Barbusse forced her eyes away from the glimpse of shimmering leg.

'Who is to say that we are not alike?' Lucy answered, the humility having fled from the voice that had once called her 'mistress'. 'We use our resources,' she added. 'We manipulate and we succeed. Was I acting out of character?'

Miss Barbusse unleashed a cold laugh from between her immaculate lips. 'If success involves theft and treason, then I want no part of it. You could have been great, but you have no discipline, Lucy, only beauty. How did you come to be so ... evil.' The last word stuck in the dean's throat and she shuddered.

Lucy laughed sarcastically and slithered on to her feet before looking into the dean's trembling face. 'Try being the heir to a fortune, and having the money that is rightfully yours filtered through a trust fund. Because you are not trusted. Because you will waste it. But life is for the living, my dean. Is that not what you said? You cannot blame me for trying to sell your story. You would have been famous too.'

Miss Barbusse shook her head with an air of tired resignation. 'You made me feel young again, Lucy, but you made me into a fool. A silly cuckold made wretched before a young flirt, a devious and spoilt little girl. You have a long way to go to pay for what you have done –'

'Don't even think about it!' Lucy shrieked. 'I have places to go. I am not stopping at this stupid Academy –'

'Wrong!' Miss Barbusse replied. 'I have spoken to your guardian this morning and told her about your deplorable behaviour and attempt to steal my life story. She has agreed that an indefinite stay at the Academy is best for all parties concerned.'

Lucy's face whitened; her lips parted; her mouth moved and shaped an unspoken no.

Miss Barbusse smiled. 'Oh, Lucy, we will have such fun together. Don't tell me that you faked every shiver and cry of delight in my room? I simply will not believe that.'

Lucy, frantic and cornered, opened her blouse and began to smile at Miss Barbusse. 'Keep your secrets. I will keep my mouth shut. I will come back now and then and you can enjoy these again.' Lucy unclipped her bra and began to massage her nipples.

Something tugged inside Miss Barbusse but she remained immobile. Lucy hiked up her skirt and flashed her stocking-tops at the dean.

'Think of me at the weekends, mistress, and my pretty legs, knowing that they will run back to you over and over again. You don't want me here all the time. You will get bored with me.'

Miss Barbusse laughed and raised her hands. 'Very clever, my dear, but just a trifle desperate. I won't get tired of having you around, even though you will be available every night and day. You see, I intend to share you, every bit of you, especially those pretty legs and delightful breasts. We shall all amuse ourselves for a very long time.'

Lucy began to shake her head and stretch her hands out as if to plead.

Miss Barbusse clapped her hands and stood back. The Celeste twins teetered through the door, whispering to each other, wobbling on their ultra-high-heeled boots, their leather waistcoats parting to reveal snow-white breasts, their long legs gripped by black nylon, their painted fingernails slowly twisting evil black riding crops.

Miss Barbusse laughed again before initiating the first of many rites. 'Let the re-education begin!'

Penny spooned the delicious apple pie into her bulging and still-flushed cheeks: it was her last Whitehead meal and she would miss the food, especially the deserts. She looked around the room; everyone seemed so happy, men and women sitting together at last amongst the silver and crystal finery, waited upon and stuffed with epicurean delights. But there was also a sense of reluctance to abandon this secret kingdom. Behind every smile Penny sensed a wistful sadness. Perhaps, she thought, this will work in our favour, making us determined to re-create the dean's enigma in our places of work, mixing business and pleasure with spectacular results.

Rupert shuffled over to Penny's table holding a cup of coffee. 'Hi, Pen.'

Penny winked and smiled her welcome, unable to speak through the mass of shortcrust pastry filling her cheeks.

'Well, you won the class of '97. Are you going to come back and give a lecture?'

'Maybe.' Penny smiled, swallowing a mouthful. 'Will you be able to visit?'

Rupert blushed before answering in a whisper, 'The dean has permitted me access to the cottage, to see Sabrina. We have developed something of a special friendship over the last week and there is just too much going on to leave behind.'

'I bet,' Penny replied, giggling.

'But listen, there is an old tradition here. That is why I have come to disturb your second helping of apple pie. On the last afternoon at Whitehead the star pupil is allowed to indulge . . . well, fulfil their wildest fantasy. That is, if they want to.'

Penny smiled, blinking with disbelief. 'You are kidding?'

'No,' Rupert replied. 'You can ask anything of the other graduates and it will be granted. The doctor told me to organise it. Just give me the word. We still have a few hours before checking out.'

Penny sat back in her chair and thought ahead to the following day, when she would be required to return to the *Inquisitor* and file her report. It had been an expensive operation and the editor would be furious with her 'alternative' story – he would have wasted ten thousand pounds. This would be, however, her last chance for some time to drink from the Academy chalice, sanctioned by tradition and untouched by the staff. Only a fool, she decided, would pass up such a tempting opportunity.

Penny turned towards Rupert and gave him her answer: 'Well, there is something I have always been curious about.'

'Name it,' Rupert replied.

'OK,' Penny said, thinking back to an incident she had observed in the maze. 'I would like you to hand-pick three men, who think I'm cute, of course –'

'That won't be hard,' Rupert interjected.

'And tell them to muster in my room in forty minutes. OK?'

'Absolutely,' Rupert replied, his eyes widening.

Rupert drifted around the table and dipped his head by certain men, to whisper in their ears. Penny took her time with a coffee and tingled when three of the male students began to look across at her and smile.

She left the table and scurried back to her room to prepare for the grand finale. Her mind drifted back to that distant but still vivid scene, when the dean had quivered beneath the bright moon, when she had informed her young lovers about the hunger in a woman. Well, Penny decided, they would feel her hunger, all of them. The situation was perfect: she may never see them again, she had a large canopied bed, the sunshine was throwing a midsummer haze across her rugs and oils, and she had three strange men to pleasure herself with.

Penny retouched her make-up and clouded her body with a new perfume: another graduation present from Miss Barbusse. She sprayed it down her long shins and dabbed it behind her little soft ears. Her stomach tingled as she prepared her outfit with trembling fingers: she wanted to look special for the send-off – as raunchy as the Celeste twins and as sultry as the dean.

Her visitors were right on time. Penny heard their muffled voices outside her bedroom door before the knock registered on the antique wood.

'Come in, it's open,' she called out, and took a deep breath.

After they had entered her room and shut the door behind them, Penny knew that she would never forget the look on all three handsome faces: each mouth opened and each pair of eyes bulged at the sight before them.

'Come in, don't be shy, and sit on the bed,' Penny

269

offered in an assertive tone – something she appeared to have developed in the last ten days.

The men shuffled past her, two of them tripping up, unable to remove their eyes from her slender corseted contours. Penny smiled, her lacquered nails planted on her hips, her little pink tongue refreshing her glossy lips. Her graduation gown had parted and she stood with one leg pushed forward, her height elevated by five-inch heels.

'Do you like my outfit?' Penny asked the three gaping faces lined up on her bed.

All three of the smartly dressed and clean-shaven men nodded their heads affirmatively.

'How about my hair?' Penny asked. 'Up or down?'

The tall dark-skinned man, who had taken the dean in the maze and on the fire-exit stairs, said, 'Down.'

Penny unhooked the little hairpins and shook her blonde hair down and across the dark shoulders of her gown. The men gasped and she pouted her fire-engine red-lips. 'Heels? On or off?' she asked, and stretched one ankle out towards them, presenting her patent stilettos from three glimmering angles.

'On, definitely on,' the blonde said.

'OK,' Penny replied. 'I never bothered with knickers, but what about the leather corset and the stockings. Will they get in the way?'

'No!'

'No way. Leave them on.'

'They are just fine, Penny.'

Penny laughed and strode past their parted knees, slowly circling a painted fingernail around her two pink nipples, which were half-exposed over soft leather cups.

'Take your clothes off, boys. We shan't bother with introductions.'

The men began an immediate and hasty unbuttoning and unzipping on the bed, rolling against each other and panting in an excitable frenzy.

'My instructions are simple and explicit,' she continued, feeling a heat throb and spread throughout her young body. 'I want you all stark-naked with a well-oiled cock. You will find the lubricant under the pillow. I am already fairly excited, but I would like you all to spend some time familiarising yourselves with my body. When you are satisfied that I am soft and compliant enough, I would like you to arrange me in such a manner that you can enter me at the same time. It can be done and the choice of entry is entirely up to you. Each option, I assure you, will be very responsive, and I can especially recommend my mouth. Shall we begin?'

Penny dropped her robe and slithered up the bed behind the three astonished men. As they turned and indented the mattress with their knees all around her, Penny took one last lingering look across the three stiff and quivering cocks before slipping her velvet sleeping-mask across her eyes.

She had guessed that her eyes would have been tightly shut from the overloading sensation and, anyway, this was an experience she wanted to feel amplified in the dark.

Penny sank her body into the soft duvet and rested her head on a pillow. She turned on her side and listened to the squeaks and rubbing motions of oil applied to erect muscle. Her heart nearly stopped when the first pair of hands slid up her legs; they were cold and rough. The second pair of hands were larger and warmer, sinking into the soft cushion of her breasts, bringing forth her first gasp of delight. The final couple of greedy, desperate palms satisfied themselves with her velveteen sex, the fingers probing right inside without any pause or restraint.

In seconds there was no way for Penny to determine which hand was partnered by any other. She had no idea either, as to which tongue belonged to which cologne-fragrant face. But they all felt good: wetting and tasting her nipples, tummy and moist sex. They pulled her back and forth across the bed, parting her shiny thighs, sucking her little tingling anus and mauling her soft breasts.

Penny gasped and moaned. She felt weightless and utterly controlled by these tides of masculine passion. Within minutes there was no controlling the foul-mouthed demon that panted inside her chest: 'Now! I am ready for you now. Take me now! Fuck –'

The thing that passed through her lips seemed much thicker than she could have imagined. It filled her cheeks and rippled across her flattened tongue, scenting her mouth and sinus passages with desperate male arousal. Penny sucked at it hard and raised a hand to find and tickle the silky balls below it.

Her legs were parted by a multitude of hands and two male chests were pressed against her back and chest. She could feel the chest hair and tiny hard nipples, the breath from two different mouths on her pale throat and goose-pimpling the back of her neck. Her buttocks were parted by something slippery and thick, while her vaginal lips were nuzzled by a round and smooth-headed pole.

It was exhilarating and excruciating: speared from two angles, pumped to the farthest recess of her body's three cavities. Never had Penny been overpowered so thoroughly and taken so ruthlessly. She had teased them deliberately; she had paraded herself in stockings and leather; she had given commands; she had fulfilled the cravings from that secret place that flushed her cheeks in sleep: her education was complete.

They were not content to take her once, banging her submissive shape across the imperial-size mattress, or to leave her damp and dishevelled body on all fours. Her lovers were satisfied only with a quick interchange of positions: each of them wanted the recommended mouth, the tight anus and sucking vagina. And Penny gave all of her treasures away, to each in turn, lovingly.

She swooned in her own private dark: eased on to her front, thrown upon her back, and occasionally removing the dewy shaft from her mouth to issue breathless suggestions. Her shoes were lost in a frenzy and her make-up ran in grey streams from her eyes. When someone raised her ankles and slipped inside her sopping orchid, one of his partners removed a stocking and sucked her little naked toes. Penny climaxed almost instantly, driven mad by so many laser-hot inspirations. When the last lover moaned and released his final hot stream across her sticky breasts, the other two gathered by Penny's contented face and kissed her forehead in thanks.

They left her in the dark, stroking her hands in farewell and whispering tender accolades after their heat had expired inside and across her body.

Penny smiled as she dozed amongst the violently disturbed sheets; she had taken a final glimpse into the heart of the dean: the patron saint of deviance. Penny said her own farewell to the Whitehead Academy, for now at least. Satisfied, she fell into a deep sleep.

Twelve

'Penny, you have to be kidding me! You ate algae and drank carrot juice for ten days? There is nothing here we can use. Nothing!'

Penny smiled and swivelled around in the leather chair, throwing her new blonde bob, cut in the French style, over her face. The fluffy blonde hair spiked around her emerald eyes and shining lips. She let the editor rant and raise his hands in frustration; she was content to just study the framed *Inquisitor* cover stories adorning the walls of the smoky office.

'Ten thousand pounds and that intricate alibi for nothing! Why all the secrecy and what about the rumours?'

'Look, chief,' Penny replied, as if he were little more than a nuisance. 'They have foreign diplomats and politicians there, heirs and high-profile executives. They need security and it is very effective. That is where the rumours come from, nothing else.'

'So I paid ten grand for you to have a holiday, playing tennis and sitting in a Jacuzzi?' the editor shouted.

'That is about the size of it,' Penny replied, raising an eyebrow.

Penny watched his expression change and he softened his tone of voice: 'I'm sorry, Pen. It's just that I am going to get heat from the board over this one. I've really messed up. I lost Sebastian to that place and his by-line alone used to double the circulation. Did he really run off with an American girl?'

'Yep,' Penny replied nonchalantly. 'You worked him to death, made him do too many things out of character, and now he lives in Fiji, catching fish and painting his girlfriend's toenails.'

The editor slumped back in his chair, shaking his head and tapping a cigarette from the crumpled packet on his messy desk.

'My head is going to roll. I will be fried,' he muttered to himself.

'Leave them to me,' Penny said, rising from the chair and approaching the editor's desk.

'Who?' he questioned, squinting through the cigarette smoke.

'The financiers and managing editor.'

'To you? What the hell can you do?' he asked, laughing sarcastically.

Penny slinked around the desk and perched her little bottom on the corner. She took the cigarette out of his hands and began to smoke it herself. She watched his eyes drifting across her tailored charcoal suit and pausing over the black satin negligée displayed between the lapels of her chic jacket. His eyes finally came to rest on her legs, which had been made extra shiny in a haze of black nylon, and tapered smoothly into her high-heeled suede slingbacks.

Penny parted her thighs, no more than an inch, and made sure he could just see a shadowy cleft beneath her hemline. She eased one foot out of a shoe and wiggled her painted toenails. Her jacket just seemed to fall open, after a subtle change in the position of her left arm, and a rustling silken breast slipped into view.

'Make me an appointment with the man upstairs and I will explain everything. Plus I can push that underground-agency story we discussed way back – the one he did not like.'

The editor heard Penny, but seemed unable to remove his eyes from her legs. His voice came softly, half-distracted: 'Sure, you can try. These clothes, Penny – where did you learn how to dress like this?'

Penny smiled; the leg nearest to the editor bent slightly and hovered against his knee, almost touching, but not quite making contact. Penny watched his fingers twitch before making her reply: 'Oh, I had some time to kick back and reflect on where my life was going, and this really pretty French girl loaned me some clothes. I also decided that I don't like the gossip column. I want to make real news. You know, bust real crims, not MPs with their pants down.'

'Don't we all,' the editor replied, his voice little more than a whisper.

'But I will. I want that art-swindle story too.'

'Already assigned it. Sorry Pen, but you are back on entertainments.'

'Is that a fact?' Penny replied, feline eyes narrowing and the icy tone in her .voice stealing the editor's attention from her legs.

He looked shocked; confusion knitted his brow and his bottom jaw quivered.

'We need a shake-up, boss,' Penny told him. 'Something new, something exciting, something exotic. It's time to be the good guys and stop rifling through rubbish bins, *comprende*?'

He shook his head, an attempt at speech disappearing in a wheeze. Penny raised one leg and inspected her knee. Her thighs rubbed together and hissed. For just a brief moment before she dropped her foot in his lap, his eyes caught the flash of pale thigh and glossy stocking-top.

He stared straight ahead, his hands fluttering and dithering in the air beside Penny's shiny calf muscle.

'So you agree,' Penny informed her employer, kneading his erection with the ball of her foot. 'I will take on the gallery story and get the agency proposition up and running.'

'Yes,' he gasped, his glasses sliding down a nose now speckled with sweat.

Penny pushed her upper body forward to switch the desk fan on, letting her braless breasts quiver close to his pursed lips. The fan whirred into life and the cool air blew Penny's soft hair off her face.

'Umm,' she cooed, 'that is much better and I am glad you agree with my future direction.' Penny glanced down, studying his hands and then the red trembling face. 'Go on,' she whispered softly. 'Have a little feel before I go to lunch. You might not get another chance.'

His hands closed around Penny's ankle and calf muscle, caressing the soft contours and fine fabric hugging her slender limbs. She stared past his rapture and looked out over the grey city. It would be nice, she decided, to have her own office with a view. She pressed her foot down harder into the editor's lap and listened to him choke.

'Make the appointment this afternoon, about three,' she instructed. 'We can lunch tomorrow and discuss the results. Somewhere quiet with a long tablecloth that falls to the floor, concealing my legs.'

The editor nodded, his fingers busy stroking the little ankle chain.

'I am off to meet the girls for a bite now – could be late back – but get things rolling upstairs. Your job will be safe, don't worry, and you really should not get so tense.'

Penny removed her silky candy from his lap and slipped her shoe back on. She eased herself off the desk and strolled towards the door, throwing a final comment over her shoulder: 'I picked up a little technique in Cornwall that will untie every one of those little stress knots. Ciao!'

The girls were waiting outside in an idling black cab,

which seemed to shudder around its occupants. Amber's sunglasses concealed her eyes, but her teeth flashed between the crimson fruit of her lips. Amanda sat close to her in the back, leafing through a magazine while the driver mopped his forehead and opened a window.

Penny slithered across the girls, her hands playing stepping stones with their exposed thighs, making them giggle and slap at her soft backside.

'Did you get the raise, Amanda?' Penny asked.

'Uh huh,' she replied, slipping her hand around Penny's back.

'How about the extra week off, Amber?' she asked the pouting beauty from New York.

'It's a done deal,' Amber replied.

'Good, then let's eat.'

'Are you sure you don't mind pitching in this evening, with this Italian clothes designer?' Amanda asked, over the noise of the cab's revving engine.

'It will be a pleasure,' Penny replied, and winked before kissing Amanda on the lips.

NEXUS BACKLIST

This information is correct at time of printing. For up-to-date information, please visit our website at www.nexus-books.co.uk

All books are priced at £6.99 unless another price is given.

ABANDONED ALICE	Adriana Arden 0 352 33969 1	☐
ALICE IN CHAINS	Adriana Arden 0 352 33908 X	☐
AMAZON SLAVE	Lisette Ashton 0 352 33916 0	☐
THE ANIMAL HOUSE	Cat Scarlett 0 352 33877 6	☐
THE ART OF CORRECTION	Tara Black 0 352 33895 4	☐
AT THE END OF HER TETHER	G.C. Scott 0 352 33857 1	☐
BARE BEHIND	Penny Birch 0 352 33721 4	☐
BELINDA BARES UP	Yolanda Celbridge 0 352 33926 8	☐
BENCH MARKS	Tara Black 0 352 33797 4	☐
THE BLACK GARTER	Lisette Ashton 0 352 33919 5	☐
THE BLACK MASQUE	Lisette Ashton 0 352 33977 2	☐
THE BLACK ROOM	Lisette Ashton 0 352 33914 4	☐
THE BLACK WIDOW	Lisette Ashton 0 352 33973 X	☐
THE BOND	Lindsay Gordon 0 352 33996 9	☐
THE BOOK OF PUNISHMENT	Cat Scarlett 0 352 33975 6	☐

- - - - - - ✂ -

Please send me the books I have ticked above.

Name   ....

Address   ....

                ....

                ....

                .... Post code ....

Send to: **Virgin Books Cash Sales, Thames Wharf Studios, Rainville Road, London W6 9HA**

US customers: for prices and details of how to order books for delivery by mail, call 1-800-343-4499.

Please enclose a cheque or postal order, made payable to **Nexus Books Ltd**, to the value of the books you have ordered plus postage and packing costs as follows:
    UK and BFPO – £1.00 for the first book, 50p for each subsequent book.
    Overseas (including Republic of Ireland) – £2.00 for the first book, £1.00 for each subsequent book.

If you would prefer to pay by VISA, ACCESS/MASTERCARD, AMEX, DINERS CLUB or SWITCH, please write your card number and expiry date here:

....

Please allow up to 28 days for delivery.

Signature ....

Our privacy policy

We will not disclose information you supply us to any other parties. We will not disclose any information which identifies you personally to any person without your express consent.

From time to time we may send out information about Nexus books and special offers. Please tick here if you do *not* wish to receive Nexus information.   ☐

- - - - - - ✂ -